LIMERICK CITY LIBRARY

Phone: 407510
Website:
www.limerickcity.ie/library
Email: citylib@limerickcity.ie

The Granary,
Michael Street,
Limerick.

**This book is issued subject to the Rules of this Library.
The Book must be returned not later than the last date
stamped below.**

Class No. ....AF........ Acc. No. .....C 98081

Date of Return	Date of Return	Date of Return	Date of Return

PRINCE OF THORNS

Book One of The Broken Empire

Mark Lawrence

HARPER
Voyager

HarperCollins*Publishers*
77–85 Fulham Palace Road,
Hammersmith, London W6 8JB

www.harpercollins.co.uk

Published by Harper*Voyager*
An imprint of HarperCollins*Publishers* 2011

1

A catalogue record for this book
is available from the British Library

ISBN: 978-0-00-742329-3

Set in Plantin and Memento

Printed and bound in Great Britain by Clays Ltd, St Ives plc

MIX
Paper from
responsible sources
FSC www.fsc.org   **FSC® C007454**

FSC is a non-profit international organisation established
to promote the responsible management of the world's forests.
Products carrying the FSC label are independently certified
to assure consumers that they come from forests that are managed
to meet the social, economic and ecological needs
of present and future generations.

Find out more about HarperCollins and the environment at
www.harpercollins.co.uk/green

Acknowledgments

I would like to thank for their help and support
Helen Mazarakis and Sharon Mack

To Celyn, the best parts were never broken.

1

Ravens! Always the ravens. They settled on the gables of the church even before the injured became the dead. Even before Rike had finished taking fingers from hands, and rings from fingers. I leaned back against the gallows-post and nodded to the birds, a dozen of them in a black line, wise-eyed and watching.

The town-square ran red. Blood in the gutters, blood on the flagstones, blood in the fountain. The corpses posed as corpses do. Some comical, reaching for the sky with missing fingers, some peaceful, coiled about their wounds. Flies rose above the wounded as they struggled. This way and that, some blind, some sly, all betrayed by their buzzing entourage.

'Water! Water!' It's always water with the dying. Strange, it's killing that gives me a thirst.

And that was Mabberton. Two hundred dead farmers lying with their scythes and axes. You know, I warned them that we do this for a living. I said it to their leader, Bovid Tor. I gave them that chance, I always do. But no. They wanted blood and slaughter. And they got it.

War, my friends, is a thing of beauty. Those as says otherwise are losing. If I'd bothered to go over to old Bovid, propped up against the fountain with his guts in his lap, he'd probably take a contrary view. But look where disagreeing got him.

'Shit-poor farm maggots.' Rike discarded a handful of fingers over Bovid's open belly. He came to me, holding out his takings, as if it was my fault. 'Look! One gold ring. One! A whole village and one fecking gold ring. I'd like to set the bastards up and knock 'em down again. Fecking bog-farmers.'

He would too: he was an evil bastard, and greedy with it. I held his eye. 'Settle down, Brother Rike. There's more than one kind of gold in Mabberton.'

I gave him my warning look. His cursing stole the magic from the scene; besides, I had to be stern with him. Rike was always on the edge after a battle, wanting more. I gave him a look that told him I had more. More than he could handle. He grumbled, stowed his bloody ring, and thrust his knife back in his belt.

Makin came up then and flung an arm about each of us, clapping gauntlet to shoulder-plate. If Makin had a skill, then smoothing things over was it.

'Brother Jorg is right, Little Rikey. There's treasure aplenty to be found.' He was wont to call Rike 'Little Rikey', on account of him being a head taller than any of us and twice as wide. Makin always told jokes. He'd tell them to those as he killed, if they gave him time. Liked to see them go out with a smile.

'What treasure?' Rike wanted to know, still surly.

'When you get farmers, what else do you always get, Little Rikey?' Makin raised his eyebrows all suggestive.

Rike lifted his visor, treating us to his ugly face. Well brutal more than ugly. I think the scars improved him. 'Cows?'

Makin pursed his lips. I never liked his lips, too thick and fleshy, but I forgave him that, for his joking and his deathly work with that flail of his. 'Well, you can have the cows, Little Rikey. Me, I'm going to find a farmer's daughter or three, before the others use them all up.'

They went off then, Rike doing that laugh of his – '*hur, hur, hur*' – as if he was trying to cough a fishbone out.

I watched them force the door to Bovid's place opposite the church, a fine house, high roofed with wooden slates and a little flower garden in front. Bovid followed them with his eyes, but he couldn't turn his head.

I looked at the ravens, I watched Gemt and his half-wit brother, Maical, taking heads, Maical with the cart and Gemt with the axe. A thing of beauty, I tell you. At least to look at. I'll agree war smells bad. But, we'd torch the place soon enough and the stink would all turn to wood-smoke. Gold rings? I needed no more payment.

'Boy!' Bovid called out, his voice all hollow like, and weak.

I went to stand before him, leaning on my sword, tired in my arms and legs all of a sudden. 'Best speak your piece quickly, farmer. Brother Gemt's a-coming with his axe. Chop-chop.'

He didn't seem too worried. It's hard to worry a man so close to the worm-feast. Still it irked me that he held me so lightly and called me 'boy'. 'Do you have daughters, farmer? Hiding in the cellar maybe? Old Rike will sniff them out.'

Bovid looked up sharp at that, pained and sharp. 'H-how old are you, boy?'

Again the 'boy'. 'Old enough to slit you open like a fat purse,' I said, getting angry now. I don't like to get angry. It makes me angry. I don't think he caught even that. I don't think he even knew it was me that opened him up not half an hour before.

'Fifteen summers, no more. Couldn't be more…' His words came slow, from blue lips in a white face.

Out by two, I would have told him, but he'd gone past hearing. The cart creaked up behind me, and Gemt came along with his axe dripping.

'Take his head,' I told them. 'Leave his fat belly for the ravens.'

Fifteen! I'd hardly be fifteen and rousting villages.

By the time fifteen came around, I'd be King!

Some people are born to rub you the wrong way. Brother Gemt was born to rub the world the wrong way.

2

Mabberton burned well. All the villages burned well that summer. Makin called it a hot bastard of a summer, too mean to give out rain, and he wasn't wrong. Dust rose behind us when we rode in; smoke when we rode out.

'Who'd be a farmer?' Makin liked to ask questions.

'Who'd be a farmer's daughter?' I nodded toward Rike, rolling in his saddle, almost tired enough to fall out, wearing a stupid grin and a bolt of samite cloth over his half-plate. Where he found samite in Mabberton I never did get to know.

'Brother Rike does enjoy his simple pleasures,' Makin said.

He did. Rike had a hunger for it. Hungry like the fire.

The flames fair ate up Mabberton. I put the torch to the thatched inn, and the fire chased us out. Just one more bloody day in the years' long death throes of our broken empire.

Makin wiped at his sweat, smearing himself all over with soot-stripes. He had a talent for getting dirty, did

Makin. 'You weren't above those simple pleasures your-self, Brother Jorg.'

I couldn't argue there. 'How old are you?' that fat farmer had wanted to know. Old enough to pay a call on his daughters. The fat girl had a lot to say, just like her father. Screeched like a barn owl: hurt my ears with it. I liked the older one better. She was quiet enough. So quiet you'd give a twist here or there just to check she hadn't died of fright. Though I don't suppose either of them was quiet when the fire reached them…

Gemt rode up and spoiled my imaginings.

'The Baron's men will see that smoke from ten miles. You shouldn'ta burned it.' He shook his head, his stupid mane of ginger hair bobbing this way and that.

'Shouldn'ta,' his idiot brother joined in, calling from the old grey. We let him ride the old grey with the cart hitched up. The grey wouldn't leave the road. That horse was cleverer than Maical.

Gemt always wanted to point stuff out. 'You shouldn'ta put them bodies down the well, we'll go thirsty now.' 'You shouldn'ta killed that priest, we'll have bad luck now.' 'If we'd gone easy on her we'd have a ransom from Baron Kennick.' I just ached to put my knife through his throat. Right then. Just to lean out and plant it in his neck. 'What's that? What say you, Brother Gemt? Bubble, bubble? Shouldn'ta stabbed your bulgy old Adam's apple?'

'Oh no!' I cried, all shocked like. 'Quick, Little Rikey, go piss on Mabberton. Got to put that fire out.'

'Baron's men will see it,' said Gemt, stubborn and red-faced. He went red as a beet if you crossed him. That red face just made me want to kill him even more. I didn't, though. You got responsibilities when you're a leader. You got a responsibility not to kill too many of your men. Or who're you going to lead?

The column bunched up around us, the way it always did when something was up. I pulled on Gerrod's reins and he stopped with a snicker and a stamp. I watched Gemt and waited. Waited until all thirty-eight of my brothers gathered around, and Gemt got so red you'd think his ears would bleed.

'Where we all going, my brothers?' I asked, and I stood in my stirrups so I could look out over their ugly faces. I asked it in my quiet voice and they all hushed to hear.

'Where?' I asked again. 'Surely it isn't just me that knows? Do I keep secrets from you, my brothers?'

Rike looked a bit confused at this, furrowing his brow. Fat Burlow came up on my right, on my left the Nuban with his teeth so white in that soot-black face. Silence.

'Brother Gemt can tell us. He knows what should be and what is.' I smiled, though my hand still ached with wanting my dagger in his neck. 'Where we going, Brother Gemt?'

'Wennith, on the Horse Coast,' he said, all reluctant, not wanting to agree to anything.

'Well and good. How we going to get there? Near forty of us on our fine oh-so-stolen horses?'

Gemt set his jaw. He could see where I was going.

'How we going to get there, if we want us a slice of the pie while it's still nice and hot?' I asked.

'Lich Road!' Rike called out, all pleased that he knew the answer.

'Lich Road,' I repeated, still quiet and smiling. 'What other way could we go?' I looked at the Nuban, holding his dark eyes. I couldn't read him, but I let him read me.

'Ain't no other way.'

Rike's on a roll, I thought, he don't know what game's being played, but he likes his part.

'Do the Baron's men know where we're going?' I asked Fat Burlow.

'War dogs follow the front,' he said. Fat Burlow ain't stupid. His jowls quiver when he speaks, but he ain't stupid.

'So…' I looked around them, real slow-like. 'So, the Baron knows where bandits such as ourselves will be going, and he knows the way we've got to go.' I let that sink in. 'And I just lit a bloody big fire that tells him and his what a bad idea it'd be to follow.'

I stuck Gemt with my knife then. I didn't need to, but I wanted it. He danced pretty enough too, bubble bubble on his blood, and fell off his horse. His red face went pale quick enough.

'Maical,' I said. 'Take his head.'

And he did.

Gemt just chose a bad moment.

Whatever broke Brother Maical left the outside untouched. He looked as solid and as tough and as sour as the rest of them. Until you asked him a question.

3

'Two dead, two wrigglers.' Makin wore that big grin of his.

We'd have camped by the gibbet in any case, but Makin had ridden on ahead to check the ground. I thought the news that two of the four gibbet cages held live prisoners would cheer the brothers.

'Two,' Rike grumbled. He'd tired himself out, and a tired Little Rikey always sees a gibbet as half empty.

'Two!' the Nuban hollered down the line.

I could see some of the lads exchanging coin on their bets. The Lich Road is as boring as a Sunday sermon. It runs straight and level. So straight it gets so as you'd kill for a left turn or a right turn. So level you'd cheer a slope. And on every side, marsh, midges, midges and more marsh. On the Lich Road it didn't get any better than two caged wrigglers on a gibbet.

Strange that I didn't think to question what business a gibbet had standing out there in the middle of nowhere. I took it as a bounty. Somebody had left their prisoners to die, dangling in cages at the roadside. A strange spot to choose, but free entertainment for my little band nonetheless. The brothers were eager, so I nudged Gerrod into a trot. A good horse, Gerrod. He shook off his weariness and clattered along. There's no road like the Lich Road for clattering along.

'Wrigglers!' Rike gave a shout and they were all racing to catch up.

I let Gerrod have his head. He wouldn't let any horse get past him. Not on this road. Not with every yard of it paved, every flagstone fitting with the next so close a blade of grass couldn't hope for the light. Not a stone turned, not a stone worn. Built on a bog, mind you!

I beat them to the wrigglers, of course. None of them could touch Gerrod. Certainly not with me on his back and them all half as heavy again. At the gibbet I turned to look back at them, strung out along the road. I yelled out, wild with the joy of it, loud enough to wake the head-cart. Gemt would be in there, bouncing around at the back.

Makin reached me first, even though he'd rode the distance twice before.

'Let the Baron's men come,' I told him. 'The Lich Road is as good as any bridge. Ten men could hold an army here. Them that wants to flank us can drown in the bog.'

Makin nodded, still hunting his breath.

'The ones who built this road … if they'd make me a castle—' Thunder in the east cut across my words.

'If the Road-men built castles we'd never get in anywhere,' Makin said. 'Be happy they're gone.'

We watched the brothers come in. The sunset turned the marsh pools to orange fire, and I thought of Mabberton.

'A good day, Brother Makin,' I said.

'Indeed, Brother Jorg,' he said.

So, the brothers came and set to arguing over the wrigglers. I went and sat against the loot-cart to read while the light stayed with us and the rain held off. The day left me in mind to read Plutarch. I had him all to myself, sandwiched between leather covers. Some worthy monk spent a lifetime on that book. A lifetime hunched over it, brush in hand. Here the gold, for halo, sun, and scrollwork. Here a blue like poison, bluer than a noon sky. Tiny vermilion dots to make a bed of flowers. Probably went blind over it, that monk. Probably poured his life in here, from young lad to grey-head, prettying up old Plutarch's words.

The thunder rolled, the wrigglers wriggled and howled, and I sat reading words that were older than old before the Road-men built their roads.

'You're cowards! Women with your swords and axes!' One of the crow-feasts on the gibbet had a mouth on him.

'Not a man amongst you. All pederasts, trailing up here after that little boy.' He curled his words up at the end like a Merssy-man.

'There's a fella over here got an opinion about you, Brother Jorg!' Makin called out.

A drop of rain hit my nose. I closed the cover on

Plutarch. He'd waited a while to tell me about Sparta and Lycurgus, he could wait some more and not get wet doing it. The wriggler had more to say and I let him tell it to my back. On the road you've got to wrap a book well to keep the rain out. Ten turns of oilcloth, ten more turns the other way, then stash it under a cloak in a saddlebag. A good saddlebag mind, none of that junk from the Thurtans, good double-stitched leather from the Horse Coast.

The lads parted to let me up close. The gibbet stank worse than the head-cart, a crude thing of fresh-cut timber. Four cages hung there. Two held dead men. *Very* dead men. Legs dangling through the bars, raven-pecked to the bone. Flies thick about them, like a second skin, black and buzzing. The lads had taken a few pokes at one of the wrigglers, and he didn't look too cheerful for it. In fact he looked as if he'd pegged it. Which was a waste, as we had a whole night ahead of us, and I'd have said as much, but for the wriggler with the mouth.

'So now the boy comes over! He's finished looking for lewd pictures in his stolen book.' He sat crouched up in his cage, his feet all bleeding and raw. An old man, maybe forty, all black hair and grey beard and dark eyes glittering. 'Take the pages to wipe your dung, boy,' he said fierce-like, grabbing the bars all of a sudden, making the cage swing. 'It's the only use you'll get from it.'

'We could set a slow fire?' Rike said. Even Rike

knew the old man just wanted us angry, so we'd finish him quick. 'Like we did at the Turston gibbets.'

A few chuckles went up at that. Not from Makin though. He had a frown on under his dirt and soot, staring at the wriggler. I held up a hand to quiet them down.

'It'd be a shameful waste of such a fine book, Father Gomst,' I said.

Like Makin, I'd recognized Gomst through all that beard and hair. Without that accent though he'd have got roasted.

'Especially an "On Lycurgus" written in high Latin, not that pidgin-Romano they teach in church.'

'You know me?' He asked it in a cracked voice, weepy all of a sudden.

'Of course I do.' I pushed both hands through my lovely locks, and set my hair back so he could see me proper in the gloom. I have the sharp dark looks of the Ancraths. 'You're Father Gomst, come to take me back to school.'

'Pr-prin…' He was blubbing now, unable to get his words out. Disgusting really. Made me feel as if I'd bitten something rotten.

'Prince Honorous Jorg Ancrath, at your service.' I did my court bow.

'Wh-what became of Captain Bortha?' Father Gomst swung gently in his cage, all confused.

'Captain Bortha, sir!' Makin snapped a salute and stepped up. He had blood on him from the first wriggler.

15

We had us a deathly silence then. Even the chirp and whir of the marsh hushed down to a whisper. The brothers looked from me, back to the old priest, and back to me, mouths hanging open. Little Rikey couldn't have looked more surprised if you'd asked him nine times six.

The rain chose that moment to fall, all at once as if the Lord Almighty had emptied his chamber pot over us. The gloom that had been gathering set thick as treacle.

'Prince Jorg!' Father Gomst had to shout over the rain. 'The night! You've got to run!' He held the bars of his cage, white-knuckled, wide eyes unblinking in the downpour, staring into the darkness.

And through the night, through the rain, over the marsh where no man could walk, we saw them coming. We saw their lights. Pale lights such as the dead burn in deep pools where men aren't meant to look. Lights that'd promise whatever a man could want, and would set you chasing them, hunting answers and finding only cold mud, deep and hungry.

I never liked Father Gomst. He'd been telling me what to do since I was six, most often with the back of his hand as the reason.

'Run Prince Jorg! Run!' old Gomsty howled, sickeningly self-sacrificing.

So I stood my ground.

Brother Gains wasn't the cook because he was good at cooking. He was just bad at everything else.

4

The dead came on through the rain, the ghosts of the bog-dead, of the drowned, and of men whose corpses were given to the mire. I saw Red Kent run blind and flounder in the marsh. A few of the brothers had the sense to take the road when they ran, most ended in the mire.

Father Gomst started praying in his cage, shouting out the words like a shield: 'Father who art in heaven protect thy son. Father who art in heaven.' Faster and faster, as the fear got into him.

The first of them came up over the sucking pool, and onto the Lichway. He had a glow about him like moonlight, something that you knew would never warm you. You could see his body limned in the light, with the rain racing through him and bouncing on the road.

Nobody stood with me. The Nuban ran, eyes wide in a dark face. Fat Burlow looking as if the blood was let from him. Rike screaming like a child. Even Makin, with a horror on him.

I held my arms wide to the rain. I could feel it beat on me. I didn't have so many years under my belt, but even to me the rain fell like memory. It woke wild nights in me when I stood on the Keep Tower, on the edge above a high fall, near drowned in the deluge and daring the lightning to touch me.

'Our Father who art in heaven. Father who art...' Gomst started to gabble when the lich came close. It burned with a cold fire and you could feel it licking at your bones.

I kept my arms wide and my face to the rain.

'My father isn't in heaven, Gomsty,' I said. 'He's in his castle, counting out his men.'

The dead thing closed on me, and I looked in its eyes. Hollow they were.

'What have you got?' I said.

And it showed me.

And I showed it.

There's a reason I'm going to win this war. Everyone alive has been fighting a battle that grew old before they were born. I cut my teeth on the wooden soldiers in my father's war-room. There's a reason I'm going to win where they failed. It's because I understand the game.

'Hell,' the dead man said. 'I've got hell.'

And he flowed into me, cold as dying, edged like a razor.

I felt my mouth curl in a smile. I heard my laughing over the rain.

A knife is a scary thing right enough, held to your throat, sharp and cool. The fire too, and the rack. And an old ghost on the Lichway. All of them might give you pause. Until you realize what they are. They're just ways to lose the game. You lose the game, and what have you lost? You've lost the game.

That's the secret, and it amazes me that it's mine and mine alone. I saw the game for what it was the night when Count Renar's men caught our carriage. There was a storm that night too, I remember the din of rain on the carriage roof and the thunder beneath it.

Big Jan had fair hauled the door off its hinges to get us out. He only had time for me though. He threw me clear; into a briar patch so thick that the Count's men persuaded themselves I'd run into the night. They didn't want to search it. But I hadn't run. I'd hung there in the thorns, and I saw them kill Big Jan. I saw it in the frozen moments the lightning gave me.

I saw what they did to Mother, and how long it took. They broke little William's head against a milestone. Golden curls and blood. And I'll admit that William was the first of my brothers, and he did have his hooks in me, with his chubby hands and laughing. Since then I've taken on many a brother, and evil ones at that, so I'd not miss one or three. But at the time, it did hurt to see little William broken like that, like a toy. Like something worthless.

When they killed him, Mother wouldn't hold her peace, so they slit her throat. I was stupid then, being only nine, and I fought to save them both. But the thorns held me tight. I've learned to appreciate thorns since.

The thorns taught me the game. They let me understand what all those grim and serious men who've fought the Hundred War, have yet to learn. You can only win the game when you understand that it *is* a game. Let a man play chess, and tell him that every pawn is his friend. Let him think both bishops holy. Let him remember happy days in the shadows of his castles. Let him love his queen. Watch him lose them all.

'What have you got for me, dead thing?' I asked.

It's a game. I will play my pieces.

I felt him cold inside me. I saw his death. I saw his despair. And his hunger. And I gave it back. I'd expected more, but he was only dead.

I showed him the empty time where my memory won't go. I let him look there.

He ran from me then. He ran, and I chased him. But only to the edge of the marsh. Because it's a game. And I'm going to win.

5

Four years earlier

For the longest time I studied revenge to the exclusion of all else. I built my first torture chamber in the dark vaults of imagination. Lying on bloody sheets in the Healing Hall I discovered doors within my mind that I'd not found before, doors that even a child of nine knows should not be opened. Doors that never close again.

I threw them wide.

Sir Reilly found me, hanging within the hook-briar, not ten yards from the smoking ruin of the carriage. They almost missed me. I saw them reach the bodies on the road. I watched them through the briar, silver glimpses of Sir Reilly's armour, and flashes of red from the tabards of Ancrath foot-soldiers.

Mother was easy to find, in her silks.

'Sweet Jesu! It's the Queen!' Sir Reilly had them turn her over. 'Gently! Show some respect—' He broke off with a gasp. The Count's men hadn't left her pretty.

'Sir! Big Jan's over here, Grem and Jassar too.' I saw them heave Jan over, then turn to the other guardsmen.

'They'd better be dead!' Sir Reilly spat. 'Look for the princes!'

I didn't see them find Will, but I knew they had by the silence that spread across the men. I let my chin fall back to my chest and watched the dark patterning of blood on the dry leaves around my feet.

'Ah, hell . . .' One of the men spoke at last.

'Get him on a horse. Easy with him,' Sir Reilly said. A crack ran through his voice. 'And find the heir!' With more vigour, but no hope.

I tried to call to them, but the strength had run from me, I couldn't even lift my head.

'He's not here, Sir Reilly.'

'They've taken him as a hostage,' Sir Reilly said.

He had part of it right, something held me against my will.

'Set him by the Queen.'

'Gentle! Gentle with him . . .'

'Secure them,' Sir Reilly said. 'We ride hard for the Tall Castle.'

Part of me wanted to let them go. I felt no pain any more, just a dull ache, and even that was fading. A peace folded me with the promise of forgetting.

'Sir!' A shout went up from one of the men.

I heard the clank of armour as Sir Reilly strode across to see.

'Piece of a shield?' he asked.

'Found it in the mud, the carriage wheel must have pushed it under.' The soldier paused. I heard scraping. 'Looks like a black wing to me . . .'

'A crow. A crow on a red field. It's Count Renar's colours,' Reilly said.

Count Renar? I had a name. A black crow on a red field. The insignia flashed across my eyes, seared deep by the lightning of last night's storm. A fire lit within me, and the pain from a hundred hooks burned in every limb. A groan escaped me. My lips parted, dry skin tearing.

And Reilly found me.

'There's something here!' I heard him curse as the hook-briar found every chink in his armour. 'Quickly now! Pull this stuff apart.'

'Dead.' I heard the whisper from behind Sir Reilly as he cut me free.

'He's so white.'

I guess the briar near bled me dry.

So they fetched a cart and took me back. I didn't sleep. I watched the sky turn black, and I thought.

In the Healing Hall Friar Glen and his helper, Inch, dug the hooks from my flesh. My tutor, Lundist, arrived while they had me on the table with their knives out. He had a book with him, the size of a Teuton shield, and three times as heavy by the look of it. Lundist had more strength in that wizened old stick of a body than anyone guessed.

24

'Those are fire-cleaned knives I hope, Friar?' Lundist carried the accent of his homelands in the Utter East, and a tendency to leave half of a word unspoken, as if an intelligent listener should be able to fill in the blanks.

'It is purity of spirit that will keep corruption from the flesh, Tutor,' Friar Glen said. He spared Lundist a disapproving glance, and returned to his digging.

'Even so, clean the knives, Friar. Holy office will prove scant protection from the King's ire if the Prince dies in your halls.' Lundist set his book down on the table beside me, rattling a tray of vials at the far end. He lifted the cover and turned to a marked page.

'"The thorns of the hook-briar are like to find the bone."' He traced a wrinkled yellow finger down the lines. '"The points can break off and sour the wound."'

Friar Glen gave a sharp jab at that, which made me cry out. He set his knife down and turned to face Lundist. I could see only the friar's back, the brown cloth straining over his shoulders, dark with sweat over his spine.

'Tutor Lundist,' he said. 'A man in your profession is wont to think all things may be learned from the pages of a book, or the right scroll. Learning has its place, sirrah, but do not think to lecture me on healing on the basis of an evening spent with an old tome!'

Well, Friar Glen won that argument. The sergeant-at-arms had to 'help' Tutor Lundist from the hall.

I guess even at nine I had a serious lack of spiritual purity, for my wounds soured within two days, and for nine weeks I lay in fever, chasing dark dreams along death's borderlands.

They tell me I raged and howled. That I raved as the pus oozed from slices where the briar had held me. I remember the stink of corruption. It had a kind of sweetness to it, a sweetness that'd make you want to hurl.

Inch, the friar's aide, grew tired of holding me down, though he had the arms of a lumberjack. In the end they tied me to my bed.

I learned from Tutor Lundist that the friar would not attend me after the first week. Friar Glen said a devil was in me. How else could a child speak such horror?

In the fourth week I slipped the bonds that held me to my pallet, and set a fire in the hall. I have no memory of the escape, or my capture in the woods. When they cleared the ruin, they found the remains of Inch, with the poker from the hearth lodged in his chest.

Many times I stood at the Door. I had seen my mother and brother thrown through that doorway, torn and broken, and in dreams my feet would take me to stand there, time and again. I lacked the courage to follow them, held on the barbs and hooks of cowardice.

Sometimes I saw the dead-lands across a black river, sometimes across a chasm spanned by a narrow bridge of stone. Once I saw the Door in the guise of the portals to my father's throne room, but edged with frost and weeping pus from every join. I had but to set my hand upon the handle . . .

The Count of Renar kept me alive. The promise of his

pain crushed my own under its heel. Hate will keep you alive where love fails.

And then one day my fever left me. My wounds remained angry and red, but they closed. They fed me chicken in soup, and my strength crept back, a stranger to me.

The spring came to paint the leaves back upon the trees. I had my strength, but I felt something else had been taken. Taken so completely I could no longer name it.

The sun returned, and, much to Friar Glen's distaste, Lundist returned to instruct me once more.

The first time he came, I sat abed. I watched him set out his books upon the table.

'Your father will see you on his return from Gelleth,' Lundist said. His voice held a note of reproach, but not for me. 'The death of the Queen and Prince William weigh heavy on him. When the pain eases he will surely come to speak with you.'

I didn't understand why Lundist should feel the need to lie. I knew my father would not waste time on me whilst it seemed I would die. I knew he would see me when seeing me served some end.

'Tell me, tutor,' I said. 'Is revenge a science, or an art?'

6

The rain faltered when the spirits fled. I'd only broken the one, but the others ran too, back to whatever pools they haunted. Maybe my one had been their leader; maybe men become cowards in death. I don't know.

As to my own cowards, they had nowhere to flee, and I found them easily enough. I found Makin first. He, at least, was headed back toward me.

'So you found a pair then?' I called to him.

He paused a moment and looked at me. The rain didn't fall so heavy now, but he still looked like a drowned rat. The water ran in rivulets over his breastplate, in and out of the dents. He checked the marsh to either side, still nervy, and lowered his sword.

'A man who's got no fear is missing a friend, Jorg,' he said, and a smile found its way onto those thick lips of his. 'Running ain't no bad thing. Leastways if you run in the right direction.' He waved a hand toward where Rike wrestled with a clump of bulrushes, the mud up to his chest already. 'Fear helps a man pick his fights. You're fighting them all, my prince.' And he bowed, there on the Lichway with the rain dripping off him.

I spared a glance for Rike. Maical had similar problems in a pool to the other side of the road. Only he'd got his problems up to the neck.

'I'm going to fight them all in the end,' I said to him.

'Pick your fights,' Makin said.

'I'll pick my ground,' I said. 'I'll pick my ground, but I'm not running. Not ever. That's been done, and we still have the war. I'm going to win it, Brother Makin, it's going to end with me.'

He bowed again. Not so deep, but this time I felt he meant it. 'That's why I'll follow you, Prince. Wherever it takes us.'

For the moment it took us to fishing brothers out of the mud. We got Maical first, even though Rike howled and cursed us. As the rain thinned, I could see the grey and the head-cart off in the distance. The grey had the sense to keep to the road, even when Maical didn't. If Maical had led the grey into the mire I'd have left him to sink.

We pulled Rike out next. When we reached him the mud had almost found his mouth. Nothing but his white face showed above the pool, but that didn't stop him shouting his foulnesses all the way. We found most of them on the road, but six got sucked down too quick, lost forever; probably getting ready to haunt the next band of travellers.

'I'm going back for old Gomsty,' I said.

We'd come a way down the road and the light had pretty much gone. Looking back you couldn't see the gibbets, just grey veils of rain. Out in the marsh the dead waited. I felt their cold thoughts crawling on my skin.

I didn't ask any of them to go with me. I knew none of them would, and it don't do for a leader to ask and be told no.

'What do you want with that old priest, Brother Jorg?' Makin said. He was asking me not to go; only he couldn't come out and say it.

'You still want to burn him up?' Even the mud couldn't hide Rike's sudden cheer.

'I do,' I said. 'But that's not why I'm getting him.' And I set off back along the Lichway.

The rain and the darkness wrapped me. I lost the brothers, waiting on the road behind. Gomst and the gibbets lay ahead. I walked in a cocoon of silence, with nothing but the soft words of the rain, and the sound of my boots on the Lichway.

I'll tell you now. That silence almost beat me. It's the silence that scares me. It's the blank page on which I can write my own fears. The spirits of the dead have nothing on it. The dead one tried to show me hell, but it was a pale imitation of the horror I can paint on the darkness in a quiet moment.

And there he hung, Father Gomst, priest to the House of Ancrath.

'Father,' I said, and I sketched him a bow. In truth though, I was in no mood for play. I had me a hollow ache behind my eyes. The kind that gets people killed.

He looked at me wide-eyed, as if I was a bog-spirit crawled out of the mire.

I went to the chain that held his cage up. 'Brace yourself, Father.'

The sword I drew had slit old Bovid Tor not twenty-four hours before. Now I swung it to free a priest. The chain gave beneath its edge. They'd put some magic, or some devilry, in that blade. Father told me the Ancraths wielded it for four generations, and took it from the House of Or. So the steel was old before we Ancraths first lay hands upon it. Old before I stole it.

The birdcage fell to the path, hard and heavy. Father Gomst cried out, and his head hit the bars, leaving a livid cross-work across his forehead. They'd bound the cage-door with wire. It gave before the edge of our ancestral sword, twice stolen. I thought of Father for a moment, imaged his face twist in outrage at the use of so high a blade for such lowly work. I've a good imagination, but putting any emotion on the rock of Father's face came hard.

Gomst crawled out, stiff and weak. As the old should be. I liked that he had the grace to feel the years on his shoulders. Some the years just toughened.

'Father Gomst,' I said. 'Best hurry now, or the marsh dead may come out to scare us with their wailing and a-moaning.'

He looked at me then, drawing back as if he'd seen a ghost, then softening.

'Jorg,' he said, all full of compassion. Brimming with it, spilling it from his eyes as if it wasn't just the rain. 'What has happened to you?'

I won't lie to you. Half of me wanted to stick the knife into him there and then, just as with red-faced Gemt. More than half. My hand itched with the need to pull that knife. My head ached with it, as if a vice were tightening against my temples.

I've been known to be contrary. When something pushes me, I shove back. Even if the one doing the pushing is me. It would have been easy to gut him then and there. Satisfying. But the need was too urgent. I felt pushed.

I smiled and said, 'Forgive me, Father, for I have sinned.'

And old Gomsty, though he was stiff from the cage, and sore in every limb, bowed his head to hear my confession.

I spoke into the rain, low and quiet. Loud enough for Father Gomst though, and loud enough for the dead who haunted the marsh about us. I told of the things I'd done. I told of the things I would do. In a soft voice I told my plans to all with ears to hear. The dead left us then.

'You're the devil!' Father Gomst took a step back, and clutched the cross at his neck.

'If that's what it takes.' I didn't dispute him. 'But I've confessed, and you must forgive me.'

'Abomination…' The word escaped him in a slow breath.

'And more besides,' I agreed. 'Now forgive me.'

Father Gomst found his wits at last, but still he held back. 'What do you want with me, Lucifer?'

A fair question. 'I want to win,' I said.

He shook his head at that, so I explained.

'Some men I can bind with who I am. Some I can bind with where I'm going. Others need to know who walks with me. I've given you my confession. I repent. Now God walks with me, and you're the priest who will tell the faithful that I am His warrior, His instrument, the Sword of the Almighty.'

A silence stood between us, measured in heartbeats.

'*Ego te absolvo.*' Father Gomst got the words past trembling lips.

We walked back along the path then, and reached the others by and by. Makin had them lined up and ready. Waiting in the dark, with a single torch, and the hooded lantern hung up on the head-cart.

'Captain Bortha,' I said to Makin, 'time we set off. We've got a ways before us till we reach the Horse Coast.'

'And the priest?' he asked.

'Perhaps we'll detour past the Tall Castle, and drop him off.'

My headache bit, hard.

Maybe it was something to do with having an old ghost haunt its way through to the very marrow of my bones, but today my headaches felt more like somebody prodding me with a stick, herding me along, and it was really beginning to fuck me off.

'I think we *will* call in at the Tall Castle.' I ground my teeth together against the daggers in my head. 'Hand old Gomsty here over in person. I'm sure my father has been worried about me.'

Rike and Maical gave me stupid stares. Fat Burlow and Red Kent swapped glances. The Nuban rolled his eyes and made his wards.

I looked at Makin, tall, broad in the shoulder, black hair plastered down by the rain. *He's my knight,* I thought. *Gomst is my bishop, the Tall Castle my rook.* Then I thought of Father. I needed a king. You can't play the game without a king. I thought of Father, and it felt good. After the dead one, I'd begun to wonder. The dead one showed me his hell, and I had laughed at it. But now I thought of Father, and it felt good to know I could still feel fear.

7

We rode through the night and the Lichway brought us from the marsh. Dawn found us at Norwood, drear and grey. The town lay in ruin. Its ashes still held the acrid ghost of smoke that lingers when the fire is gone.

'The Count of Renar,' said Makin at my side. 'He grows bold to attack Ancrath protectorates so openly.' He shed the roadspeak like a cloak.

'How can we know who wrought such wickedness?' Father Gomst asked, his face as grey as his beard. 'Perhaps Baron Kennick's men raided down the Lichway. It was Kennick's men who caged me on the gibbet.'

The brothers spread out among the ruins. Rike elbowed Fat Burlow aside, and vanished into the first building, which was nothing but a roofless shell of stone.

'Shit-poor bog-farmers! Just like fecking Mabberton.' The violence of his search drowned out any further complaint.

I remembered Norwood on fete day, hung with ribbons. Mother walked with the burgermeister. William and I had treacle-apples.

'But these were *my* shit-poor bog-farmers,' I said. I turned to look at old Gomsty. 'There are no bodies. This is Count Renar's work.'

Makin nodded. 'We'll find the pyre in the fields to the west. Renar burns them all together. The living and the dead.'

Gomst crossed himself and muttered a prayer.

War is a thing of beauty, as I've said before, and those who say otherwise are losing. I put a smile on, though it didn't fit me. 'Brother Makin, it seems the Count has made a move. It behoves us, as fellow soldiers, to appreciate his artistry. Have yourself a ride around. I want to know how he played his game.'

Renar. First Father Gomst, now Renar. As though the spirit in the mire had turned a key, and the ghosts of my past were marching through, one by one.

Makin gave a nod and cantered off. Not into town but out along the stream, following it up to the thickets beyond the market field.

'Father Gomst,' I said in my most polite court-voice. 'Pray tell, where were you when Baron Kennick's men found you?' It made no sense that our family priest should be taken on a raid.

'The hamlet of Jessop, my prince,' Gomst replied, wary and looking anywhere but at me. 'Should we not ride on? We'll be safe in the homelands. The raids won't reach past Hanton.'

True, I thought, *so why would you come out into danger?*

'The hamlet of Jessop? Can't say I've even heard of it, Father Gomst,' I said, still nice as nice. 'Which means it won't be much more than three huts and a pig.'

Rike stormed out of the house, blacker than the Nuban with all the ash on him, and spitting mad. He made for the next doorway. 'Burlow, you fat bastard! You set me up!' If Little Rikey couldn't find himself some loot then somebody else would pay. Always.

Gomst looked glad of the diversion, but I drew his attention back. 'Father Gomst, you were telling me about Jessop.' I took the reins from his hands.

'A bog-town, my prince. A nothing. A place where they cut peat for the protectorate. Seventeen huts and perhaps a few more pigs.' He tried a laugh, but it came out too sharp and nervy.

'So you journeyed there to offer absolution to the poor?' I held his eye.

'Well…'

'Out past Hanton, out to the edge of the marsh, out into danger,' I said. 'You're a very holy man, Father.'

He bowed his head at that.

Jessop. The name rang a bell. A bell with a deep voice, slow and solemn. *Send not to ask for whom the bell tolls…*

'Jessop is where the marsh-tide takes the dead,' I said. I saw the words on the mouth of old Tutor Lundist as I spoke them. I saw the map behind him, pinned to the study wall, currents marked in black ink. 'It's a slow current but sure. The marsh keeps her secrets, but not forever, and Jessop is where she tells them.'

'That big man, Rike, he's strangling the fat one.' Father Gomst nodded toward the town.

'My father sent you to look at the dead.' I didn't let Gomst divert me with small talk. 'Because you'd recognize me.'

Gomst's mouth framed a 'no', but every other muscle in him said 'yes'. You'd think priests would be better liars, what with their job and all.

'He's still looking for me? After four years!' Four weeks would have surprised me.

Gomst edged back in his saddle. He spread his hands helplessly. 'The Queen is heavy with child. Sageous tells the King it will be a boy. I had to confirm the succession.'

Ah! The 'succession'. That sounded more like the father I knew. And the Queen? Now that put an edge on the day.

'Sageous?' I asked.

'A heathen bone-picker, newly come to court.' Gomst spat the words as if they tasted sour.

The pause grew into a silence.

'Rike!' I said. Not a shout, but loud enough to reach him. 'Put Fat Burlow down, or I'll have to kill you.'

Rike let go, and Burlow hit the ground like the three hundred pound lump of lard that he was. I guess that of the two, Burlow looked slightly more purple in the face, but only a little. Rike came toward us with his hands out before him, twisting as though he already had them around my neck. 'You!'

No sign of Makin, and Father Gomst would be as useful as a fart in the wind against Little Rikey with a rage on him.

'You! Where's the fecking gold you promised us?' A score of heads popped out of windows and doors at that. Even Fat Burlow looked up, sucking in a breath as if it came through a straw.

I let my hand slip from the pommel of my sword. It doesn't do to sacrifice too many pawns. Rike had only a dozen yards to go. I swung off Gerrod's saddle and patted his nose, my back to the town.

'There's more than one kind of gold in Norwood,' I said. Loud enough but not too loud. Then I turned and walked past Rike. I didn't look at him. Give a man like Rike a moment, and he'll take it.

'Don't you be telling me about no farmers' daughters this time, you little bastard!' He followed me roaring, but I'd let the heat out of him. He just had wind and noise now. 'That fecker of a count staked them all out to burn already.'

I made for Midway Street, leading up to the burgermeister's house from the market field. As we passed him, Brother Gains looked up from the cook-fire he'd started. He clambered to his feet to follow and watch the fun.

The grain-store tower had never looked like much. It looked less impressive now, all scorched, the stones split in the heat. Before they burned them all away, the grain sacks would have hidden the trapdoor. I found it with a little prodding. Rike huffed and puffed behind me all the time.

'Open it up.' I pointed to the ring set in the stone slab.

Rike didn't need telling twice. He got down and heaved the slab up as if it weighed nothing. And there they were, barrel after barrel, all huddled up in the dusty dark.

'The old burgermeister kept the festival beer under the grain-tower. Every local knows that. A little stream runs down there to keep it all nice and cool-like. Looks like, what, twenty? Twenty barrels of golden festival beer.' I smiled.

Rike didn't smile back. He stayed on his hands and knees, and let his eye wander up the blade of my sword. I imagined how it must tickle against his throat.

'See now, Jorg, Brother Jorg, I didn't mean...' he started. Even with my sword at his neck he had a mean look to him.

Makin clattered up and came to stand at my shoulder. I kept the blade at Rike's throat.

'I may be little, Little Rikey, but I ain't a bastard,' I said, soft, in my killing voice. 'Isn't that right, Father Gomst? If I was a bastard you wouldn't have to risk life and limb to search the dead for me, now would you?'

'Prince Jorg, let Captain Bortha kill this savage.' Gomst must have found his composure somewhere. 'We'll ride on to the Tall Castle and your father—'

'My father can damn well wait!' I shouted. I bit back the rest, angry at being angry.

Rike forgot about the sword for a moment. 'What the feck is all this "prince" shit? What the feck is all this "Captain Bortha" shit? And when do I get to drink the fecking beer?'

We had ourselves as full an audience then as we'd get, all the brothers about us in a circle.

'Well,' I said. 'Since you ask so nice, Brother Rike, I'll tell you.'

Makin raised his brows at me and he took a grip on his sword. I waved him down.

'The Captain Bortha shit is Makin being Captain Makin Bortha of the Ancrath Imperial Guard. The prince shit is me being the beloved son and heir of King Olidan of the House of Ancrath. And we can drink the beer now, because today is my fourteenth birthday, and how else would you toast my health?'

Every brotherhood has a pecking order. With brothers like mine you don't want to be at the bottom of that order. You're liable to get pecked to death. Brother Jobe had just the right mix of whipped cur and rabies to stay alive there.

8

So we sat on the tumbled stones of the burgermeister's house and drank beer. The brothers drank deep and called out my name. Some had it 'Brother Jorg', some had it 'Prince Jorg', but all of them saw me with new eyes. Rike watched me, beer-foam in his stubbled beard, the line of my sword across his neck. I could see him weighing the odds, a slow ballet of possibilities working their way across his low forehead. I didn't wait for the word 'ransom' to bubble to the surface.

'He wants me dead, Little Rikey,' I said. 'He sent Gomsty out to find proof I was dead, not to find me. He's got a new queen now.'

Rike gave a grin that had more scowl than grin in it, then belched mightily. 'You ran from a castle with gold and women, to ride with us? What idiot would do that?'

I sipped my beer. It tasted sour, but that seemed right somehow. 'An idiot who knows he won't win the war with the King's guard at his side,' I said.

'What war, Jorg?' The Nuban sat close by, not drinking. He always spoke slow and serious. 'You want to beat the Count? Baron Kennick?'

'The War,' I said. 'All of it.'

Red Kent came over from the barrels, his helm brimming with ale. 'Never happen,' he said. He lifted the helm and half-drained it in four swallows. 'So you're Prince of Ancrath? A copper-crown kingdom. Must be dozens with as good a claim on the high throne. Each of them with their own army.'

'More like fifty,' Rike growled.

'Closer to a hundred,' I said. 'I've counted.'

A hundred fragments of empire grinding away at each other in a never-ending cycle of little wars, feuds, skirmishes, kingdoms waxing, waning, waxing again, lifetimes spent in conflict and nothing changing. Mine to change, to end, to win.

I finished my beer and got up to find Makin.

I didn't have to look far. I found him with the horses, checking his stallion, Firejump.

'What did you find?' I asked him.

Makin pursed his lips. 'I found the pyre. About two hundred, all dead. They didn't light it though – probably scared off.' He waved toward the west. 'They came in on foot, up the marsh road, and over the ridge yonder. Had about twenty archers in the thicket by the stream, to pick off folks that tried to run.'

'How many men altogether?' I asked.

'Probably a hundred. Foot soldiers most of them.' He yawned and ran a hand from forehead to chin. 'Two days gone now. We're safe enough.'

I felt invisible thorns scratching at me, sharp hooks in my skin. 'Come with me,' I told him.

Makin followed me back to the steps and fallen pillars at the burgermeister's doors. The brothers had Maical staving in a second barrel.

'What ho, Captain!' Burlow called out at Makin, his voice still hoarse from Rike's strangling. A laugh went up at that, and I let it run its course. I felt the thorns again, sharp and deep. Sharpening me up for something. Two hundred bodies in a heap. All dead.

'Cap'n Makin tells me we're going to have company,' I said.

Makin's brows rose at that but I ignored him. 'Twenty swords, rough men, bandits of the lowest order. Not the sort you'd like to meet,' I told them. 'Idling along in our direction, weighed down with loot.'

Rike got to his feet all sudden like, his flail rattling at his hip. 'Loot?'

'Slugs, I tell you. Growing rich off the destruction of others.' I showed them my smile. 'Well, my brothers, we're going to have to show them the error of their ways. I want them dead. Every last one. And we'll do it without a scratch. I want trip-pits in the main street. I want brothers hidden in the grain-tower and the Blue Boar tavern. I want Kent, Row, Liar and the Nuban here, behind these walls to shoot them down when they come between tower and tavern.'

The Nuban hefted his crossbow, a monstrous feat of engineering, worked in the old metal and embellished with the faces of strange gods. Kent tossed the dregs from his helm and set it on his head, ready with his longbow.

'Now they might come over the ridge instead, so Rike's going to take Maical and six others to hide in the tannery ruins. Anyone comes that way, let them past you, then gut them. Makin will be our scout to give us warning. The good father here and you five there, you're going to stand with me to tempt them in.'

The brothers needed no telling. Well, Jobe did, but Rike hauled him out of the beer quick enough and he wasn't gentle about it.

'Loot!' Rike shouted the words in his face. 'Get digging trip-pits, shit-brains.'

They knew how to set up an ambush those lads. No mistake there. No one knew better how to fight in the ruins. Half the time they'd make the ruins themselves, half the time they'd fight in somebody else's.

'Burlow, Makin,' I called them to me as the others set about their tasks. 'I don't need you to scout, Makin,' I said, keeping my voice low. 'I want you two to go to the thicket by the stream. I want you to hide yourselves. Hide so a bastard could sit on you and still not know you were there. You hide down there and wait. You'll know what to do.'

'Prince— Brother Jorg,' Makin said. He had a big frown on, and his eyes kept straying down the street to old Gomsty praying before the burned-out church. 'What's this all about?'

'You said you'd follow wherever I led, Makin,' I answered. 'This is where it starts. When they write the legend, this will be the first page. Some old monk will go blind illuminating this page, Makin. This is where it all starts.' I didn't say how short the book might be though.

Makin did that bow of his that's half a nod, and off he went, Fat Burlow hurrying behind.

So, the brothers dug their traps, laid out their arrows, and hid themselves in what little of Norwood remained. I watched them, cursing their slowness, but holding my peace. And by and by only Father Gomst, my five picked men, and I remained on show. All the rest, a touch over two dozen, lay lost in the ruins.

Father Gomst came to my side, still praying. I wondered how hard he'd pray if he knew what was really coming.

I had an ache in my head now, like a hook inserted behind both eyes, tugging at me. The same ache that started up when the sight of old Gomsty made me think of going home. A familiar pain, one I'd felt at many a turn on the road. Oft times I'd let that pain lead me. But I felt tired of being a fish on a line. I bit back.

I saw the first scout on the marsh road an hour later. Others came soon enough, riding up to join him. I made sure they'd seen the seven of us standing on the burger-meister's steps.

'Company,' I said, and pointed the riders out.

'Shitdarn!' Brother Elban spat on his boots. I'd chosen Elban because he didn't look like much, a grizzled old streak in his rusty chainmail. He had no hair and no teeth, but he had a bite on him. 'They's no brigands, look at them ponies.' He lisped the words a bit, having no teeth and all.

'You know Elban, you might be right,' I said, and I gave him a smile. 'I'd say they looked more like house-troops.'

'Lord have mercy,' I heard old Gomsty murmur behind me.

The scouts pulled back. Elban picked up his gear and started for the market field where the horses stood grazing.

'You don't want to do that, old man,' I said, softly.

He turned and I could see the fear in his eyes. 'You ain't gonna cut me down is you, Jorth?' He couldn't say Jorg without any teeth; I suppose it's a name you've got to put an edge on.

'I won't cut you down,' I said. I almost liked Elban; I wouldn't kill him without a good reason. 'Where you going to run to, Elban?'

He pointed over the ridge. 'That's the only clear way. Get snarled up elsewise, or worse, back in the marsh.'

'You don't want to go over that ridge, Elban,' I said. 'Trust me.'

And he did. Though maybe he trusted me because he didn't trust me, if you get my meaning.

We stood and waited. We sighted the main column on the marsh road first, then moments later, the soldiers showed over the ridge. Two dozen of them, housetroops, carrying spears and shields, and above them the colours of Count Renar. The main column had maybe three score soldiers, and following on behind in a ragged line, well over a hundred prisoners, yoked neck to neck. Half a dozen carts brought up the rear. The covered ones would be loaded with provisions, the others held bodies, stacked like cord-wood.

'House Renar doesn't leave the dead unburned. They don't take prisoners,' I said.

'I don't understand,' Father Gomst said. He'd gone past scared, into stupid.

I pointed to the trees. 'Fuel. We're on the edge of a swamp. There's no trees for miles in this peat bog. They want a good blaze, so they're bringing everyone back here to have a nice big bonfire.'

I had an explanation for Renar's actions but as to my own, like Father Gomst, I wasn't sure I understood either. Whatever strength I had on the road, it came to me through a willingness to sacrifice. It came on the day I set aside my vengeance on Count Renar as a thing without profit. And yet here I was, in the ruins of Norwood, with a thirst that couldn't be quenched by any amount of festival beer. Waiting for that self-same count. Waiting with too few men, and with every instinct telling me to run. Every instinct, except for that one to hold or break, but never bend.

I could see individual figures at the head of the column quite clearly now. Six riders, chain-armoured, and a knight in heavy plate. The device on his shield came into view as he turned to signal his command. A black crow on a red field, a field of fire, Count Osson Renar wouldn't lead a hundred men into an Ancrath protectorate, so this would be one of his boys. Marclos or Jarco.

'The brothers won't fight this lot,' Elban said. He put a hand on my shoulder-plate. 'We might fight a path out through the trees if we get to the horses, Jorth.'

Already twenty of the Renar men hastened toward the tree line, holding their longbows before them so they wouldn't snag.

'No.' I let out a long sigh. 'I'd best surrender.'

I held out my hand. 'White flag if you please.'

The house-troops had deployed by the time I made my way down toward the main column. My 'flag' should properly be described as grey. An unwholesome grey at that, torn from Father Gomst's hassock.

'Noble born!' I shouted. 'Noble born under flag of truce!'

That surprised them. The house-troops, fanned out behind our horses, let me cross the market field unhindered. They looked to be a sorry lot, the metal scales falling from their leathers, rust on their swords. Homebodies they were, too long on the road and not hardened to it.

'The lad wants to be first on the fire,' one of them said. A skinny bastard with a boil on each cheek. He got a laugh with that.

'Noble born!' I called out. 'Flag o' truce.' I didn't expect to get this far with my sword.

I caught the stink of the column and could hear the weeping. The prisoners turned blank eyes upon me.

Two of Renar's riders came forward to intercept me. 'Where'd you steal the armour, boy?'

'Go fuck yourself,' I said. I kept it pleasant. 'Who've you got leading this show then? Marclos?'

They exchanged a look at that. A wandering hedge-knight probably wouldn't know one son of the House Renar from the next.

'It doesn't do to kill a noble prisoner without orders,' I said. 'Best let the Count-ling decide.'

Both riders dismounted. Tall men, veterans by the look of them. They took my sword. The older one, dark bearded with a white scar under both eyes, found my knife. The cut had taken the top of his nose too.

'You're a bit of an ugly mess aren't you?' I asked.

He found the knife in my boot as well.

I had no plan. The pain in my head hadn't left any room for one. I'd ignored the wordless voice that had led me for so long. Ignored it for the joy of being stubborn. And here I was unarmed amongst too many foes, stupid and alone.

I wondered if my brother William was watching me. I hoped my mother wasn't.

I wondered if I was going to die. If they'd burn me, or leave me as a maimed thing for Father Gomst to cart back to the Tall Castle.

'Everyone has doubts,' I said as Scar-face finished his search. 'Even Jesu had his moment, and I ain't him.'

The man looked at me as if I were mad. Maybe I was, but I'd found my peace. The pain left me and I saw things clear once again.

They led me to where Marclos sat on his horse, a monstrous stallion, twenty hands if it was one. He lifted his visor then and showed a pleasant face, a bit fat in the cheeks, quite jolly really. Looks, of course, can be deceiving.

'Who the hell are you?' he asked.

He had a nice bit of plate on, acid etched with a silver inlay and burnished so it shone even in the dreariest of light.

'I said who the hell are you?' He got some red in his cheeks then. Not so jolly. 'You'll sing on the fire, boy, so you may as well tell me now.'

I leaned forward as if to hear him. The bodyguards reached for me but I did the old shake and twist. Even with me in armour they were too slow. I used Marclos's foot as a step, where it stuck out from the stirrup, and got up alongside him in no time at all. He had a nice stiletto in a sheath set handy in the saddle, so I had that out and stuck it in his eye. Then we were off. The pair of us galloping out across the market field. How to steal a horse is the first thing you learn on the road.

We bounced along, with him howling and shaking behind me. A couple of the house-troops tried to bar the way but I rode them down. They weren't going to get up again either; that stallion was fearsome big. The archers might have taken a shot or three, but they couldn't make sense of it from that distance, and we were headed into town.

I could hear the bodyguard thundering along behind. It sounded as if they knocked a few men down themselves. They came close, but we'd taken them by surprise, me and Marclos, and got a start on them. And as we reached the outskirts of Norwood they drew up short.

At the first building I wheeled sharply, and Marclos obliged by falling off. He hit the ground face first. Another one that wouldn't be getting up again. It felt good, I won't lie about that. I imagined the Count getting the news as he broke his fast. I wondered how he'd like the taste of it. Would he finish his eggs?

'Men of Renar!' I shouted it hard enough to hurt my lungs. 'This town stands under the Prince of Ancrath's protection. It will not be surrendered.'

I turned the horse again and rode on. A few arrows clattered behind me. At the steps I drew up and dismounted.

'You came back...' Father Gomst looked confused.

'I did,' I said. I turned to face Elban. 'No fighting a retreat now eh, brother?'

'You're insane.' The words escaped in a whisper. For some reason he didn't lisp when he whispered.

The riders, Marclos's personal guard, led the charge. Now that they had fifty foot soldiers around them, they had found their courage. Up on the ridge the two dozen house-troops took their cue and began to run with the slope. The archers started to emerge from the thicket for better aim.

'These bastards will burn you alive if they take you that way,' I said to the five brothers I had with me. Then I paused and I looked them in the eye, each one. 'But they don't want to die. They won't want to go back to the Count either way. Would you take old bonfire-Renar his dead son back, and smooth it over with an "oh yes, but we killed scavengers … there was this boy … and an old man with no teeth…"?'

'So mark me now. You fight these tame soldiers, and you show them hell. Show them enough of it and the bastards'll break and run.' I paused and caught Brother Roddat's eye, for he was a weasel and like to run, sense or no sense. 'You stick with me, Brother Roddat.'

I looked to the thicket, over the heads of the men surging up from the market field and saw an archer fall among the trees. Then another. An armoured figure emerged from the undergrowth. The archers in front of him still had their eyes on the advance. He took the head from the first one with a clean swing. *Thank you, Makin,* I thought. Fat Burlow came out at a run then, barrelling his armoured bulk into the bowmen.

The troops from the ridge passed by Rike's position and his lads set to gutting them from behind. Not the sort of odds Little Rikey favoured, but the word 'loot' always did have an uncanny effect on him.

ChooOm! The Nuban's crossbow shot its load. He couldn't really miss with so many targets, but by rights he shouldn't be able to pick his man with that thing. Even so, both bolts hit the lead rider in the chest and lifted him out of his saddle. Kent and the other two rose from behind the burgermeister's walls. They did a double-take when they saw what was coming, but choices were in short supply and they had plenty of arrows.

The Renar troops hit our trip-pits at full tilt. I swear I heard the first ankle snap. After that it was all yelling as man went over man. Kent and Liar and Row took the opportunity to send a dozen more arrows into the main mass of the attack. The Nuban loaded his monster again and this time nearly took the head off a horse. The rider went over the top, and the beast fell onto him, brains spilling on the ground.

Some of those soldier boys didn't like the road so much any more and took to finding a way through the ruins. Of course they found more than a way, they found the brothers who were waiting there.

The archers broke first. There isn't much a man in

a padded tunic, with a knife at his hip, can do against a decent swordsman in plate armour. And even Burlow was more than decent.

Three of the riders reached us. We didn't stay on the street to meet them. We fell back into the skeleton of what used to be Decker's Smithy. So they rode in, slowly, ash crunching under hoof. Elban leapt the first one from an alcove over the furnaces. Took that rider down sweet as sweet he did, his sharp little knife hitting home over and over. If you recall, I said Elban had a bite to him.

Two brothers pulled the second rider down, feinting in and out until they got an opening. He had no room to move his horse around. Should have got off.

That left me and Scar-face. He had a bit more to him, and had dismounted before he followed us. He came at me slow and easy, the tip of his sword waving before him. He wasn't in a hurry: there's no rush when the best part of fifty men are hard on your heels.

'Flag o' truce?' I said, trying to goad him.

He didn't speak. His lips pressed together in a tight line and he stepped forward, real slow. That's when Brother Roddat stepped up behind him and stuck a sword through the back of his neck.

'Should have taken your moment, Scar-face,' I said.

I got back onto the street just in time to meet some huge red-faced bastard of a house-trooper who'd run his way up the hill. He pretty much exploded as the Nuban's bolts hit him. Then they were on us. The Nuban picked up his mattock and Red Kent grabbed his axe. Roddat came past me with his spear and found a man to pin with it.

They came in two waves. There were the dozen or so who'd kept up with Marclos's bodyguard and then behind them, another twenty coming at a slower pace. The rest lay strewn along the main street or dead in the ruins.

I ran past Roddat and the man he'd skewered. Past a couple of swordsmen who didn't want me bad enough, and I was through the first wave. I could see that skinny bastard with the boils on his cheeks, there in the second wave, the one who'd joked about me on the fire.

Me charging the second wave, howling for Boil-cheeks's blood. That's what broke them. And the men from the ridge? They never reached us. Little Rikey thought they might be carrying loot.

I reckon more than half of the Count's men ran. But they weren't the Count's men any more. They couldn't go back.

Makin came up the hill, blood all over him. He looked like Red Kent the day we found him! Burlow came with him, but he stopped to loot the dead, and of course that involves turning the injured into the dead.

'Why?' Makin wanted to know. 'I mean, superb victory, my prince … but why in the name of all the hells run such a risk?'

I held my sword up. The brothers around me took a step back, but to his credit, Makin didn't flinch. 'See this sword?' I said. 'Not a drop of blood on it.' I showed it around then waved it at the ridge. 'And out there there's fifty men who'll never fight for the Count of Renar again. They work for me now. They're carrying a story about a prince who killed the Count's son. A prince who would not retreat. A prince who never retreats. A prince who didn't have to blood his sword to beat a hundred men with thirty.

'Think about it, Makin. I made Roddat here fight like a madman because I told him if they think you're not going to give up, they'll break. Now I've got fifty enemies who're out there telling everyone who'll listen, "That Prince of Ancrath, he's not going to break". It's a simple sum. If they think we won't break, they give up.'

All true. It wasn't the reason, but it was all true.

9

Four years earlier

The baton struck my wrist with a loud crack. My other hand caught hold as it rose. I tried to twist it free, but Lundist held tight. Even so, I could see his surprise.

'I see you were paying attention after all, Prince Jorg.'

In truth I had been somewhere else, somewhere bloody, but my body has a habit of keeping watch for me at such times.

'Perhaps you can summarize my points thus far?' he said.

'We are defined by our enemies. This holds true for men, and by extension, their countries,' I said. I'd recognized the book Lundist brought to the lesson. That our enemies shape us was its central thesis.

'Good.' Lundist pulled his baton free and pointed to the table-map. 'Gelleth, Renar, and the Ken Marshes. Ancrath is a product of her environs; these are the wolves at her door.'

'The Renar highlands are all I care about,' I said. 'The rest can go hang.' I rocked my chair onto the back two legs. 'When Father orders the Gate against Count Renar, I'm going too. I'll kill him myself if they let me.'

Lundist shot me a look, a sharp one, to see if I meant it. There's something wrong about such blue eyes in an old man, but wrong or not he could see to the heart with them.

'Boys of ten are better occupied with Euclid and Plato. When we visit war, Sun Tzu will be our guide. Strategy and tactics, these are of the mind, these are the tools of prince and king.'

I did mean it. I had a hunger in me, an aching for the Count's death. The tight lines around Lundist's mouth told me that he knew how deep the hunger ran.

I looked to the high window where sunlight fingered into the schoolroom and turned the dust to dancing motes of gold. 'I will kill him,' I said. Then, with a sudden need to shock, 'Maybe with a poker, like I killed that ape Inch.' It galled me to have killed a man and have no memory of it, not even a trace of whatever rage drove me to it.

I wanted some new truth from Lundist. Explain me, to me. Whatever the words, that was my question, youth to old age. But even tutors have their limits.

I rocked forward, set my hands upon the map, and looked to Lundist once more. I saw the pity in him. A part of me wanted to take it, wanted to tell him how I'd struggled against those hooks, how I'd watched William die. A part of me longed to lay it all down, that weight I carried, the acid pain of memory, the corrosion of hate.

Lundist leaned across the table. His hair fell around his face, long in the fashion of Orient, so white as to be almost silver. 'We are defined by our enemies – but also we can choose them. Make an enemy of hatred, Jorg. Do that and you could be a great man, but more importantly, maybe a happy one.'

There's something brittle in me that will break before it bends. Something sharp that puts an edge on all the soft words I once owned. I don't think the Count of Renar put it there that day they killed my mother, he just drew the razor from its sheath. Part of me longed for a surrender, to take the gift Lundist held before me.

I cut away that portion of my soul. For good or ill, it died that day.

'When will the Gate march?' I left nothing in my voice to say I'd heard his words.

'The Army of the Gate won't march,' Lundist said. His shoulders held a slump, tiredness or defeat.

That hit me in the gut, a surprise shot passing my guard. I jumped up toppling the chair. 'They will!' How could they not?

Lundist turned toward the door. His robes made a dry sound as he moved, like a sigh. Disbelief pinned me to the spot, my limbs strangers to me. I could feel the heat rising in my cheeks. 'How could they not?' I shouted at his back, angry for feeling like a child.

'Ancrath is defined by her enemies,' he said, walking still. 'The Army of the Gate must guard the homeland, and no other army would reach the Count in his halls.'

'A queen has died.' Mother's throat opened again and coloured my vision red. The hooks burned in my flesh once more. 'A prince of the realm, slain.' Broken like a toy.

'And there is a price to pay.' Lundist paused, one hand against the door, leaning as if for support.

'The price of blood and iron!'

'Rights to the Cathun River, three thousand ducats, and five Araby stallions.' Lundist wouldn't look at me.

'What?'

'River trade, gold, horses.' Those blue eyes found me over his shoulder. An old hand took the door-ring.

The words made sense one at a time, not together.

'The army . . .' I started.

'Will not move.' Lundist opened the door. The day streamed in, bright, hot, laced with the distant laughter of squires at play.

'I'll go alone. That man will die screaming, by my hand.' Cold fury crawled across my skin.

I needed a sword, a good knife at least. A horse, a map – I snatched the one before me, old hide, musty, the borders tattooed in Indus ink. I needed . . . an explanation.

'How? How can their deaths be purchased?'

'Your father forged his alliance with the Horse Coast kingdoms through marriage. The strength of that alliance threatened Count Renar. The Count struck early, before the links grew too strong, hoping to remove both the wife, and the heirs.' Lundist stepped into the light, and his hair became golden, a halo in the breeze. 'Your father hasn't the strength to destroy Renar and keep the wolves from Ancrath's doors. Your grandfather on the Horse Coast will not accept that, so the alliance is dead, Renar is safe. Now Renar seeks a truce so he may turn his strength to other borders. Your father has sold him such a truce.'

Inside I was falling, pitching, tumbling. Falling into an endless void.

'Come, Prince.' Lundist held out a hand. 'Let's walk in the sunshine. It's not a day for desk-learning.'

I bunched the map in my fist, and somewhere in me I found a smile, sharp, bitter, but with a chill to it that held me to my purpose. 'Of course, dear tutor. Let us walk in the sun. It's not a day for wasting – oh no.'

And we went out into the day, and all the heat of it couldn't touch the ice in me.

Knife-work is a dirty business, yet Brother Grumlow is always clean.

10

We had ourselves a prisoner. One of Marclos's riders proved less dead than expected. Bad news for him all in all. Makin had Burlow and Rike bring the man to me on the burgermeister's steps.

'Says his name is Renton. "Sir" Renton, if you please,' Makin said.

I looked the fellow up and down. A nice black bruise wrapped itself halfway round his forehead, and an over-hasty embrace with Mother Earth had left his nose some-what flatter than he might have liked. His moustache and beard could have been neatly trimmed, but caked in all that blood they looked a mess.

'Fell off your horse did you, Renton?' I asked.

'You stabbed Count Renar's son under a flag of truce,' he said. He sounded a little comical on the 'stabbed' and 'son'. A broken nose will do that for you.

'I did,' I said. 'I can't think of anything I wouldn't have stabbed him under.' I held Renton's gaze; he had squinty little eyes. He wouldn't have been much to look at in court finery. On the steps, covered in mud and blood, he looked like a rat's leavings. 'If I were you, I'd be more worried about my own fate than whether Marclos was stabbed in accordance with the right social niceties.'

That of course was a lie. If I were in his place, I'd have been looking for an opportunity to stick a knife in me. But I knew enough to know that most men didn't share my priorities. As Makin said, something in me had got broken, but not so broken I didn't remember what it was.

'My family is rich, they'll ransom me,' Renton said. He spoke quickly, nervous now, as if he'd just realized his situation.

I yawned. 'No they're not. If they were rich you wouldn't be riding in chain armour as one of Marclos's guards.' I yawned again, stretching my mouth until my jaw cracked. 'Maical, get me a cup of that festival beer, will you?'

'Maical's dead,' Rike said, from behind Sir Renton.

'Never?' I said. 'Idiot Maical? I thought God had blessed him with the same luck that looks after drunkards and madmen.'

'Well he's near enough dead,' Rike said. 'Got him a gut-full of rusty iron from one of Renar's boys. We laid him out in the shade.'

'Touching,' I said. 'Now get my beer.'

Rike grumbled and slapped Jobe into taking the errand.

I turned back to Sir Renton. He didn't look happy, but he didn't look as sad as you might expect a man in such a bad place to look. His eyes kept sliding over to Father Gomst. Here's a man with faith in a higher source, I thought.

'So, Sir Renton,' I said. 'What brings young Marclos to Ancrath's protectorates? What does the Count think he's up to?'

Some of the brothers had gathered around the steps for the show, but most were still looting the dead. A man's coin is nice and portable, but the brothers wouldn't stop there. I expected the head-cart to be heaped with arms and armour when we left. Boots too; there's three coppers in a well-made pair of boots.

Renton coughed and wiped at his nose, spreading black gore across his face. 'I don't know the Count's plans. I'm not privy to his private council.' He looked up at Father Gomst. 'As God is my witness.'

I leaned in close to him. He smelled sour, like cheese in the sun. 'God is your witness, Renton, he's going to watch you die.'

I let that sink in. I gave old Gomsty a smile. 'You can look after this knight's soul, Father. The sins of the flesh though – they're all mine.'

Rike handed me my cup of beer, and I had a sip. 'The day you're tired of looting, Little Rikey, is the day you're tired of life,' I said. It got a chuckle from the brothers on the steps. 'Why're you still here when you could be cutting up the dead in search of a golden liver?'

'Come to see you put the hurt on Rat-face,' Rike said.

'You're going to be disappointed then,' I said. 'Sir Rat-face is going to tell me everything I want to know, and I'm not even going to have to raise my voice. When I'm done, I'm going to hand him over to the new burger-meister of Norwood. The peasants will probably burn him alive, and he'll count it the easy way out.' I kept it conversational. I find it's the coldest threats that reach the deepest.

Out in the marshes I'd made a dead man run in terror, with nothing more than what I keep inside. It occurred to me that what scared the dead might worry the living a piece too.

Sir Renton didn't sound too scared yet though. 'You stabbed the better man today, boy, and there's a better man before you. You're nothing more than shit on my shoe.' I'd hurt his pride. He was a knight after all, and here was a beardless lad making mock. Besides, the best I'd offered was an 'easy' burning. Nobody considers that the soft option.

'When I was nine, the Count of Renar tried to have me killed,' I said. I kept my voice calm. It wasn't hard. I was calm. Anger carries less horror with it, men understand anger. It promises resolution; maybe bloody resolution, but swift. 'The Count failed, but I watched my mother and my little brother killed.'

'All men die,' Renton said. He spat a dark and bloody mess onto the steps. 'What makes you so special?'

He had a good point. What made my loss, my pain, any more important than everyone else's?

'That's a good question,' I said. 'A damn good question.'

It was. There weren't but a handful of the prisoners we'd taken from Marclos's train who hadn't seen a son, or a husband, a mother or a lover, killed. And killed in the past week. And this was my soft option, the mercies of these peasants compared to the attention of a young man whose hurt stood four years old.

'Consider me a spokesman,' I said. 'When it comes to stage-acting, some men are more eloquent than others. It's given to particular men to have a gift with the bow.' I nodded to the Nuban. 'Some men can knock the eye out of a bull at a thousand paces. They don't aim any better for wanting it, they don't shoot straighter because they're justified. They just shoot straighter. Now me, I just … avenge myself better than most. Consider it a gift.'

Renton laughed at that and spat again. This time I saw part of a tooth in the mess. 'You think you're worse than the fire, boy?' he asked. 'I've seen men burn. A lot of men.'

He had a point. 'You've a lot of good points, Sir Renton,' I said.

I looked around at the ruins. Tumbled walls in the most, and blackened timber skeletons where roofs had kept a lid on folk's lives for year after year. 'It's going to take a lot of rebuilding,' I said. 'A lot of hammers and a lot of nails.' I sipped my beer. 'A strange thing – nails will hold a building together, but there's nothing better for taking a man apart.' I held Sir Renton's rat-like eyes, dark and beady. 'I don't enjoy torturing people, Sir Renton, but I'm good at it. Not world-class you understand. Cowards make the best torturers. Cowards understand fear and they can use it. Heroes on the other hand, they make terrible torturers. They don't see what motivates a normal man. They misunderstand everything. They can't think of anything worse than besmirching your honour. A coward on the other hand; he'll tie you to a chair and light a slow fire under you. I'm not a hero or a coward, but I work with what I've got.'

Renton had the sense to pale at that. He reached out a muddy hand to Father Gomst. 'Father, I've done nothing but serve my master.'

'Father Gomst will pray for your soul,' I said. 'And forgive me the sins I incur in detaching it from your body.'

Makin pursed those thick lips of his. 'Prince, you've spoken about how you'd break the cycle of revenge. You could start here. You could let Sir Renton go.'

Rike gave him a look as if he'd gone mad. Fat Burlow covered a chuckle.

'I have spoken about that, Makin,' I said. 'I will break the cycle.' I drew my sword and laid it across my knees. 'You know how to break the cycle of hatred?' I asked.

'Love,' said Gomst, all quiet-like.

'The way to break the cycle is to kill every single one of the bastards that fucked you over,' I said. 'Every last one of them. Kill them all. Kill their mothers, kill their brothers, kill their children, kill their dog.' I ran my thumb along the blade of my sword and watched the blood bead crimson on the wound. 'People think I hate the Count, but in truth I'm a great advocate of his methods. He has only two failings. Firstly he goes far, but not far enough. Secondly he isn't me. He taught me valuable lessons though. And when we meet, I will thank him for it, with a quick death.'

Old Gomsty started at that. 'Count Renar did you wrong, Prince Jorg. Forgive him, but don't thank him. He'll burn in Hell for what he did. His immortal soul will suffer for eternity.'

I had to laugh out loud at that. 'Churchmen, eh? Love one minute, forgiveness the next, and then it's eternity on fire. Well rest at ease, Sir Renton, I've no designs on your immortal soul. Whatever happens between us, it will all be over in a day or two. Three at most. I'm not the most patient of men, so it will end when you tell me what I want to know, or I get bored.'

I got up from my step and went to crouch by Sir Renton. I patted his head. They'd tied his hands behind him, and I had my chainmail gauntlets on, so if he had a mind to bite, it'd do him no good.

'I swore to Count Renar,' he said. He tried to pull away, and he craned his neck to look at old Gomsty. 'Tell him, Father, I swore before God. If I break my vow I'll burn in Hell.'

Gomst came to lay his hand on Renton's shoulder. 'Prince Jorg, this knight has made a holy vow. There are few oaths more sacred than that of a knight to his liege lord. You should not ask him to break it. Nor should any threat against the flesh compel a man to betray a covenant and forever place his soul in the fires of the Devil.'

'Here's a test of faith for you, Sir Renton,' I said. 'I'll tell you my tale and we'll see whether you want to tell me the Count's plans when I'm done.' I settled down on the step beside him and swigged my beer. 'When I first took to the road I was, oh, ten years of age. I'd a lot of anger in me then, and a need to know how the world worked. You see, I'd watched the Count's men kill my brother, William, and slit Mother open. So I knew that the way I'd thought things were supposed to work was wrong. And of course, I fell in with bad sorts – didn't I Rikey?'

Rike gave that laugh of his: '*hur hur hur*'. I think he just made the sound when he thought we expected a laugh. It didn't have any joy in it.

'I tried my hand at torture then. I wondered if I was supposed to be evil. I thought maybe I'd had a message from God to take up the Devil's work.'

I heard Gomst muttering at that one, prayers or condemnation. It was true too. For the longest time I looked

72

for a message in it all, to work out what I was supposed to be doing.

I laid my hand on Renton's shoulder. He sat there with my hand on his left shoulder, and Gomst's hand on his right. We could have been the Devil and the angel from those old scrolls, whispering in his ears.

'We caught Bishop Murillo down by Jedmire Hill,' I said. 'I'm sure you heard about the loss of his mission? Anyhow, the brothers let me have the bishop. I was something of a mascot to them back then.'

The Nuban stood and walked off down the hill. I let him go. The Nuban didn't have the stomach for this kind of thing. That made me feel – I don't know – dirty? I liked the Nuban, though I didn't let it show.

'Now, Bishop Murillo was full of harsh words and judgement. He had plenty to tell me about hellfire and damnation. We sat a while and discussed the business of souls. Then I hammered a nail into his skull. Just here.' I reached out and touched the spot on Renton's greasy head. He flinched back like he'd been stung. 'The bishop changed his tune a bit after that,' I said. 'In fact every time I knocked a new nail into him, he changed his tune. After a while he was a very different man. Did you know you can break a man into his parts like that? One nail will bring back memories of childhood. Another will make him rage, or sob, or laugh. In the end it seems we're just toys, easy to break and hard to mend.

'I hear that the nuns at Saint Alstis still have Bishop Murillo in their care. He's a very different person now. He clutches at their habits and slurs awful things at them, so they say. Where the soul of that proud and pious man we took from the papal caravan is – well, I can't tell you.'

With that, I 'magicked' a nail into my fingers. A rusty spike, three inches long. The man wet himself. There on the steps. Burlow gave an oath and kicked him, hard. When Renton got his breath back, he told me everything he knew. It took almost an hour. Then we gave him to the peasants and they burned him.

I watched the good folk of Norwood dance around their fire. I watched the flames lick above their heads. There's a pattern in fire, as if something's written there, and there's folk who say they can read it too. Not me, though. It would have been nice to find some answers in the flames. I had questions: it was a thirst for the Count's blood that had set me on the road. But somehow I'd given it up. Somehow I set it aside and told myself it was a sacrifice to strength.

I sipped my beer. Four years on the road. Always going somewhere, always doing something, but now, with my feet pointed towards home, it felt like I'd been lost all that time. Lost or led.

I tried to remember when I'd given up on the Count, and why. Nothing came to me, just the glimpse of my hand on a door, and the sensation of falling into space.

'I'm going home,' I said.

The dull ache between my eyes became a rusty nail, driven deep. I finished my beer, but it did nothing for me. I had an older kind of thirst.

11

Four years earlier

I followed Lundist out into the day.

'Wait.' He held his baton to my chest. 'It never pays to walk blind. Especially not in your own castle where familiarity hides so much – even when we have the eyes to see.'

We stood for a moment on the steps, blinking away the sunlight, letting the heat soak in. Release from the gloom of the schoolroom held no great surprise. Four days in seven my studies kept me at Lundist's side, sometimes in the schoolroom, the observatory, or library, but as often as not the hours would pass in a hunt for wonders. Whether it was the mechanics of the siege machinery held in the Arnheim Hall, or the mystery of the Builder-light that shone without flame in the salt cellar, every part of the Tall Castle held a lesson that Lundist could tease out.

'Listen,' he said.

I knew this game. Lundist held that a man who can observe is a man apart. Such a man can see opportunities where others see only the obstacles on the surface of each situation.

'I hear wood on wood. Training swords. The squires at play,' I said.

'Some might not call it play. Deeper! What else?'

'I hear birdsong. Skylarks.' There it was, a silver chain of sound, dropped from on high, so sweet and light I'd missed it at first.

'Deeper.'

I closed my eyes. What else? Green fought red on the back of my eyelids. The clack of swords, the grunts, panting, muted scuffle of shoe on stone, the song of skylarks. What else?

'Fluttering.' On the edge of hearing – I was probably imagining it.

'Good,' Lundist said. 'What is it?'

'Not wings. It's deeper than that. Something in the wind,' I said.

'There's no wind in the courtyard,' Lundist said.

'Up high then.' I had it. 'A flag!'

'Which flag? Don't look. Just tell me.' Lundist pressed the baton harder.

'Not the festival flag. Not the King's flag, that's flown from the north wall. Not the colours, we're not at war.' No, not the colours. Any curiosity in me died at that reminder of Count Renar's purchase. I wondered, if they'd slain me also, would the price of a pardon have been higher? An extra horse?

'Well?' Lundist asked.

'The execution flag, black on scarlet,' I said.

It's always been that way with me. Answers come when I stop trying to think it through and just speak. The best plan I'll come up with is the one that happens when I act.

'Good.'

I opened my eyes. The light no longer pained me. High above the courtyard the execution flag streamed in a westerly breeze.

'Your father has ordered the dungeons cleared,' Lundist said. 'There will be quite a crowd come Saint Crispin's Day.'

I knew that to be understatement. 'Hangings, beheadings, impalement, oh my!'

I wondered if Lundist would seek to shield me from the proceedings. The corner of my mouth twitched, hooked on the notion that he might imagine I'd not seen worse already. For the mass executions of the previous year, Mother had taken us to visit Lord Nossar at his estates in Elm. William and I had the fort of Elm almost to ourselves. Later I learned that most of Ancrath had converged on the Tall Castle to watch the sport.

'Terror and entertainment are weapons of statehood, Jorg.' Lundist kept his tone neutral, his face inscrutable save for a tightness in the lips suggesting that the words carried a bad taste. 'Execution combines both elements.' He gazed at the flag. 'Before I journeyed and fell slave to your mother's people, I dwelt in Ling. In the Utter East pain is an artform. Rulers make their reputations, and that of their land, on extravagances of torture. They compete at it.'

We watched the squires spar. A tall knight gave instruction, sometimes with his fist.

For several minutes I said nothing. I imagined Count Renar at the mercy of a Ling torture-master.

No – I wanted his blood and his death. I wanted him to die knowing why he died, knowing who held the sword. But his pain? Let him do his burning in Hell.

'Remind me not to go to Ling, Tutor,' I said.

Lundist smiled, and led off across the courtyard. 'It's not on your father's maps.'

We passed close by the duelling square, and I recognized the knight by his armour, a dazzling set of field plate with silver inlaid into acid-etched scrollwork across the breastplate.

'Sir Makin of Trent,' I said. I turned to face him. Lundist walked on for a few paces before realizing I'd left his side.

'Prince Honorous.' Sir Makin offered me a curt bow. 'Keep that guard up, Cheeves!' A barked instruction to one of the older boys.

'Call me Jorg,' I said. 'I hear my father has made you Captain of the Guard.'

'He found fault with my predecessor,' Sir Makin said. 'I hope to fulfil my duties more to the King's pleasing.'

I'd not seen Sir Grehem since the attack on our coach. I suspected that the incident cost the former Captain of the Guard rather more than it cost Count Renar.

'Let us hope so,' I said.

Makin ran a hand through his hair, dark and beaded with sweat from the heat of the day. He had a slightly fleshy face, expressive, but you wouldn't mistake him for someone without mettle.

'Won't you join us, Prince Jorg? A good right feint will serve you better in times of trouble than any amount of book learning.' He grinned. 'If your wounds are recovered sufficiently, of course.'

Lundist settled a hand on my shoulder. 'The Prince is still troubled by his injuries.' He fixed those too-blue eyes of his on Sir Makin. 'You might consider reading Proximus's thesis on the defence of royals. If you wish to avoid Sir Grehem's fate, that is. It's in the library.' He moved to steer me away. I resisted on nothing more than principle.

'I think the Prince knows his own mind, Tutor.' Sir Makin flashed Lundist a broad smile. 'Your Proximus can keep his advice. A knight trusts in his own judgement, and the weight of his sword.'

Sir Makin took a wooden sword from the cart on his left, and offered it to me, hilt first. 'Come, my prince. Let's see what you've got. Care to spar against young Stod here?' He pointed out the smallest of the squires, a slight lad maybe a year my senior.

'Him.' I pointed to the biggest of them, a hulking lout of fifteen with a shock of ginger hair. I took the sword.

Sir Makin raised an eyebrow, and grinned all the wider. 'Robart? You'll fight Robart, will you now?'

He strode to the boy's side and clapped a hand to the back of his neck. 'This here is Robart Hool, third son of the House of Arn. Of all this sorry lot, he's the one who might have a chance to earn his spurs one day. Got himself a way with the blade has our Master Hool.' He shook his head. 'Try Stod.'

'Try none of them, Prince Jorg.' Lundist kept the irritation from his voice, almost. 'This is foolishness. You are not yet recovered.' He shot a look at the grinning guard captain. 'King Olidan will not take kindly to a relapse in his only heir.'

Sir Makin frowned at that, but I could see it had gone too far for his pride to let him take instruction. 'Go easy on him, Robart. Really easy.'

'If this ginger oaf doesn't do his level best, I'll make sure the closest he gets to being a knight is clearing the horse dung after the joust,' I said.

I advanced on the squire, my head craned to look him in the face. Sir Makin stepped between us, a training sword in his left hand. 'A quick test first, my prince. I've got to know you've enough of the basics not to get yourself hurt.'

The point of his blade clacked against mine, and slipped away, angled for my face. I slapped it aside, and made a half-lunge. The knight tamed my thrust easily enough; I tried to slide to his guard but he cut to my legs and I barely held him.

'Not bad. Not bad.' He inclined his head. 'You've had decent instruction.' He pursed his lips. 'You're what, twelve?'

'Ten.' I watched him return the trainer to the cart. He was right-handed.

'All right.' Sir Makin motioned the squires into a circle around us. 'Let's have us a duel. Robart, show the Prince no mercies. He's good enough to lose without serious injury to anything but his pride.'

Robart squared up to me, all freckles and confidence. The moment seemed to come into focus. I felt the sun on my skin, the grit between the soles of my shoes and the flagstones.

Sir Makin held his hand up. 'Wait for it.'

I heard the silver voices of the skylarks, invisible against the blue vaults above us. I heard the flapping of the execution flag.

'Fight!' The hand dropped.

Robart came in fast, swinging low. I let my sword fall to the ground. His blow caught me on the right side, just below the ribs. I'd have been cut in two . . . if it hadn't been made of wood. But it was. I hit him in the throat, with the edge of my hand, an eastern move that Lundist had showed me. Robart went down as if a wall had dropped on him.

I watched him writhe, and for an instant I saw Inch in the Healing Hall on his hands and knees with the fire all around us and the blood pulsing from his back. I felt the poison in my veins, the hooks in my flesh, the simple need to kill – as pure an emotion as I have ever known.

'No.' I found Lundist's hand on my wrist, stopping me as I reached for the boy. 'It's enough.'

It's never enough. Words in my head, spoken by a voice not my own, a voice remembered from the briar and the fever-bed.

For several moments we watched the lad choke on the floor, and turn crimson.

The strangeness left me. I picked up my sword and returned it to Sir Makin.

'Actually, Proximus is yours, Captain, not Lundist's,' I said. 'Proximus was a Borthan scholar, seventh century. One of your ancestors. Perhaps you should read him after all. I'd hate to have nothing but Robart here, and his judgement, between me and my enemies.'

'But . . .' Sir Makin chewed his lip. He seemed to have run out of objections after 'but'.

'He cheated.' Young Stod found the words for all of them.

Lundist had already started walking. I turned to follow him, then looked back.

'It's not a game, Sir Makin. You teach these boys to play by the rules, and they're going to lose. It's not a game.'

And when we make a mistake, we can't buy our way out of it. Not with horses, not with gold.

We reached the Red Gate on the far side of the courtyard.

'That boy could die,' Lundist said.

'I know,' I said. 'Take me to see these prisoners that Father's to have killed.'

12

Four years earlier

More of the Tall Castle lies below the ground than above. It should be called the Deep Castle, really. It took us a while to reach the dungeons. We heard the shrieks from a level up, through walls of Builder-stone.

'This visit is, perhaps, a bad idea,' Lundist said, pausing before an iron door.

'It's my idea, Tutor,' I said. 'I thought you wanted me to learn by my mistakes?'

Another scream reached us, guttural with a hoarse edge to it, an animal sound.

'Your father wouldn't approve of this visit,' Lundist said. He pressed his lips in a tight line, troubled.

'That's the first time you've called on Father's wisdom to resolve an issue. Shame on you, Tutor Lundist.' Nothing would turn me back now.

'There are things that children—'

'Too late, that horse already bolted. Stable burned.'

I brushed past him and rapped on the door with the hilt of my dagger. 'Open up.'

A rattle of keys, and the door slid inward on oiled hinges. The wave of stench that hit me nearly took my breath. A warty old fellow in warder's leathers leaned into view and opened his mouth to speak.

'Don't,' I said, holding the business end of my dagger toward his tongue.

I walked on, Lundist at my heels.

'You always told me to look and make my own judgement, Lundist,' I said. I respected him for that. 'No time to get squeamish.'

'Jorg . . .' He was torn, I could hear it in his voice, wracked between emotions I couldn't understand, and logic that I could. 'Prince—'

The cry rang out again, much louder now. I'd heard the sound before. It pushed at me, trying to force me away. The first time I heard that kind of pain, my mother's pain, something held me back. I'll tell you it was the hook-briar which held me fast. I'll show you the scars. But in the night, before the dreams come, a voice whispers to me that it was fear that held me back, terror that rooted me in the briar, safe while I watched them die.

Another scream, more terrible and more desperate than any before. I felt the hooks in my flesh.

'Jorg!'

I shook Lundist's hands from me, and ran toward the sound.

I didn't have far to run. I pulled up short at the entrance to a wide room, torch-lit, with cell doors lining three sides. At the centre, two men stood on opposite sides of a table, to which a third man had been secured with chains. The larger of the two warders held an iron poker, one end in a basket of glowing coals.

None of the three noted my arrival, nor did any of the faces pressed to the barred windows in the cell doors turn my way. I walked in. I heard Lundist arrive at the entrance and stop to take in the scene, as I had.

I drew close and the warder without the iron glanced my way. He jumped as if stung. 'What in the—' He shook his head to clear his vision. 'Who? I mean ...'

I'd imagined the torturers would be terrifying men with cruel faces, thin lips, hooked noses, the eyes of soulless demons. I think I found their ordinariness more of a shock. The shorter of the two looked a touch simple, but in a friendly way. Mild I'd call him.

'Who're you?' This one had a more brutish cast to him, but I could picture him at ale, laughing, or teaching his son pitch-ball.

I hadn't any of my court weeds on, just a simple tunic for the schoolroom. There was no reason for warders to recognize me. They would enter the vaults through the Villains' Gate and had probably never walked in the castle above.

'I'm Jorg,' I said, in a servant's accent. 'My uncle paid old Wart-face at the door to let me see the prisoners.' I pointed toward Lundist. 'We're going to the executions tomorrow. I wanted to see criminals close up first.'

I wasn't looking at the warders now. The man on the table held my gaze. I'd seen only one black skin before, a slave to some noble visiting Father's court from the south. But that man was brown. The fellow on the table had skin blacker than ink. He turned his head to face my way, slow as if it weighed like lead. The whites of his eyes seemed to shine in all that blackness.

'Wart-face? Heh, I like that.' The big warder relaxed and took up his iron again. 'If there's two ducats in it for me and Grebbin here, then I reckon you can stay and watch this fellow squeal.'

'Berrec, it don't seem right.' Grebbin furrowed his broad forehead. 'He's a young-un an' all.'

Berrec pulled the poker from the coals and held it toward Grebbin. 'You don't want to stand between me and a ducat, my friend.'

The black man's naked chest glistened below the glowing point. Ugly burns marked his ribs, red flesh erupting like new-ploughed furrows. I could smell the sweet stench of roasted meat.

'He's very black,' I said.

'He's a Nuban is what he is,' Berrec said, scowling. He gave the poker a critical look and returned it to the fire.

'Why are you burning him?' I asked. I didn't feel easy under the Nuban's scrutiny.

The question puzzled them for a moment. Grebbin's frown deepened.

'He's got the devil in him,' Berrec said at last. 'All them Nubans have. Heathens, the lot of them. I heard that Father Gomst, him as leads the King himself in prayer, says to burn the heathen.' Berrec laid a hand on the Nuban's stomach, a disturbingly tender touch. 'So we're just crisping this one up a bit, before the King comes to watch him killed on the morrow.'

'Executed.' Grebbin pronounced the word with the precision of one who has practised it many times.

'Executed, killed, what's the difference? They all end up for the worms.' Berrec spat into the coals.

The Nuban kept his eyes on me, a quiet study. I felt something I couldn't name. I felt somehow wrong for being there. I ground my teeth together and met his gaze.

'What did he do?' I asked.

'Do?' Grebbin snorted. 'He's a prisoner.'

'His crime?' I asked.

Berrec shrugged. 'Getting caught.'

Lundist spoke from the doorway. 'I believe . . . Jorg, that all of the prisoners for execution are bandits, captured by the Army of the March. The King ordered the action to prevent raids across the Lichway into Norwood and other protectorates.'

I broke my gaze from the Nuban's, and let it slide across the marks of his torture. Where the skin remained unburned, patterns of raised scars picked out symbols, simple in design but arresting to the eye. A soiled loincloth hung across his hips. His wrists and ankles were bound with iron shackles secured with a basic pin-lock. Blood oozed along the short chains anchoring them to the table.

'Is he dangerous?' I asked. I moved close. I could taste the burned meat.

'Yes.' The Nuban smiled as he said it, his teeth bloody.

'You shut your heathen hole, you.' Berrec yanked the iron from the coals. A shower of sparks flew up as he lifted the white-hot poker to eye-level. The glow made something ugly of his face. It reminded me of a wild night when the lightning lit the faces of Count Renar's men.

I turned to the Nuban. If he'd been watching the iron I'd have left him to it.

'Are you dangerous?' I asked him.

'Yes.'

I pulled the pin from the manacle on his right wrist.

'Show me.'

13

Four years earlier

The Nuban moved fast, but it wasn't his speed that impressed, it was his lack of hesitation. He reached for Berrec's wrist. A sudden heave brought the warder sprawling across him. The poker in Berrec's outstretched hand skewered Grebbin through the ribs, deep enough so that Berrec lost his grip on it as Grebbin twisted away.

Without pause, the Nuban lifted himself halfway to sitting, as close to upright as his manacled wrist would let him. Berrec slid down the Nuban's chest, sliding on sweat and blood, into his lap. He started to raise himself. The Nuban's descending elbow put an end to the escape attempt. It caught Berrec on the back of the neck, and bones crunched.

Grebbin screamed of course, but screams were common enough in the dungeon. He tried to run, but somehow lost his sense of direction and slammed into a cell door, with enough force to drive the point of the poker out below his shoulder blade. The impact knocked him over and he didn't get up again. He twisted for a moment, mouthing something, with only wisps of smoke or steam escaping his lips.

A cheer went up from those cells containing occupants too stupid to know when to stay silent.

Lundist could have run. He had plenty of time. I expected him to go for help, but he was halfway to me by the time Grebbin hit the ground. The Nuban pushed Berrec clear, and freed his other wrist.

'Run!' I shouted at Lundist in case it hadn't occurred to him.

Actually, he was running, only in the wrong direction. I knew the years lay less heavy on him than an old man had a right to expect, but I didn't think he could sprint.

I moved to put the table, and the Nuban, between Lundist and me.

The Nuban unpinned both ankles as Lundist reached him. 'Take the boy, old man, and go.' He had the deepest voice I'd ever heard.

Lundist fixed the Nuban with those disconcerting blue eyes of his. His robes settled, forgetting the rush from the doorway. He held hands to his chest, one atop the other. 'If you go now, man of Nuba, I will not stop you.'

That brought a scatter of laughter from the cells.

The Nuban watched Lundist with the same intensity I'd seen earlier. He had a few inches on my tutor, but it was the difference in bulk that made it seem a contest between

David and Goliath. Where Lundist stood slender as a spear, the Nuban had as much weight again, and more, corded into thick slabs of muscle over heavy bone.

The Nuban didn't laugh at Lundist. Perhaps he saw more than the prisoners did. 'I'll take my brothers with me.'

Lundist chewed on that, then took a pace back. 'Jorg, here.' He kept his gaze on the Nuban.

'Brothers?' I asked. I couldn't see any black faces at the bars.

The Nuban gave a broad smile. 'Once I had hut-brothers. Now they are far away, maybe dead.' He spread his arms, the smile becoming half grimace as he felt his burns. 'But the gods have given me new brothers, road-brothers.'

'Road-brothers.' I rolled the words across my tongue. An image of Will flickered in my mind, blood and curls. There was power here. I felt it.

'Kill them both, and let me out.' A door to my left rattled as if a bull were worrying at it. If the speaker matched his voice, there was an ogre in there.

'You owe me your life, Nuban,' I said.

'Yes.' He jerked the keys from Berrec's belt and stepped toward the cell on my left. I stepped with him, keeping him between Lundist and myself.

'You'll give me a life in return,' I said.

He paused, glancing at Lundist. 'Go with your uncle, boy.'

'You'll give me a life, brother, or I'll take yours as forfeit,' I said.

More laughter from the cells, and this time the Nuban joined in. 'Who do you want killed, Little Brother?' He set the key in the lock.

'I'll tell you when we see him,' I said. To specify Count Renar now would raise too many questions. 'I'm coming with you.'

Lundist rushed forward at that. He pivoted past the Nuban, delivering a kick to the back of his knee. I heard a loud click as the black man went down.

The Nuban twisted as he fell, and lunged for Lundist. Somehow the old man evaded him, and when the Nuban sprawled at his feet, Lundist kicked him in the neck, a blow that cut off his oath and left him limp on the stone floor.

I almost skipped free, but Lundist's fingers knotted in my hair as it streamed behind me. 'Jorg! This is not the way!'

I fought to escape, snarling. 'It's exactly the way.' And I knew it to be true. The wildness in the Nuban, the bonds between these men, the focus on what will make the difference – no matter what the situation – all of it echoed in me.

From the corner of my eye I caught sight of the cell door opening. The click had been the key turning.

Lundist held my shoulders and made me face him. 'You've no place with these men, Jorg. You can't imagine the life they lead. They don't have the answers you want.' He had such intensity to him, I could almost believe he cared.

A figure emerged from the cell, stooping to come through the doorway. I'd never seen a man so big, not Sir Gerrant of the Table Guard, not Shem the stablehand, nor the wrestlers from The Slavs.

The man came up behind Lundist, quick, a rolling storm.

'Jorg, you think I don't understand—' The sweep of a massive arm cut off Lundist's words and sent him to the stone floor with such force I'd have winced even if he hadn't taken a handful of my hair with him.

The man towered over me, an ugly giant in stinking rags, with his hair hanging down in matted curtains. The scale of him mesmerized me. He reached for me, and I moved too slow. The hand that caught me could almost close around my waist. He lifted me level with his face, and his filthy mane parted as he looked up.

'Jesu, but you're one hideous offence to the eye.' I could tell he was going to kill me, so no point in being tactful. 'I can see why the King wants to execute you.'

Even from the anonymity of the cells the laughter was hesitant. Not a man to mock, then. Nothing soft in his face, just brute lines, scar, and the jut of bone beneath coarse skin. He lifted me, as if to dash me on the stone, like throwing down an egg.

'No!'

I could see under the giant's arm, an old man and a red-haired youth had followed him out and were now helping the Nuban to his feet.

'No,' the Nuban said again. 'I owe him a life, Brother Price. And besides, without him, you'd still be in that cell waiting on the pleasures of the morrow.'

Brother Price gave me a look of impersonal malice, and let me fall as though I'd ceased to exist. 'Let them all out.' He growled the words.

The Nuban gave the keys to the old man. 'Brother Elban.' Then he came across to where I'd landed. Lundist lay close by, face to the floor, blood pooling around his forehead.

'The gods sent you, boy, to loose me from that table.' The Nuban glanced at the torture rack, then at Lundist. 'You come with the brothers now. If we find the man you want dead; I kill him, maybe.'

I narrowed my eyes. I didn't like that 'maybe'.

I looked to Lundist for a moment. I couldn't tell if he were still breathing. I sensed a ghost of the guilt I should perhaps have felt, the itch from an amputated limb, still niggling though the flesh has long since gone.

I stood beside the Nuban, with Lundist at my feet, and watched as the outlaws released their comrades. I found myself staring into the orange heat of the coals, remem-bering.

I remembered a time when I lived in the lie. I lived in a world of soft things, mutable truths, gentle touches, laughter for its own sake. The hand that pulled me from the carriage that night, from the warmth of my mother's side, into a night of rain and screaming, that hand pulled me out by a doorway that I can't go back through. We all of us pass through that door, but we tend to exit of our own volition, and by degrees, sniffing the air, torn and tentative.

In the days following my escape and illness, I saw my old dreams grow small and wither. I saw my child's life yellow on the tree and fall, as if a harsh winter had come to haunt the spring. It was a shock to see how little my life had meant. How mean the dens and forts in which William and I had played with such fierce belief, how foolish our toys without the intensity of an innocent imagination to animate their existence.

Every waking hour I felt an ache, a pain that grew each time I turned the memory over in my hand. And I returned to it, time and again, like a tongue to the socket of a missing tooth, drawn by the absence.

I knew it would kill me.

The pain became my enemy. More than the Count Renar, more than my father's bartering with lives he should have held more precious than crown, or glory, or Jesu on the cross. And, because in some hard core of me, in some stubborn trench of selfish refusal, I could not, even at ten years of age, surrender to anything or anyone, I fought that pain. I analysed its offensive, and found its lines of attack. It festered, like the corruption in a wound turned sour, drawing strength from me. I knew enough to know the remedy. Hot iron for infection, cauterize, burn, make it pure. I cut from myself all the weakness of care. The love for my dead,

I put aside, secure in a casket, an object of study, a dry exhibit, no longer bleeding, cut loose, set free. The capacity for new love, I burned out. I watered it with acid until the ground lay barren and nothing there would sprout, no flower take root.

'Come.'

I looked up. The Nuban was speaking to me. 'Come. We're ready.'

The brothers were gathered around us in ragged and ill-smelling array. Price had one of the warders' swords. The other gleamed in the hand of a second giant of a man, just a shade shorter, a shade lighter, a shade younger, and so similar in form that he could only have been squeezed from the same womb as Price.

'We're going to cut a way out of here.' Price tested the edge of his sword against the short beard along his jawline. 'Burlow, up front with Rike and me. Gemt and Elban, take the rear. If the boy slows us down, kill him.'

Price threw a look around the chamber, spat, and made for the corridor.

The Nuban put a hand on my shoulder. 'You should stay.' He nodded to Lundist. 'But if you come, don't fall behind.'

I looked down at Lundist. I could hear the voices telling me to stay, familiar voices, but distant. I knew the old man would walk through fire to save me, not because he feared my father's wrath, but just . . . because. I could feel the chains that bound me to him. The hooks. I felt the weakness again. I felt the pain seeping through cracks I'd thought sealed.

I looked up at the Nuban. 'I won't fall behind,' I said.

The Nuban pursed his lips, shrugged, and set off after the others. I stepped over Lundist, and followed.

Assassination is just murder with a touch more precision. Brother Sim is precise.

14

So we rode out from Norwood. The peasants watched us, all sullen and dazed, and Rike cursed them. As if it had been his idea to keep them from a Renar bonfire and now they owed him a cheer as he left. We left them the ruins of their town, decorated with the corpses of the men that ruined it. Poor compensation, especially after Rike and the brothers had stripped the dead of anything of worth. I reckoned we could make Crath City by nightfall, riding hard, and be banging on the gates of the Tall Castle before the moon rose.

I shouldn't have been turning for home, picking up my old ways, and thinking once more about vengeance upon the Count of Renar. That's what instinct told me. But today instinct spoke with an old and dry voice and I no longer trusted it. I wanted to go home, perhaps because it felt as though something else required that I did not. I wanted to go home and if Hell rose up to stop me, it would make me desire it the more. We took the Castle Road, up through the garden lands of Ancrath.

Our path ran alongside gentle streams, between small woods and quiet farms. I'd forgotten how green it was. I'd grown used to a world of churned mud, burnt fields, smoke-grey skies, and the dead rotting on the ground. The sun found us, pushing its way through high cloud. In the warmth our column slowed until the clatter of hooves broke into lazy thuds. Gerrod paused where a three-bar gate led through the hedgerow. Beyond it, a field, golden with wheat, rolled out before us. He tore at the long grass around the gatepost. It felt as if God had poured honey over the land, sweet and slow, holding everything at peace. Norwood lay fifteen miles, and a thousand years, behind us.

'Good to be back eh, Jorg?' Makin pulled up beside me. He leaned forward in his stirrups and drank in the air. 'Smells of home.'

And it did. The scent of warm earth took me back, back to times when my world was small, and safe.

'I hate this place,' I said. He looked shocked at that, and Makin was never an easy man to shock. 'It's a poison men take willingly, knowing it will make them weak.'

I gave Gerrod my heels and let him hurry up the road. Makin caught me up and cantered alongside. We passed Rike and Burlow at the crossroads, throwing rocks at a scarecrow.

'Men fight for their homeland, Prince,' Makin said. 'It's the land they defend. The King and the land.'

I turned to holler at the stragglers. 'Close the line!'

Makin kept pace, waiting for an answer. 'Let the soldiers die for their land,' I said to him. 'If the time comes to sacrifice these fields in the cause of victory, I'll let them burn in a heartbeat. Anything that you cannot sacrifice pins you. Makes you predictable, makes you weak.'

We rode on at a trot, west, trying to catch the sun.

Soon enough we found the garrison at Chelny Ford. Or rather they found us. The watchtower must have seen us on the trail, and fifty men came out along the Castle Road to block our way.

I pulled up a few yards short of the pikemen, strung across the road in a bristling hedge, double-ranked. The rest of the squad waited behind the pike-wall, with drawn swords, save for a dozen archers arrayed amongst the corn in the field to our right. A score of heifers, in the field opposite, saw our approach and idled over to investigate.

'Men of Chelny Ford,' I called out. 'Well met. Who leads here?'

Makin came up behind me, the rest of the brothers trailing in after him, easy in their saddles.

A tall man stepped forward between two pikemen, but not too far forward, no idiot this one. He wore the Ancrath colours over a long chain shirt, and an iron pot-helm low on his brow. To my right a dozen sets of white knuckles strained on bowstrings. To my left the heifers watched from behind the hedge, complacent and chewing on the cud.

'I'm Captain Coddin.' He had to raise his voice as one of the cows let out a low moo. 'The King signs mercenaries at Relston Fayre. Armed bands are not permitted to roam into Ancrath. State your business.' He kept his eyes on Makin, looking for his answer there.

I didn't care for being dismissed as a child, but there's a time and place for taking offence. Besides, old Coddin seemed to know his stuff. Putting Brother Gemt out of his misery was one thing, but wasting one of Father's captains quite another.

I had my visor up already, so I used it to pull my helm off. 'Father Gomst!' I called for the priest, and the brothers shuffled their horses aside with a few mutters to let the old fellow past. He wasn't much to look at. He'd hacked off that beard he grew in the gibbet-cage, but grey tufts still decorated his face in random clusters, and his priestly robes seemed more mud than cloth.

'Captain Coddin,' I said. 'Do you know this priest, Father Gomst?'

Coddin raised an eyebrow at that. He had a pale face, and now it went paler. His mouth took on a hard edge, like a man who knows he's the butt of a joke that he hasn't worked out yet. 'Aye,' he said. 'The King's priest.' He snapped his heels together and inclined his head, as if he were in court. It seemed funny out there in the road, with the birds tweeting overhead and the stink of the cows washing over us.

'Father Gomst,' I said. 'Pray tell Captain Coddin who I am.'

The old fellow puffed himself up a bit. He'd been listless and grey since Norwood, but now he tried to find a crumb or two of authority.

'Prince Honorous Jorg Ancrath sits before you, Captain. Lost and now returned, he is bound for his royal father's court, and you would do well to see that he gets there with proper escort...' He glanced at me, screwing up what courage he had behind the foolish remnants of his beard. 'And a bath.'

A little snigger went up at that, on both sides of our standoff. It doesn't pay to underestimate a cleric. They know the power of words and they'll use them to their own ends. My palm ached for the hilt of my sword. I saw old Gomst's head falling from his shoulders, bouncing once, twice, and rolling to a halt by the hooves of a black-and-white heifer. I pushed the vision away.

'No bath. It's about time for a little road-stink at court. Soft words and rose-water may please the gentry, but those that fight the war live dirty. I return to my father as a man who has shared the soldier's lot. Let him know the truth of it.' I let my words carry on the still air, and kept my eyes on Gomsty. He had the wit to look away.

My speech earned no rousing cheer, but Coddin bowed his head and we had no further mention of baths. A shame, truth be told, because I'd been looking forward to a hot tub ever since I decided to turn for home.

So Coddin left his second to command the garrison, and rode with us. His escort of two dozen riders swelled our numbers to nearly sixty. Makin carried a lance from the Ford armoury now, flying the Ancrath colours and royal crest. The garrison riders spread word through the villages as we passed. 'Prince Jorg, Prince Jorg returned from the dead.' The news stole ahead of us, until each town presented a larger and better prepared reception. Captain Coddin sent a rider to the King before we left Chelny Ford, but even without his message, they would know of us in the Tall Castle well before we got there.

At Bains Town the bunting stretched across Main Street, six minstrels, sporting lute and clavichord, played 'The King's Sword' with more gusto than skill, jugglers exchanged twirling fire-brands and a bear danced before the mill pond. And the crowds! People packed in so tight we'd no hope of riding through. A fat woman in a tent of a dress which was striped like a tourney pavilion, saw me amid the van. She pointed and gave a shriek that drowned the minstrels out, 'Prince Jorg! The Stolen Prince!' The whole place went mad at that, cheering and crying. They surged forward like mad things. Coddin had his men in quick, though. I forgave him his earlier slight for that. If peasants had reached Rike we'd have had red slaughter.

On the Lich Road the brothers were more scared, but that's the only time I've seen more fear in them than there at Bains Town. They none of them knew what to make of it. Grumlow's left hand never left his dagger.

Red Kent grinned like a maniac, terror in his eyes. Still, they'd learn fast enough. When they figured out the welcome that lay ahead. When they'd seen the taverns and the whores. Well, there'd be no dragging them out of Bains Town in a week.

One of the minstrels found a horn, and a harsh note cut through the tumult. Guards, red-robed with black chain beneath, cleared a path, and no less a man than Lord Nossar of Elm emerged before us. I recognized the man from court. He looked slightly fatter in his gilded show-plate and velvets, rather more grey in the beard spilling down over his breastplate, but pretty much the same jolly old Nossar who rode me on his shoulders once upon a time.

'Prince Jorg!' The old man's voice broke for a moment. I could see tears shining in his eyes. It caught at me, that did. I felt it hook something in my chest. I didn't like it.

'Lord Nossar,' I gave back, and let a smile curl my lip. The same smile I gave Gemt before I let him have my knife. I saw a flicker in Nossar's eyes then. Just a moment of doubt.

He rallied himself. 'Prince Jorg! Beyond all hope, you've returned to us. I cursed the messenger for a liar, but here you are.' He had the deepest voice, rich and golden. Old Nossar spoke and you knew it was truth, you knew he liked you, it wrapped you up all warm and safe, that voice did. 'Will you honour my house, Prince Jorg, and stay a night?'

I could see the brothers exchanging glances, eyeing women in the crowd. The mill pond burned crimson with the dying sun. North, above the dark line of Rennat Forest, the smoke of Crath City stained a darkening sky.

'My Lord, it's a gracious invitation, but I mean to sleep in the Tall Castle tonight. I've been away too long,' I said.

I could see the worry on him. It hung on every crag of the man's face. He wanted to say more, but not here. I wondered if Father set him to detain me.

'Prince…' He lifted a hand, his eyes seeking mine.

I felt that hook in my chest again. He would set me down in his high hall and talk of old times in that golden voice. He'd speak of William, and Mother. If there was a man who could disarm me, Nossar was that man.

'I thank you for the welcome, Lord Nossar.' I gave him court formality, curt and final.

I had to haul on the reins to turn Gerrod. I think even horses liked Nossar. I led the brothers around by the river trail, trampling over some farmer's autumn turnips. The peasants cheered on, not sure what was happening, but cheering all the same.

We came to the Tall Castle by the cliff path, avoiding the sprawl of Crath City. The lights lay below us. Streets beaded with torch-light, the glow of fire and lamp rising from windows not yet shuttered against the cool of the night. The watchmen's lanterns picked out the Old City wall, a skewed semi-circle, tapering down to the river where the houses spilled out beyond the walls, into the valley, reaching out along the river. We came to the West Gate, the one place we could reach the High City without trailing up through the narrow streets of the Old City. The guards raised the portcullises for us, first one, then the next, then the next. Ten minutes of creaking windlass and clanking chain. I wondered why the three gates were down. Did our foes truly press so close we must triple-gate the High Wall?

The gate captain came out whilst his men sweated to raise the last portcullis. Archers watched from the battlements high above. No bunting here. I recognized the man vaguely, as old as Gomst, salt-and-pepper hair. It was his sour expression I recalled best, pinched around the mouth as if he'd just that moment sucked a lemon.

'Prince Jorg, we are told?' He peered up at me, raising his torch almost to my face. Evidently I had enough of the King's look about me to satisfy his curiosity. He lowered the torch fast enough and took a step back. I'm told I have my father's eyes. Maybe I do, though mine are darker. We could both give a stare that made men think again. I've always thought I look too girlish. My mouth too much the rosebud, my cheekbones too high and fine. It's of no great consequence. I've learned to wear my face as a mask, and generally I can write what I choose on it.

The captain nodded to Captain Coddin. He passed his gaze over Makin without a flicker, missed Father

Gomst in the crowd, and lingered instead on the Nuban, before casting a dubious eye over Rike.

'I can find accommodation for your men in the Low City, Prince Jorg,' he said. By the Low City he meant the sprawl beyond the walls of Old City.

'My companions can board with me at the castle,' I said.

'King Olidan requires only your presence, Prince Jorg,' the gate captain said. 'And that of Father Gomst, and Captain Bortha if he is with you?'

Makin raised a mailed hand. Both the gate captain's eyebrows vanished up beneath his helm at that. 'Makin Bortha? No…?'

'One and the same,' Makin said. He gave the man a broad grin, showing altogether too many teeth. 'Been a while, Relkin, you old bastard.'

King Olidan requires … no room for manoeuvre there. A polite little 'get your road-scum down to the slums'. At least Relkin made it clear enough from the start, rather than letting me lose face by arguing the odds before over-ruling me with King Olidan requires.

'Elban, take the brothers down to the river and find some rooms. There's a tavern, The Falling Angel, should be big enough for you all,' I said.

Elban looked surprised at having been chosen, surprised but pleased. He smacked his lips over his toothless gums and glared back at the rest of them. 'You heard Jorth! Prince Jorth I mean. Move it out!'

'Killing peasants is a hanging offence,' I said as they turned their horses. 'Hear me, Little Rikey? Even one. So no killing, no pillage, and no raping. You want a woman, let the Count of Renar buy you one with his coin. Hell, let him buy you three.'

All three gates stood open. 'Captain Coddin, a pleasure. Enjoy your ride back to the Ford,' I said.

Coddin bowed in the saddle and led his troops off. That left just me, Gomst and Makin. 'Lead on,' I said. And Gate Captain Relkin led us through the West Gate into the High City.

We had no crowds to contend with. The hour was well past midnight and the moon rode high now. The wide streets of the High City lay deserted save for the occasional servant scurrying from one great house to the next. Maybe a merchant's daughter or two watched us from behind the shutters, but in the main the noble houses slept sound and showed no interest in a returning prince.

Gerrod's hooves sounded too loud on the flagstones leading up to Tall Castle. Four years ago I left in velvet slippers, quieter than any mouse. The clatter of iron shoes on stone hurt my ears. Inside, a small voice still whispered that I'd wake Father. Be quiet, be quiet, don't breathe, don't even let your heart beat.

Tall Castle is of course anything but tall. In four years on the road I had seen taller castles, even bigger castles, but never anything quite like Tall Castle. The place seemed at once familiar and strange. I remembered it as bigger. The castle may have shrunk from the unending vastness I'd carried with me in memory, but it still seemed huge. Tutor Lundist told me the whole place once served as foundations for a castle so tall it would scrape the sky. He said that when men first built this, all we see now lay under the ground. The Road-men didn't build Tall Castle, but those who did had artifice almost to equal that of the Road-men. The walls weren't quarry-hewn, but seemingly crushed rock that had once poured like water. Some magic set metal bars through the stone of the wall, twisted bars of a metal tougher even than the black iron from the East. So Tall Castle brooded squat and ancient, and the King sat within its metal-veined walls, watching over the High City, the Old City, the Low City. Watching over the city of Crath and all the dominions of his line. My line. My city. My castle.

15

Four years earlier

We left the Tall Castle by the Brown Gate, a small door on the lower slopes of the mount, out past the High Wall. I came last, with the ache of all those steps in my legs.

Faint red footprints marked the top stair. The owners of that blood were probably still bleeding, far behind us.

For a moment I saw Lundist, lying as I'd left him.

We'd climbed from the very bowels of the castle vaults, to the least ostentatious of all the castle's exits. Dung men came this way a dozen times a day, carrying off the treasures of the privy. And I'll tell you, royal shit stinks no less than any other.

The brother ahead of me turned at the archway, and showed me his teeth by way of a grin. 'Fresh air! Take a breath o' that, Castle Boy.'

I'd heard the Nuban call this one Row, a wire of a man, gristle and bone, old scars and a mean eye. 'I'll lick a leper's neck before I take a lung-full o' your stench, Brother Row.' I pushed past him. It'd take more than talking like a road-brother to earn a place with these men, and giving an inch wasn't the way to start.

Ancrath stretched out on our right. To the left, the smoke and spires of Crath City rose behind the Old Wall. A storm light covered it all. The kind that falls when thunderclouds gather in the day. A flat light that makes a stranger of even the most familiar landscape. It felt appropriate.

'We travel fast and we travel hard,' Price said.

Price and Rike, the only true brothers among us, stood shoulder to shoulder at the head of the column, Rike bee-tling his brow while Price told us how it would be. 'We put as many miles between us and this shit-hole as it takes. The storm will hide our tracks. We'll find horses as we go, roust a village or two if need be.'

'You think the King's hunters can't track two dozen men through a bit of rain?' I wished my voice didn't ring so pure and high as I said it.

They all turned round at that. The Nuban flashed me a look, eyes wide, and patted down at the air as if to shut me up.

I pointed to the sprawl of roofs edging toward the river where Father's loving citizens had built beyond the safety of the city walls in their passion to be near him.

'By ones and twos a brother could find his way to a warm hearth, bit of roast beef, and an ale maybe,' I said. 'I hear there's a tavern or three to be found down there. A brother could be toasting by a fire before the rain even got to wash-ing his trail away.

'The King's men would be riding back and forth on those fine horses of theirs, getting wet, looking for the kind of rut that twenty men put in a road or across a field, looking for the kind of trouble a band of brothers stir up. And we'd be sitting comfortable in the shadow of the Tall Castle, waiting for the weather to clear.

'You think there's a man we left behind who could tell the Criers what we look like? You think the good folk of Crath City will notice a score added to their thousands?'

I could see I'd won them. I could see the light of that warm hearth reflecting in their eyes.

'And how the feck are we to pay for roast beef and a roof to hide under?' Price shoved through the brothers, setting the redhead, Gemt, on his rear. 'Start robbing in the shadow of the Tall Castle?'

'Yeah, how we a-gonna pay, Castle Boy?' Gemt scrambled to his feet, finding me a better target than Price for his anger. 'How we gonna?'

I brought up two ducats from my purse, and rubbed them together.

'I'll take that!' A sharp-faced man to my left lunged for the purse, still fat with coin.

I flipped the dagger from my belt and stuck it through his outstretched hand.

'Liar,' I said. I shoved a little more, until the hilt slapped up against his palm, the blade glistening red behind.

'Out the way, Liar.' Price grabbed him by the neck and tossed him down the slope.

Price loomed over me. Any full-grown man loomed over me, but Price added a new dimension to it. He took a handful of my jerkin and hauled me up, eye to eye, careless of the bloody knife I still had hold of.

'You're not scared of me, are you, boy?' The stink of him was something awful. Dead dog comes close.

I thought about stabbing him, but I knew there wasn't a wound that would stop him breaking me in two before he died.

'Are you scared of me?' I asked him.

We had us a moment of understanding then. Price didn't so much as twitch, but I saw it in him, and he saw it in me. He let me fall.

'We'll stay a day in the city,' Price said. 'The drinks are on Brother Jorg. Any of you whoresons start trouble before we leave, and I'll hurt you, bad.'

He held a hand out to me where I lay. I half-reached for it, before understanding. I tossed the purse to him.

'I'll go with the Nuban,' I said.

Price nodded. A black face lost from the dungeons would be remembered. A black face found in a Crath tavern would be remarked on.

The Nuban shrugged, and set off, east toward the open fields. I followed.

It wasn't until we'd lost ourselves in the maze of tracks and hedgerows that the Nuban spoke again.

'You should be afraid of Price, boy.'

The first breath of storm wind set the hawthorn rustling

to either side. I could smell the electricity, mixed in with the richness of the earth.

'Why?' I wondered if he thought I lacked the imagination for fear. Some men are too dull to feel what might happen. Others torture themselves with maybes and populate their dreams with horrors more terrible than their worst enemy could inflict upon them.

'Why would the gods care what happens to a child who doesn't care about himself?' the Nuban asked.

He paused before a turn in the road and moved close to the hedge. The wind shook again and white petals fell among the thorns. He looked back along the way we'd come.

'Maybe I'm not afraid of the gods either,' I said.

Fat drops of rain began to land around us.

The Nuban shook his head. Raindrops sparkled in the tight curls of his hair. 'You're a fool to make a fist at the gods, boy.' He flashed me a grin, and edged to the corner. 'Who knows what they might send you?'

Rain appeared to be the answer. It seemed to fall faster than normal, as if the sheer weight of water waiting to fall hurried the raindrops down. I moved in beside the Nuban. The hedge offered no shelter. The rain came through my tunic, cold enough to steal my breath. I thought then of the comforts I'd left behind, and wondered if perhaps I should have taken Lundist's counsel after all.

'Why are we waiting?' I asked. I had to raise my voice above the roar of the rain.

The Nuban shrugged. 'The road feels wrong.'

'Feels more like a river – but why are we waiting?'

He shrugged again. 'Maybe I need a rest.' He touched a hand to his burns, and a wince showed me his teeth, very white where most of the brothers had a mouthful of grey rot.

Five minutes passed and I kept my peace. We couldn't get wetter if we'd fallen down a well.

'How did you all get taken?' I asked. I thought of Price and Rike, and the notion of them surrendering to the King's guard seemed somehow comical.

The Nuban shook his head.

'How?' I asked again, louder, above the rain.

The Nuban glanced back along the road, then bent in close. 'A dream-witch.'

'A witch?' I made a face at him and spat water to the side.

'A dream-witch.' The Nuban nodded. 'The witch came in our sleep and kept us tied in dreams while the King's men took us.'

'Why?' I asked. If I took the witch seriously, and I didn't, I knew for certain that my father didn't employ any.

'I think he was seeking to please the King,' the Nuban said.

He stood without announcement and set off through the mud. I followed, but I held my tongue. I'd seen children tag after grown men throwing question after question, but I had put childhood aside. My questions could wait, at least until the rain stopped.

We sploshed along at a good pace for the best part of an hour before he stopped again. The rain had graduated from deluge to a steady soak that fell with the promise of lasting the night and through the next morning. This time our pause in the hedgerow proved well judged. Ten horsemen thundered by, kicking up mud left and right.

'Your king wants us back in his dungeons, Jorg.'

'He's not my king any more,' I said. I made to stand, but the Nuban caught my shoulder.

'You left a rich life in the King's own castle, and now you're hiding in the rain.' He kept a close watch on me. He read too much with his eyes and I didn't like it. 'Your uncle sacrificed himself to keep you safe. A good man I think. Old, strong, wise. But you came.' He shook a clot of mud from his free hand. A silence stretched between us, the kind that invites you to fill it with confession.

'There's a man I want dead.'

The Nuban frowned. 'Children shouldn't be this way.' The rain ran in trickles over the furrows on his brow. 'Men shouldn't be this way.'

I shook loose and set off. The Nuban fell in beside me and we covered another ten miles before the light failed entirely.

Our path took us by farmhouses and the occasional mill, but as night came we saw a cluster of lights below a wooded ridge a little south of us. From memory of Lundist's maps I guessed it to be the village of Pineacre, until now nothing more to me than a small green dot on old parchment.

'A bit of dry would be nice.' I could smell the wood-smoke. All of a sudden I understood how easily I'd sold the brothers my plan on the strength of warmth and food.

'We should spend the night up there.' The Nuban pointed to the ridge.

The rain fell soft now. It wrapped us in a cold blanket that leeched my strength away. I cursed my weakness. A day on the road had left me dead on my feet.

'We could sneak into one of those barns,' I said. Two stood isolated, just below the treeline.

The Nuban started to shake his head. In the east thunder rumbled, low but sustained. The Nuban shrugged. 'We could.' The gods loved me!

We made our way through fields turned half to swamp, stumbling in the darkness, me tripping over my exhaustion.

The door to the barn groaned a protest then squealed open as the Nuban heaved on it. A dog barked somewhere in the distance, but I doubted any farmer would dare the rain on the strength of a hound's opinion. We reeled in and fell into the hay. Each limb felt leaden, I would have sobbed with the tiredness if I'd let it have its way.

'You're not worried the dream-witch will come after you again?' I asked. 'She's hardly going to be pleased if her present to the King has escaped.' I stifled a yawn.

'He,' said the Nuban. 'I think it's a he.'

I pursed my lips. In my dreams the witches were always women. They'd hide in a dark room I'd never noticed before. A room whose open doorway stood off the corridor I had to follow. I'd pass the entrance and the skin on my back would crawl, invisible worms would tingle their way across the backs of my arms. I'd see her, sketched by shadows, her pale hands like spiders writhing from black sleeves. In that moment, when I tried to run, I'd become mired, as if I ran through molasses. I'd struggle, trying to shout, vomiting silence, a fly in the web, and she would advance, slow, inevitable, her face inching into the light. I'd see her eyes . . . and wake screaming.

'So you're not worried he'll come after you again?' I asked.

Thunder came in a sudden clap, shaking the barn.

'He has to be close,' the Nuban said. 'He has to know where you are.'

I let go of a breath I hadn't realized I'd been keeping.

'He'll send his hunter after us instead,' the Nuban said. I heard the rustle as he pulled the hay down on himself.

'That's a pity,' I said. It had been a long time since I'd dreamed of my own dream-witch. I rather liked the idea that she might be chasing us here, to this barn, in the jaws of the storm. I settled back into the prickle of the hay. 'I'll see if I can dream a witch tonight, yours or mine, I don't care. And if I do, this time I'm not running anywhere. I'm going to turn around and gut the bitch.'

16

Four years earlier

Thunder again. It held me for a moment. I felt it in my chest. Then the lightning, spelling out the world in harsh new shapes. I saw visions in the afterimages. A baby shaken until the blood came from its eyes. Children dancing in a fire. Another rumble rattled the boards, and the darkness returned.

I sat in the confusion between sleep and the waking world, surrounded by the creak of wood, the shake and rattle of the wind. Lightning stabbed again and I saw the interior of the carriage, mother opposite, William beside her, curled upon the bench-seat, his knees to his chest.

'The storm!' I twisted and caught the window. The slats resisted me, spitting rain as the wind whistled outside.

'Shush, Jorg,' Mother said. 'Go back to sleep.'

I couldn't see her in the dark, but the carriage held her scent. Roses and lemon-grass.

'The storm.' I knew I'd forgotten something. That much I remembered.

'Just rain and wind. Don't let it frighten you, Jorg, love.'

Did it frighten me? I listened as the gusts ran their claws across the door.

'We have to stay in the carriage,' she said.

I let the roll and rock of the carriage take me, hunting for that memory, trying to jog it loose.

'Sleep, Jorg.' It was more of a command than a recommendation.

How does she know I'm not asleep?

Lightning struck so close I could hear the sizzle. The light crossed her face in three bars, making something feral of her eyes.

'We have to stop the carriage. We have to get off. We have to—'

'Go to sleep!' Her voice carried an edge.

I tried to stand, and found myself weighed down, as if I were wading in the thickest mud . . . or molasses.

'You're not my mother.'

'Stay in the carriage,' she said, her voice a whisper.

The tang of cloves cut the darkness, a breath of myrrh beneath it, the perfume of the grave. The stink of it smothered all sound. Except the slow rasp of her breath.

I hunted the door handle with blind fingers. Instead of cold metal I found corruption, the softness of flesh turned sour in death. A scream broke from me, but it couldn't pierce the silence. I saw her in the next flash of the storm, skin peeled from the bone, raw pits for eyes.

Fear took my strength. I felt it running down my leg in a hot flood.

'Come to mother.' Fingers like twigs closed around my arm and drew me forward in the blackness.

No thoughts would form in the terror that held me. Words trembled on my lips but I had no mind to know what they would be.

'You're . . . not her,' I said.

One more flash, revealing her face an inch before mine. One more flash, and in it I saw my mother dying, bleeding in the rain of a wild night, and me hung on the briar, helpless in a grip made of more than thorns. Held by fear.

A cold rage rose in me. From the gut. I drove my forehead into the ruin of the monster's face, and took the door handle with a surety that needed no sight.

'No!'

And I leapt into the storm.

The thunder rolled loud enough to wake even the deepest buried. I jerked into a sitting position, confused by the stink of hay and the prickle of straw all around me. The barn! I remembered the barn.

A single point of illumination broke the night. A lantern's glow. It hung from a beam close by the barn door. A figure, a man, a tall one, stood in the fringes of the light. The Nuban lay at his feet, caught in a troubled sleep.

I made to cry out, then bit my cheek hard enough to stop myself. The copper tang of the blood sharpened away the remnants of my dream.

The man held the biggest crossbow I'd ever seen. With one hand he began to wind back the cable. He took his time. When you're hunting on behalf of a dream-witch I guess you're never in a rush. Unless one of your victims escapes whatever dreams have been sent to keep them sleeping . . .

I reached for my knife, and found nothing. I guessed it lost along whatever path my nightmare had led me through the hay. The lantern struck a gleam from something metal by my feet. A bailing hook. Three more turns on that crank and he'd be done. I took the hook.

The storm howl covered my approach. I didn't sneak. I walked across slow enough to be sure of my footing, fast enough to give ill fortune no time to act against me.

I'd thought to reach around and cut the bastard's throat, but he was tall, too tall for a ten-year-old's reach.

He lifted the crossbow to sight down at the Nuban.

Wait when waiting is called for. That's what Lundist used to tell me. But never hesitate.

I hooked the hunter between the legs and yanked up as hard as I could.

Where the crash of thunder and the roar of the wind had failed, the hunter's scream succeeded. The Nuban woke up. And to his credit there was no wondering where he was or what was happening. He surged to his feet and had a foot of steel through the man's chest in two heartbeats.

We stood with the hunter lying between us, each with our weapon blooded.

The Nuban wiped his blade on the hunter's cloak.

124

'That's a big old crossbow!' I toed it across the floor and marvelled at the weight of it.

The Nuban lifted the bow. He ran his fingers over the metalwork inlaid on the wood. 'My people made this.' He traced the symbols and the faces of fierce gods. 'And now I owe you another life.' He hefted the crossbow and smiled, his teeth a white line in the lantern glow.

'One will be enough.' I paused. 'It's Count Renar that has to die.'

And the smile left him.

17

The old corridors enfolded me and four years became a dream. Familiar turns, the same vases, the same suits of armour, the same paintings, even the same guards. Four years and everything was the same, except me.

In the niches small silver lamps burned oil squeezed from whales in distant seas. I walked from one pool of light to the next, behind a guard whose armour beggared my own. Makin and Gomst had been led to separate destinations, and I went alone to whatever reception awaited. The place still made me feel small. Doors built for giants, ceilings soaring so high that a man with a lance could scarcely touch them. We came to the west wing, the royal quarters. Would Father meet me here? Man to man in the arboretum? Souls bared beneath the planetarium dome? I had imagined him seated in the black claw of his throne, brooding above the court, and me led toward him between the men of the Imperial Guard.

I followed the single guard, feeling vaguely cheated. Did I want to be surrounded by armed men? Had I grown so dangerous? To be heaped with chains? Did I want him to fear me? Fourteen years old, and the King of Ancrath quaking behind his bodyguard?

I felt foolish for a moment. I brushed a hand over the hilt of my sword. They'd cast the blade from the metal that ran through the castle walls. A true heirloom, with a heritage at the Tall Castle predating mine by a thousand years at least. I ached for a confrontation then. Voices rose at the back of my mind, clamouring, fighting one against the other. The skin on my back tingled, the muscle beneath twitched for action.

'A bath, Prince Jorg?'

It was the guardsman. I nearly drew on him.

'No,' I said. I forced myself to calmness. 'I'll see the King now.'

'King Olidan has retired, Prince,' the guard said. Was he smirking at me? His eyes held an intelligence I didn't associate with the palace guard.

'Asleep?' I would have given a year of my life to take the surprise from those words. I felt like Captain Coddin must have: the butt of a joke I had yet to comprehend.

'Sageous awaits you in the library, my prince,' the man said. He turned to go, but I had him by the throat.

Asleep? They were playing with me, Father and this pet magician of his.

'This game,' I said. 'I expect it will provide amusement to somebody, but, if you … worry me … one more time, I will kill you. Think on it. You're a piece in

127

somebody else's game, and all you'll earn from it is a sword through the stomach, unless you redeem yourself in the next twenty seconds.'

It was a defeat, resorting to crude threats in a game of subtlety, but sometimes one must sacrifice a battle to win the war.

'Prince, I … Sageous is waiting for you…' I could see I'd turned his smug superiority into terror. I'd stepped outside the rules of play. I squeezed his throat a little. 'Why would I want to speak to this … Sageous? What's he to me?'

'He-he holds the King's favour. Pl-please, Prince Jorg.'

He got the words out past my fingers. It takes no great strength to throttle a man if you know where to grip.

I let him go and he fell, gasping. 'In the library you say? What's your name, man?'

'Yes, my prince, in the library.' He rubbed at his neck. 'Robart. My name is Robart Hool.'

I strode out across the Hall of Spears, angling for the leathered door to the library. I paused before it, turning back to Robart. 'There are turning points, Robart. Forks in the path we follow through our lives. Times that we look back to and say, "If only". This is one of those times. It's not often we get them pointed out to us. At this point you'll either decide to hate me, or to serve me. Consider the choice carefully.' I threw the library door open. It slammed back into the wall and I walked through.

In my mind the library walls stretched to the very heavens, thick with books, pregnant with the written word. I learned to read at three years of age. I was talking with Socrates at seven, learning form and thing from Aristotle. For the longest time I had lived in this library. Memory dwarfed reality: the place looked small now, small and dusty.

'I've burned more books than this!' I said.

Sageous stepped out from the aisle given over to ancient philosophy. He was younger than I expected, forty at the most, wearing just a white cloth, like the Roman togara. His skin held the dusky hue of the middle-lands, maybe Indus or Persia, but I could see it only in the rare spots the tattooist's needle hadn't found. He wore the text of a small book on his living hide, cut there in the flowing script of the mathmagicians. His eyes – well I know we're supposed to cower beneath the gaze of potent men, but his eyes were mild. They reminded me of the cows on the Castle Road, brown and placid. His scrutiny was the thing that cut. Somehow those mild eyes dug in. Perhaps the script beneath them bore the power. All I can say is that, for a time uncounted, I could see nothing but the heathen's eyes, hear nothing but his breath, stir no muscle but my heart.

He let me go, like a fish thrown back into the river, too small for the pot. We stood face to face, inches apart, and I'd no memory of closing the gap. But I'd come to him. We stood among the books. Among the wise words

129

of ten thousand years. Plato to my left, copied, copied and copied again. The 'moderns' to my right, Russell, Popper, Xiang, and the rest. A small voice inside me, deep inside, called for blood. But the heathen had taken the fire from me.

'Father must depend upon you, Sageous,' I said. I twisted my fingers, wanting to want my sword. 'To have a pagan at court must vex the priests. If the pope dared leave Roma these days, she'd be here to curse your soul to eternal hellfire!' I had nothing but dogma with which to beat him.

Sageous smiled, a friendly smile, like I'd just run an errand for him. 'Prince Jorg, welcome home.' He had no real accent, but he ran his words out fluid and musical, like a Saracen or a Moor.

He stood no taller than me, in fact I probably had an inch on him. He was lean too, so I could have taken him to the floor there and then, and choked the life out of him. One murderous thought bubbled up after another, and leaked away.

'There's a lot of your father in you,' he said.

'Have you got him tamed too?' I asked.

'One doesn't tame a man like Olidan Ancrath.' His friendly smile took an edge of amusement. I wanted to know the joke. He could manage me but not my father? Or he could manipulate the King and chose to cover the fact with a smirk?

I imagined the heathen's tattooed head shorn from his

shoulders, his smile frozen and blood pumping from the stump of his neck. In that instant I reached for my sword and threw all my will behind the action. The pommel felt cold beneath my touch. I curled my fingers around the hilt, but before I could squeeze them tight, my hand fell away like a dead thing.

Sageous raised a brow at that. He'd had them shaved like his head, and drawn back in. He took a step backward.

'You're an interesting young man, Prince Jorg.' His eyes hardened. Mild one moment, and in the next, dead as flint. 'We shall have to find out what makes you tick, yes? I'll have Robart escort you to your chamber, you must be tired.' All the time he spoke, the fingers of his right hand traced words in the flowing script across his left arm, brushing over one symbol jumping higher to a black crescent moon, underlining a phrase, underlining it again. I did feel tired. I felt lead in every limb, pulling me down.

'Robart!' he called out loud enough for the corridor.

He looked back to me, mild again. 'I expect you'll have dreams, Prince, after so long away.' His fingers moved over new lines, left hand, right arm. He traced words blacker than night across the veins in his wrist. 'Dreams tell a man who he is.'

I struggled to keep my eyes open. On Sageous's neck, just to the left of his Adam's apple, amid all the tight-packed scrawl, was a letter, bigger than the rest, curled and recurled so it looked like a flower.

Touch the flower, I thought. *Touch the pretty flower*. And as if by magic, my treacherous hand moved. It took him by surprise, my fingers at his throat. I heard the door open behind me.

He's skinny, I thought. *So skinny*. I wonder if I could close my hand around his neck. I admitted no hint of violence, just curiosity. And there it was, my hand around his neck. I heard Robart's sudden intake of breath. Sageous stood frozen, his mouth half open, as if he couldn't believe it.

I could barely stand, I could hardly keep the yawning from my voice, but I held his eye and let him think that the pressure I put on him was a threat, and not to keep me from falling.

'My dreams are my own, heathen,' I said. 'Pray you're not in them.'

I turned then, before I fell, and strode past Robart. He caught up in the Hall of Spears.

'I've never seen anyone lay hand on Sageous, my prince.'

My prince. That was better. There was admiration in his voice, maybe genuine, maybe not, I was too tired to care.

'He's a dangerous man, his enemies die in their sleep. That or they're broken. Lord Jale left the court two days after disagreeing with the pagan in front of your father. They say he can't feed himself now, and spends his days singing an old nursery rhyme over and over.'

I reached the West Stair, Robart prattling beside me. He broke off all of a sudden. 'Your chamber is off the Red Corridor, my prince.' He stopped and studied his boots. 'The Princess has your former chamber.'

Princess? I didn't care. Tomorrow, tomorrow I would find out. I let him lead me to my room. One of the guest rooms off the Red Corridor. The chamber could have housed many a tavern I'd slept in, but it was a studied insult none the less. A room for a country baron or distant cousin visiting from the protectorates.

I stopped at the door, reeling with exhaustion. Sageous's spell bit deeper and my strength left me like blood from sliced veins.

'I told you it was time to choose, Robart,' I said. I forced the words out one by one. 'Get Makin Bortha here. Let him guard my door this night. Time to choose.'

I didn't wait for a reply. If I had, he'd have had to carry me to bed. I pushed the door and half-staggered, half-fell, into the chamber. I collapsed back against the door, closing it, and slid to the floor. It felt like I kept on sliding, deeper and deeper, into an endless well.

18

I woke up with that sudden convulsion you get when every muscle you own suddenly realizes it's dropped off on duty. Next came the shock of realizing how deeply I'd been asleep. You don't sleep like that on the road, not if you want to wake up again. For a moment the darkness would yield nothing to my confusion. I reached for my sword and found only soft sheets. The Tall Castle! It came back to me. I remembered the pagan and his spell.

I rolled to the right. I always left my gear on my right side. Nothing but more mattress, soft and deep. I might have been blind for all the help my eyes gave. I guessed the shutters were shut tight, for not the slightest whisper of starlight reached me. It was quiet too. I reached out for the edge of the bed, and didn't find it. *A wide bed*, I thought, trying to find some humour in the situation.

I let go the breath I'd been holding, the one I sucked in so fast when I woke. What was it that made me start?

What dragged me out of the pagan's spell in this oh so comfortable bed? I pulled my hand back, drew my knees to my chest. Somebody had put me to bed and taken my clothes. Not Makin, he'd not leave me naked against the night. That somebody and I would be having a discussion soon enough. But it could wait until morning. I just wanted to sleep, to let the day come.

Only sleep had kicked me out, and it wasn't about to let me back in. So I lay there, naked in the strange bed, and wondered where my sword was.

The noise came so quiet at first I could believe I imagined it. I stared blind into the darkness and let my ears suck in the silence. It came again, soft as the whisper of flesh on stone. I could hear the ghost of a sound, a breath being drawn. Or maybe just a night breeze fingering its way through the shutters.

Ice ran up my spine, tingling on my shoulders. I sat up, biting back the urge to speak, to show bravado to the unseen terrors. *I'm not six years old*, I told myself. *I've made the dead run*. I threw the sheets back and stood up. If the pagan's horror was waiting in the darkness then sheets would be no shield. With my hands held up before me, I walked forward, finding first the elusive edge of the bed, and then the wall. I turned and followed it, fingers trailing the stonework. Something went tumbling and broke with an expensive crash. I barked my shins on an unseen obstacle, nearly groined myself on a sideboard of some kind, then found the shutter slats.

I fumbled with the shutter catch. It defied me maddeningly, as though my fingers were frost-clumsy. The skin on my back crawled. I heard footsteps drawing closer. I hauled on the shutters with all my strength. Every move I made seemed slow and feeble, as though I moved through molasses, like in those dreams where the witch chases you and you can't run.

The shutters gave without warning. They flew back and I found that I was standing high above the execution yard, drenched in moonlight. I spun around. Slow, too slow. And found nothing. Just a room of silver and shadows.

The window threw the moonlight on the wall to my right. My shadow reached forward in the arch of the window and fell at the feet of a tall portrait. A full length picture of a woman. I went numb: my face felt like a mask. I knew the picture. Mother. Mother in the great hall. Mother in a white dress, tall and icy in her perfection. She said she never liked that picture, that the artist had made her too distant, too much the queen. Only William softened it, she said. If she'd not had William hugging to her skirts she would have given the picture away, she said. But she couldn't throw little William away.

I pulled my eyes from her face, pale in the silver light. She loomed above me, tall in life, taller in the portrait. Her dress fell in cascades of lace-froth: the artist had caught it well. He made it look real.

The open shutters let in a chill and I felt a cold beyond any autumn frost. My skin rose in tiny bumps. She couldn't throw William away. Only William wasn't there any more … I took a step back toward the open window.

'Sweet Jesu…' I blinked away tears.

Mother's eyes followed me.

'Jesu wasn't there, Jorg,' she said. 'Nobody came to save us. You watched us, Jorg. You watched, but you didn't come to help.'

'No.' I felt the window sill cold against the back of my knees. 'The thorns … the thorns held me.'

She looked at me, eyes silver with the moon. She smiled and I thought for a moment she would forgive me. Then she screamed. She didn't scream the screams she'd made when the Count's men raped her. I could have stood that. Maybe. She screamed the screams she made when they killed William. Ugly, hoarse, animal screams, torn from her perfect painted face.

I howled back. The words burst from me. 'The thorns! I tried, Mother. I tried.'

He rose up from behind the bed then. William, sweet William with the side of his head caved in. The blood clotted black on his golden hair. The eye that side was gone, but the other held me.

'You let me die, Jorg,' he said. He spoke it past a bubbling in his throat.

'Will.' I couldn't say any more.

He lifted a hand to me, white with the trickles of blood darkest crimson.

The window yawned behind me and I made to throw

myself back through it, but as I did something jolted me forward. I staggered and righted myself. Will stood there, silent now.

'Jorg! Jorg!' A shout reached me, distant but somehow familiar.

I looked back toward the window and the dizzying fall.

'Jump,' said William.

'Jump!' Mother said.

But Mother didn't sound like Mother any more.

'Jorg! Prince Jorg!' The shout came louder now, and a more violent jolt threw me to the floor.

'Get out of the fucking way, boy.' I recognized Makin's voice. He stood framed in the doorway, lamplight behind. And somehow I lay on the floor at his feet. Not by the window. Not naked, but in my armour still.

'You were jammed up against the door, Jorg,' Makin said. 'This Robart fellow told me to come running, and here you are screaming behind the door.' He glanced around, looking for the danger. 'I ran from the South Wing for your blasted nightmare did I?' He shoved the door open wider and added a belated, 'Prince.'

I got to my feet, feeling as if I'd been rolled on by Fat Burlow. There was no painting on the wall, no Mother, no Will behind the bed.

I drew my sword. I needed to kill Sageous. I wanted it so badly I could taste it, like blood, hot and salt in my mouth.

'Jorg?' Makin asked. He looked worried, as if he was wondering if I'd gone mad.

I moved toward the open door. Makin stepped to block me. 'You can't go out there with a drawn sword, Jorg, the guard would have to stop you.'

He didn't stand as tall or as wide as Rike, but Makin was a big man, broad in the shoulder and stronger than a man should be. I didn't think I could take him down without killing him.

'It's all about sacrifice, Makin,' I said. I let my sword drop.

'Prince?' He frowned.

'I'm going to let that tattooed bastard live,' I said. 'I need him.' I glimpsed my mother again, fading. 'I need to understand what game is being played out here. Who exactly the pieces are and who the players are.'

Makin's frown deepened. 'You get some sleep, Jorg. In the bed this time.' He glanced back into the corridor. 'Do you want some light in there?'

I smiled at that. 'No,' I said. 'I'm not afraid of the dark.'

19

I woke early. A grey light through the shutters showed me the room for the first time: big, well-furnished, hunting tapestries on the walls. I uncoiled my fingers from my sword hilt, stretched and yawned. It didn't feel right, this bed. It was too soft, too clean. When I threw the covers back they knocked the servant-bell from the bedside table. It hit the flagstones with a pretty tinkling then bounced onto a rug and lost its voice. Nobody came. That suited me fine: I'd dressed myself for four years. Hell, I'd rarely undressed! And what rags I had would be put to shame by the meanest of servant smocks. Even so. Nobody came.

I wore my armour over the grey tatters of my shirt. A looking-glass lay on the sideboard. I let it lie there face down. A quick run of fingers through hair in search of any louse fat enough to be found, and I was ready to break my fast.

First I threw the shutters open. No fumbling with the catch this time. I looked out over the execution yard, a square bounded by the blank walls of the Tall Castle. Kitchen-boys and maids hastened across the bleak courtyard, going about their various quests, blind to the pale wash of the sky so high above them.

I turned from the window and set off on my own little quest. Every prince knows the kitchens better than any other quarter of his castle. Where else can so much adventure be found? Where else is the truth spoken so plain? William and I learned a hundred times more in the kitchens of the Tall Castle than from our books on Latin and strategy. We'd steal ink-handed from Lundist's study and sprint through long corridors, leaping down the stairs too many at a time, to reach the refuge of the kitchens.

I walked those same corridors now, ill at ease in the confined space. I'd spent too long under wide skies, living bloody. We learned about death in the kitchens too. We watched the cook turn live chickens to dead meat with a twist of his hands. We watched Ethel the Bread pluck the fat hens, leaving them naked in death, ready for gutting. You soon learn there's no elegance or dignity in death if you spend time in the castle kitchens. You learn how ugly it is, and how good it tastes.

I turned the corner at the end of the Red Corridor, too full of memories to pay attention. All I saw was a figure bearing down on me. Instincts learned on the road took over. Before I had time to register the long hair and silks, I had her against the wall, a hand across her mouth and my knife to her throat. We were face by face and my captive held my stare, eyes an unreal green like stained glass. I let my snarl relax into a smile and unclenched my teeth. I stepped back, letting her off the wall.

'Your pardon, my lady,' I said, and sketched her a shallow bow. She was tall, nearly my height, and surely not many years my senior.

She gave me a fierce grin and wiped her mouth with the back of her hand. It came away bloody, from a bitten tongue. Gods but she was good to look at. She had a strong face, sharp in the nose and cheekbones but rich in the lips, all framed by the darkest red hair.

'Lord how you stink, boy,' she said. She stepped around me, as if she was checking a horse at market. 'You're lucky Sir Galen isn't with me, or a skivvy would be picking your head off the ground about now.'

'Sir Galen?' I asked. 'I'll be sure to watch out for him.' She had diamonds around her neck on a complex web of gold. Spanard work: none on the Horse Coast could make a thing like that. 'It wouldn't do for the King's guests to go about killing one another.' I took her for the daughter of a merchant come a-toadying to the King. A very rich merchant, or maybe the daughter of some count or earl from the east: there was a eastern burr to her voice.

'You're a guest?' She raised a brow at that, and very pretty it looked too. 'I think not. You look to have stolen in. By the privy chute to judge by the smell. I don't think you could have climbed the walls, not in that clunky old armour.'

I clicked my heels together, like the table knights, and offered her an arm. 'I was on my way to break fast in the kitchens. They know me there. Perhaps you'd like to accompany me and check my credentials, lady?'

She nodded, ignoring my arm. 'I can send a kitchen-boy for the guards and have you arrested, if we don't meet any on the way.'

So we walked side by side through the corridors and down one flight of stairs after another.

'My brothers call me Jorg,' I said. 'How are you called, lady?' I found the court-speak awkward on the tongue, especially with my mouth so unaccountably dry. She smelled like flowers.

'You can call me "my lady",' she said, and wrinkled her nose again. We passed two of the house guards in their fire-bronze plate and plumes. Both of them studied me as if I was a turd escaped from the privy, but she said nothing and they let us pass.

We passed the storerooms where the salt beef and pickled pork lay in barrels, stacked to the ceiling. 'My lady' seemed to know the way. She shot me a glance with those emerald eyes of hers.

'So did you come here to steal, or for murder with that dagger of yours?' she asked.

'Perhaps a bit of both.' I smiled.

A good question though. I couldn't say why I'd come, other than I felt somebody didn't want me to. Ever since that moment when I found Father Gomst in his cage, ever since that ghost ran its course through me and my thoughts turned to the Tall Castle, it felt as though someone were steering me away. And I don't take direction.

We passed Short Bridge, little more than three mahogany planks over the great iron valves that could seal the lower levels from the castle main. The doors, steel and three feet thick, would slide up from the gaping slot in the corridor floor, so Tutor Lundist told me. Lifted on old magic. I'd never seen them close. Torches burned here, no silver lamps for the servant levels. The stink of tar-smoke made me more at home than anything yet.

'Perhaps I'll stay,' I said.

The kitchen arch lay just ahead of us. I could see Drane, the assistant cook, wrestling half a hog through the doors.

'Wouldn't your brothers miss you?' she asked, playful now. She touched her fingers to the corner of her mouth, where the red pattern of my fingers had started to rise. Something in her gesture made me rise too.

I shrugged, then paused as I worked the straps of the vambrace over my left forearm. 'There are plenty of brothers on the road,' I said. 'Let me show you the kind of brothers I meant...'

'Here,' she said, impatient.

The torch-light burned in the red of her hair. She undid the clasps with deft fingers. The girl knew armour. Perhaps Sir Galen was for more than just beheading ill-mannered louts?

'What then?' she asked. 'I've seen arms before, though maybe not one so dirty.'

I grinned at that and turned my arm over so she could see the Brotherhood brand across my wrist. Three ugly bands of burn-scar. A look of distaste furrowed her brow. 'You're a sell-sword? You take your pride in that?'

'More pride in that than in what true family I have left.' I felt a bite of anger. I felt like sending this distracting merchant's daughter on her way, making her run.

'What are these?' She reached out to run her fingers from the brand up to the small of my elbow where the armour stopped her. 'Jesu! There's more scar than boy under this dirt!'

At her touch a thrill ran through me, and I pulled away. 'I fell in a thorn bush when … when I was a child,' I said, my voice too sharp.

'Some thorn bush!' she said.

I shrugged. 'A hook-briar.'

She twisted her mouth into an 'ouch'. 'You've got to lie still in one of those,' she said, her eyes still on my arm. 'Everyone knows that. Looks as if it tore you to the bone.'

'I know that. *Now.*' I set off for the kitchen doors, walking fast.

She ran to catch me, silks swirling. 'Why did you struggle? Why didn't you stop?'

'I was stupid,' I said. 'I wouldn't struggle now.' I wanted the silly bitch to leave. I didn't even feel hungry any more.

My arm burned with the memory of her fingers. She was right, the thorns had cut me deep. Every few weeks for more than a year the poison would flare in the wounds and run through my blood. When the poison ran in me I'd done things that scared even the brothers.

Drane lumbered out through the doors just as I reached them. He pulled up short, and wiped his hands on the soiled white apron stretched over his belly. 'Wh—' He looked past me and his eyes widened. 'Princess!' He seemed suddenly terrified, quivering like a blob of jelly. 'Princess! Wh-what are you doing in the kitchens? It's no place for a lady in silks and all.'

'Princess?' I turned to stare at her. I'd left my mouth open, so I closed it.

She gave me a smile that left me wondering if I wanted to slap it off her, or kiss it. Before I could decide, a heavy hand landed on my shoulder, and Drane turned me round. 'And what's a ruffian like you doing leading her highness astray...' The question died in his throat. His fat face crinkled up and he tried to speak again, but the words wouldn't come. He let me go and found his voice. 'Jorg? Little Jorg?' Tears streamed down his cheeks.

Will and I had watched the man throttle a few chickens and bake a few pies: there was no call for him to start blubbing over me. I let him off the embarrassment though, he'd given me the chance to see her royal highness look surprised. I grinned at her and gave a court bow.

'Princess, eh? So I guess that means the road-trash you wanted to have the palace guards arrest is in fact your step-brother.'

She recovered her composure quickly. I'll give her that.

'Actually, that would make you my nephew,' she said. 'Your father married my older sister two months ago. I'm your Aunt Katherine.'

20

We sat at the long trestle where the kitchen skivvies ate their meals, Aunt Katherine and I. The servants cleared the low vault and brought in more light, candles of every length and girth in clay holders. They watched from the doorways at either end, a shabby crowd grinning and bobbing as though it was a holy day or a high day, and we were the mummers to entertain them. Drane hove into view and crested through the skivvies like a barge through water. He brought fresh bread, honey in a bowl, golden butter, and silver knives.

'This is the place to eat,' I said. I kept my eyes on Katherine. She didn't seem to mind. 'Bread hot from the oven.' It steamed when I tore it open. Heaven must smell like fresh bread. 'I knew I missed you for a reason, Drane.' I called the words over my shoulder. I knew the fat cook would bask in that for a year. I hadn't missed him. I hadn't spared him but one thought for every hundred times I dreamed of his pies. In fact I'd struggled to remember his name when I saw him in the doorway. But something about the girl made me want to be the kind of man who would remember.

The first bite woke my hunger and I tore at the loaf as though it were a haunch of venison and me huddled on the road with the brothers. Katherine paused to watch, her knife suspended above the honey bowl, her lips twitching with a smile.

'Mmmfflg.' I chewed and swallowed. 'What?' I demanded.

'She's probably wondering if you'll go under the table when the bread's gone and wrestle the dogs for bones.' Makin had come up behind me unnoticed.

'Damn but you'd make a good footpad, Sir Makin.' I swung round to find him standing over me, his armour gleaming. 'A man in plate-mail should have the decency to clank.'

'I clanked plenty, Prince,' he said. He showed me an annoying smile. 'You had your mind on more pressing matters maybe?' He bowed toward Katherine. 'My lady. I haven't had the honour?'

She extended a hand to him. 'Princess Katherine Ap Scorron.'

Makin raised a brow at that. He took her hand and bowed again, much more deeply, lifting her fingers to his lips. He had thick lips, sensuous. He'd washed his face and his hair gleamed as much as his armour, coal-black and curled. He cleaned up well, and for the smallest moment I hated him without reservation.

'Take a seat,' I said. 'I'm sure the excellent Drane can find more bread.'

He let go of her hand. Too slowly for my liking. 'Sadly, my prince, duty rather than hunger brings me to the kitchens. I thought I might find you here. You're summoned to the throne-room. There must be a hundred squires hunting the halls for you. You also, Princess.' He favoured her with an appreciative stare. 'I met a fellow named Galen searching for you.' Something tight laced those last words. Makin didn't like Sir Galen any more than I did. And he'd met the man.

I took the bread with me. It was too good to leave.

We found our way back above ground. The Tall Castle appeared to have woken up during my trip to the kitchens. Squires and maids ran this way and that. Plumed guards passed by in twos and fives, bound for their duties. We skirted a lord in his furs and gold chain, girded by flunkies, leaving him with his astonishment, his bowing, and his 'Good morning, Princess!'.

By corridor and hall we reached Torrent Vault, the antechamber before the throne-room where the tourney armour of past kings lined the walls like hollow knights standing silent vigil.

'Prince Honorous Jorg Ancrath, and the Princess Katherine,' Makin announced us to the guards before the doors. He placed me before the princess. A small matter on the road, but a touch that spoke volumes in the Torrent Vault. *Here is the heir to the throne, let him in.*

The crested guardsmen flanking the hallway stood as still as the armour on the stands behind them. They followed us only with their eyes, gauntleted hands kept folded on the pommels of their greatswords, set point to floor. The two table knights at the throne-room doors exchanged a glance. They paused for a moment to bow to Katherine, then set to work drawing the great doors open wide enough to admit us. I recognized one of them by the coat of arms on his breastplate, horns above an elm. Sir Reilly. He'd turned grey in the years I'd been gone. He struggled with his door, straining to move the oak in its bronze cladding. The doors parted. Our narrow view grew from a sliver of warm light to a window on a world I once knew. The Court of the Ancrath kings.

'Princess?' I took her hand, holding it high, and we walked through.

The men that built the Tall Castle lacked nothing in skill, and everything in imagination. Their walls might remain for ten thousand years, but they would hold no artistry. The throne-room was a windowless box. A box one hundred feet on every side maybe, and with a twenty-foot ceiling to dwarf the courtiers, but a box none the less. Elaborate wooden galleries for the musicians muted the harsh corners, and the King's dais added a certain splendour. I kept my eyes from the throne.

'The Princess Katherine Ap Scorron,' the herald called.

No mention of poor Jorgy. No herald would dare such a slight without instruction.

We crossed the wide floor, our pace measured, watched by the guardsmen at the walls. Men with cross-bows by the walls to left and right, swordsmen at the plinth and by the door.

I might have been nameless, but my arrival had certainly roused some interest. In addition to the guardsmen and despite the early hour, at least a hundred courtiers formed our audience. They waited attendance on the throne, milling around the lowest steps in their velvets. I let my eyes stray across the glittering crowd, pausing to linger on the finest jewels. I still had my road-habits and made mental tally of their worth. A new charger on that countess's fat bosom alone. That lord's chain of office could buy ten suits of scale armour. There was surely a fine longbow and a pony in each of his rings. I had to remind myself I played for new stakes now. Same old game, new stakes. Not higher, but different.

The gentle chatter of the court rose and fell as we approached. The soft hubbub of knife-edged comments, damaging sarcasm, honeyed insults. Here the sharp intake of breath at the Prince coming to court still wearing the road, there the mocking laughter half-hidden behind a silk handkerchief.

I let myself look at him then.

Four years had wrought no change in my father. He sat on the high-backed throne, hunched in a wolf-skin robe edged with silver. He'd worn the same robe on the day I left. The Ancrath crown rested on his brow: a warrior crown, an iron band set with rubies, confining black hair streaked with the same grey as the iron. To his left, in the consort chair, the new queen sat. She had Katherine's looks, though softer, with a web of silver and moonstones to tame her hair. Any sign of her pregnancy lay hid beneath the ivory froth of her gown.

Between the thrones grew a magnificent tree, wrought all of glass, its leaves the emerald of Katherine's eyes, wide and thin and many. It reached a slender nine feet in height, its twigs and branches gnarled and vitreous, brown as caramel. I'd never seen the like before. I wondered if it might be the Queen's dowry. Surely it had the worth.

Sageous stood beside the glass tree, in the dappled green light beneath its leaves. He'd abandoned the simple white he'd worn when first we met in favour of black robes, high in the collar, with a rope of obsidian plates about his neck. I met his eyes as we approached, and manufactured a smile for him.

The courtiers drew back before us, Makin to the fore, Katherine and me hand in hand. The perfumes of lords and ladies tickled at my nose: lavender and orange oil. On the road, shit has the decency to stink.

Only two steps down from the throne a tall knight stood in magnificent plate, the iron worked over with fire-bronze, twin dragons coiling on his breastplate in a crimson inferno.

'Sir Galen.' Makin hissed the words back at me.

I glanced at Katherine and found her smile unreadable. Galen watched us with hot blue eyes. I liked him a little better for wearing his hostility so plainly. He had the blonde hair of a Teuton, his features square and handsome. He was old though. As old as Makin. Thirty summers at the least.

Sir Galen made no move to let Makin past. We stopped five steps down.

'Father,' I said. In my head, I'd made my speech a hundred times but somehow the old bastard managed to steal the words from my tongue. The silence stretched between us. 'I hope—' I started again but he cut over me.

'Sir Makin,' Father said, not even looking at me. 'When I send the captain of the palace guard out to retrieve a ten-year-old child, I expect him to return by nightfall. Perhaps a day or three might suffice if the child proved particularly elusive.' Father raised his left hand from the arm of the throne, just by an inch or two but enough to cue his audience. A scattered tittering sounded among the ladies, cut off when his fingers returned to the ironwood of the chair.

Makin bowed his head and said nothing.

'A week or two on such a task would signify incompetence. More than three years speaks of treason.'

Makin looked up at that. 'Never, my king! Never treason.'

'We once had reason to consider you fit for high office,

154

Sir Makin,' Father said, his voice as cold as his eyes. 'So, you may explain yourself.'

The sweat gleamed on Makin's brow. He'd have gone through this speech as many times as I had mine. He'd probably lost it just as profoundly.

'The Prince has all the resourcefulness one might hope for in the heir to the throne,' Makin began. I saw the Queen frown at his turn of phrase. Even Father's mouth tightened and he glanced at me, fleeting and unreadable. 'When at last I found him we were in hostile lands … Jaseth … more than three hundred miles to the south.'

'I know where Jaseth is, Sir Makin,' Father said. 'Do not presume to lecture me on geography.'

Makin inclined his head. 'Your majesty has many enemies, as do all great men in these times of trouble. No single blade, even one as loyal as my own, could protect your heir in such lands as Jaseth. Prince Jorg's best defence lay in anonymity.'

I glanced over the court. It seemed that Makin's speech had not deserted him after all. His words had an impact.

Father ran a hand over his beard. 'Then you should have ridden back to the castle with a nameless charge, Sir Makin. I wonder that this journey took four years.'

'The Prince had taken up with a band of mercenaries, your majesty. By his own skill he won their allegiance. He told me plain that if I moved to take him they would kill me and that if I stole him away, he would announce himself to every passer by. And I believed him, for he has the will of an Ancrath.'

Time to be heard, I thought. 'Four years on the road have given you a better captain,' I said. 'There's more to learn about making war than can be discovered in this castle. We—'

'You lack enterprise, Sir Makin,' Father said. His eyes never flickered from Makin. I wondered if I'd spoken at all. Anger tinged his voice now. 'Had I ridden out after the boy, I would have found a way to return with him from Jaseth within a month.'

Sir Makin bowed deeply. 'That is why you deserve your throne, majesty, whilst I am merely captain of your palace guard.'

'You are the captain of my guard no longer,' Father said. 'Sir Galen serves in that capacity now, as he served the House of Scorron.'

Galen offered Makin the slightest of bows, a mocking smile on his lips.

'Perhaps you would like to challenge Sir Galen for your old office?' Father asked. Again he fingered his salt-and-pepper beard.

I sensed a trap here. Father didn't want Makin back.

'Your majesty has chosen his captain,' Makin said. 'I would not presume to over-write that decision with my sword.' He sensed the trap too.

'Indulge me.' Father smiled then, for the first time since our entrance, and it was a cold thing. 'The court has been quiet in your absence. You owe us some entertainment. Let us have a show.' He paused. 'Let us see what you have learned on the road.' So he did hear me.

'Father—' I started. And again he cut me off. I couldn't seem to rise above him.

'Sageous, take the boy,' he said.

And that was that. The heathen had his eyes on me and led me mild as a sheep to stand with him between the thrones. Katherine shot me a pale glance and hastened to her sister's side.

Makin and Galen bowed to the King. They went out through the press of courtiers, breaking free and crossing to where an inlaid marble star, some ten feet across, marked the middle of the throne-room floor. They faced each other, bowed, and drew steel.

Makin bore the longsword Father gave him when he took captaincy of the palace guard. A good weapon, Indian steel woven dark and light, acid-etched with old runes of power. Our time on the road had left its history recorded in notches along the blade. I'd never seen a better swordsman than Makin. I didn't want to see one here.

Sir Galen made no move. He held his longsword ready, but in a lazy grip. I could see no marking on the weapon, a simple blade, forged from the black iron of the Turkmen.

'Never trust a Turkman sword…' I spoke in a whisper.

'For Turkman iron sucks up spells like a sponge and holds a bitter edge.' Sageous finished the old line for me.

I had a sharp reply for the heathen, but the clash of swords rang out over it. Makin advanced on the Teuton, feinting low then swinging high. Makin had an elemental way with a sword. The blade was part of him, a living thing from tip to hilt. In a wild fight he knew where every danger lay, and where his cover waited.

Sir Galen blocked and delivered a sharp riposte. Their swords flickered and the play of metal rang out high and sharp. I could barely follow the exchange. Galen fought with technical precision. He fought like a man who rose at dawn every day to train and duel. He fought like a man who expected to win.

A hundred narrow escapes from death counted out the first minute of their duel. I found my right hand gripping the trunk of the glass tree, the crystal slick and cool under my fingers. By the end of that first minute I could tell Galen would win. This was his game. Makin had his brilliance but, like me, he fought in real fights. He fought in the mud. He fought through burning villages. He used the battlefield. But this dry little game, so narrow in its scope, this was all Galen lived for.

Makin swung at Galen's legs. A touch too tight in the curve, and Galen made him pay. The tip of the Turkman blade sketched a red line across Makin's forehead. A quarter of an inch more reach in Galen's arm and the blow would have shattered Makin's skull.

'So, you open your game by sacrificing your knight, Prince Jorg.' Sageous spoke close to my ear.

I startled. I'd forgotten about the man. My gaze wandered to the green canopy above us. 'I have no problems with sacrifice, heathen.' The tree trunk slipped glassy smooth under my fingers as my left hand moved up along the trunk. The clash of swords punctuated our conversation. 'But I sacrifice only when there is something to be gained.'

The tree was heavier than I had imagined and for a moment I didn't think I could topple it. I braced my legs and put my shoulder to the task. The thing fell without a sound, then exploded into a million pieces against the steps. I could have blinded half of Ancrath's aristocracy had their eyes been on the throne rather than the fight before them. As it was I peppered their backs with shards of glass. The costumed throng at the base of the royal dais turned into a screaming mass. Noble-born women ran their hands through hair confined by diamond tiaras, and brought them out sliced and bloody. Lords in thread-of-gold slippers, coiled in the latest fashions, hopped howling on a carpet of broken glass.

Sir Makin and Sir Galen lowered their swords and watched in amazement.

When Father stood, everyone fell silent, cuts or no cuts.

Everyone except me. He opened his mouth to speak and I spoke first.

'The lessons Makin learned on the road did not include tourney games. Wars are not won with jousting

159

or chivalry. The lessons Makin learned are the same lessons I learned. Unfortunately Sir Makin would rather die than offend his king by demonstrating them.' I didn't raise my voice. That kept them quiet. 'Father,' I turned to face him direct. 'I'll show you what I've learned. I'll fight your pet Teuton. If a man of my little experience can defeat your champion then you should be happy to reinstate Sir Makin, neh?' I fell back into road-speak, hoping to stir his anger.

'You're not a man, boy, and your challenge is an insult to Sir Galen, not worthy of consideration.' He spoke through clenched teeth. I'd never seen him so angry. In fact, I'd never seen him angry.

'An insult? Maybe.' I felt a smile bubbling up and let it show. 'But I am a man. I came of age three days ago, Father. I'm fit for marriage now. A valuable commodity. And I claim this fight as my Year Gift. Or would you turn your back on three centuries of Ancrath tradition and deny me my coming of age boon?'

The veins in his neck stood proud and his hands flexed as if hungry for a sword. I didn't think it safe to count on his good will.

'If I die the succession will be clear,' I said. 'Your Scorron whore will give you a new son, and you'll be rid of me. Gone for good, like Mother and William. And you won't have to send dear old Father Gomst trawling the mire to prove it.' I took a moment to bow toward the Queen. 'No offence, your majesty.'

'Galen!' Father's voice was a roar. 'Kill this devil, for he's no son of mine!'

I ran then, crunching emerald leaves under hard leather. Sir Galen charged from the centre star, trailing his black sword behind him, shouting for my blood. He came fast enough, but the fight with Makin had taken some of his wind. I knocked an old woman from my path, she went down spitting teeth, pearls spilling from her broken necklace.

I won free of the courtiers and kept on running, angled away from Galen. He'd given up the shouting but I could hear him behind me, the thud of his boots and the rasp of his breath. He must have been a hand above six foot, but lighter armour and fresher wind made up for my shorter legs. As we ran, I pulled out my sword. There were charms enough in its edge to put a notch in that Turkman blade. I threw it away. I didn't need the weight.

Little space remained to me. The left wall loomed just yards ahead, Galen moments behind.

I'd been aiming for one guardsman in particular, a younger fellow with fair sideburns and an open mouth. By the time he realized I wasn't veering away, it was too late. I hit him with the vambrace over my right forearm. The blow hammered his head back against the wall and he slid down it with no further interest in the proceedings. I caught the crossbow in my left hand, turned, and shot Galen through the bridge of the nose.

The bolt barely made it through his skull. It's one of the drawbacks in keeping them loaded, but still it should have been tightened only hours before. In any event, most of the Teuton's brain left by the back of his head and he fell down very dead.

The silence would have been utter but for the whimpering of the old woman on the floor back by the dais. I looked back over the crowd of nobles, cut and bloody, at Galen lying with his arms flung out, at the sparkling ruins of the glass tree reaching toward the throne-room doors.

'Was the show to your liking, Father?' I asked. 'I've heard that the court has been quiet in Sir Makin's absence.'

And for the first time in my life I heard my father laugh. A chuckle at first, then louder, then a howling gale such that he had to hold his throne to stand.

21

'Get out.' Father's laughing fit left him without warning, snuffed like a candle. He spoke into the silence. 'Get out. I'll talk to the boy now.' The boy, not 'my son'. I didn't miss that edge.

And they went. The high and the mighty, the lords and the ladies, the guards helping the injured, two of them dragging Galen's corpse. Makin followed after Galen, crunch, crunch, crunch, across the broken glass, as if to make sure no life remained in him. Katherine let herself be led by a table knight. She stopped though, at the base of the dais, and gave me a look as if she'd just that moment seen me for what I was. I sketched her a mocking bow, a reflex, like reaching for a blade. It hurt to see the hatred on her face, pure and astonished, but sometimes a bit of pain's just what we need: to cauterize the wound, burn out the infection. She saw me and I saw her, both of us stripped of pretence in that empty moment, newlyweds naked for their conjugals. I saw her for the same weakness I'd recognized when first we rode back into the green fields of Ancrath. That soft seduction of need and want, an equation of dependence that eases under the skin, so slow and sweet, only to lay a man open at the very time he most needs his strength. Oh, it hurt right enough, but I finished my bow and watched her back as they led her out.

The Queen went too, flanked by knights right and left, slightly awkward down the steps, a hint of a waddle. I could see the swell of her belly now, as she walked. My half-brother if Sageous's prediction held true. Heir to the throne should I die. Just a swelling now, just a hint, but sometimes that's all it takes. I recalled Brother Kane from the road, cut on the bicep when we took the village of Holt.

''T'ain't nothing, little Jorgy,' he'd said when I offered to heat a knife. 'Some farm boy with a rusty hoe. It don't go deep.'

'It's swelling,' I told him. 'Needs hot iron.' If it's not too late already.

'Fuck that, not for some farm boy with a hoe,' Kane said.

He died hard, did Kane. Three days later and his arm lay as thick as my waist, weeping pus greener than snot, and with a stench so bad we left him screaming to die alone. *It don't go deep* – but sometimes the shallow cut bites to the bone if you don't deal with it hard and fast.

Just a swelling. I watched the Queen go.

Sageous stayed. His eyes kept returning to the shattered ruin of the tree. You'd have thought he'd lost his lover.

'Pagan, see to the Queen,' Father said. 'She may need calming.'

A dismissal, plain and simple, but Sageous was too distracted to see it. He looked up from the glittering remains of the trunk I'd toppled. 'Sire, I…'

You what, heathen? You want something? It's not your place to want.

'I…' This was new to Sageous, I could see that: he was used to control. 'You should not be left unattended, Sire. The b—'

The boy? Say it man, spit it out.

'It may not be safe.'

Wrong thing to say. I guessed the heathen had relied on his magics too long. If he'd truly learned my father's mind he'd know better than to suggest he needed protection from me.

'Out.'

Whatever else I might think of my dear father I always did admire his way with words.

The look Sageous gave me held more than hate. Where Katherine channelled a pure emotion the tattooed magician offered bewildering complexity. Oh there was hate there, sure enough, but admiration too, respect maybe, and other flavours, all mixed in those mild brown eyes.

'Sire.' He bowed and started toward the doors.

We watched him in silence, watched him pace across the sparkling carpet of debris, spotted here with a discarded fan, there with a powdered wig. The doors closed behind him with a dull clang of bronze on bronze. A scar on the wall behind the throne caught my attention. I threw a hammer once, hard, and missed my target. It hit there. It seemed to be a day for old scars, old feelings.

'I want Gelleth,' Father said.

I had to admire his ability to wrong-foot me. I stood there armed with accusations, burdened with all my yesterdays, and he'd turned away from me, to the future.

'Gelleth hinges on the Castle Red,' I said. It was a test. That was just how we spoke. Every conversation a game of poker, every line a bet or a raise, bluff or call.

'Party tricks are well and good. You killed the Teuton. I didn't think you had it in you. You scandalized my court – well we both know what they are, and what they're worth. But can you do it when it counts? Can you give me Gelleth?'

I met his stare. I didn't inherit his blue eyes, I followed Mother in that department. There was a whole winter in those eyes of his, and nothing else. Even in Sageous's placid gaze I could dig deeper and find a subtext, but Father's eyes held nothing but a cold season. I think that was where the fear lay, in the lack of curiosity. I've seen malice many a time and hate in all its colours. I've seen the gleam in the torturer's eyes, the sick-light, but even there was the comfort of interest, the slightest touch of salvation in shared humanity. He might have the hot irons, but at least he was curious, at least he cared how much it hurt.

'I can give you Gelleth,' I said.

Could I? Probably not. Of all Ancrath's neighbours, Gelleth stood unassailable above the rest. The Lord of Gelleth probably had better claim to the Empire Throne than Father did. In the Hundred, Merl Gellethar had few equals.

I found my hand on the hilt of my dagger. I itched to draw the tempered steel, to lay it across his neck, to scream at him, to bring some heat into those cold eyes. *You traded my mother's death away, you bastard! Your own son's blood. Sweet William dead and barely cold, and you traded them away. A pax for the rights to river trade.*

'I'll need an army,' I said. 'Castle Red won't fall easy.'

'You will have the Forest Watch.' Father spread his hands over the throne's armrests and leaned back, watching.

'Two hundred men?' I felt my fingers tighten on the pommel of my knife. Two hundred men against the Castle Red. Ten thousand might not be enough.

'I'll take my brothers too,' I said. I watched his eyes. No flicker in the winter, no start at 'brother'. The weakness in me wanted to speak of Will. 'You'll have Gelleth. I will give you the Castle Red. I'll give you the head of the Lord Gellethar. Then you'll give the heathen to me.'

And you'll call me 'son'.

22

So we sat, Makin and I, at a table in the Falling Angel tavern with a jug of ale between us, and the song of a cracked-voice bard struggling to be heard against the din. Around us the brothers mixed with the lowest of the Low Town, gaming, whoring, and gorging. Rike sat close at hand, his face buried in a roast chicken. He appeared to be attempting to inhale it.

'Have you even seen the Castle Red, Jorg?' Makin asked.

'No.'

Makin looked at his ale. He hadn't touched it. For a few moments we listened to the sound of Rike crunching chicken bones.

'Have you?' I asked.

He nodded slowly and leaned back in his chair, eyes on the lanterns above the street-door. 'When I was a squire to Sir Reilly, we took a message to the Lord Gellethar. We stayed a week in the guest halls at the Castle Red before Merl Gellethar deigned to see us. His throne-room puts your father's to shame.'

Brother Burlow staggered by, belly escaping over his sturdy belt, a haunch of meat in one hand and two flagons in the other, foaming over his knuckles.

'What about the castle?' I could care less about a pissing contest over throne-rooms.

Makin toyed with his ale, but didn't drink. 'It's suicide, Jorg.'

'That bad?'

'Worse,' he said.

A painted whore, hennaed hair, and red-mouthed, backed into Makin's lap. 'Where's your smile, my handsome?' She had good tits, full and high, pushed into an inviting sandwich in a bodice of lace and whalebone. 'I'm sure I could find it.' Her hands vanished into the froth of her skirts where they bunched around Makin's waist. 'Sally will make it all good. My handsome knight doesn't need no boys to keep him warm.' She flicked a jealous glance my way.

Makin pitched her to the floor.

'It's built into a mountain. What shows above the rock are walls so high it hurts your neck to look up at the battlements.' Makin reached for his ale and fastened both hands around the flagon.

'Ow!' The whore picked herself up from the wet boards and wiped her hands on her dress. 'You didn't have to do that now!'

Makin didn't spare her a glance. He turned his dark

eyes on me. 'The doors are iron, thick as a sword is long. And what's above the ground isn't but a tenth part of it. There's provisions in those deep vaults to last years.'

Sally proved to be a true professional. She transferred her attentions to me, so smooth you'd think I'd been the object of her affection all along. 'And who might you be, now?' She came in close, running her fingers into my hair. 'You're too pretty for that grumpy sell-sword,' she said. 'You're old enough to learn how it works with girls, and Sally will show you.'

She had her mouth close to my ear now, sending tickles down my neck. I could smell her cheap lemon-grass scent, cutting through the ale stink, and the dream-weed on her breath.

'How many men would it take? To bring the place down around Lord Gellethar's ears?' I asked.

Makin's eyes returned to the lanterns and his knuckles went white around his flagon. Somewhere behind us Rike gave a roar, quickly followed by the splintering sound of a body meeting a table at high speed.

'If you had ten thousand men,' Makin said, raising his voice above the crashing sounds. 'Ten thousand men, well supplied, and with siege machines, lots of siege engines, then you might have him in a year. That's if you could keep his allies off your back. With three thousand you might starve him out eventually.'

I caught hold of Sally's hand as it slipped across my belly to the buckle of my belt. I twisted her wrist a little, and she came front and centre, sharpish, with a high-pitched gasp. She had green eyes, like Katherine's but more narrow and not so clear. Under the paint she had fewer years on me than I first thought, she might be twenty, certainly no more.

'And what if I found us a way in? What then, Brother Makin? How many men to take the Castle Red if I opened us a door?' I spoke to Sally's face, inches before mine.

'The garrison stands at nine hundred. Veterans mostly. He sends his fresh meat to the borders and takes it back when it's been seasoned.' I heard Makin's chair scrape back. 'Which son of a whore threw that?' he yelled.

I kept the whore's wrist turned. I took her throat in my other hand and drew her closer. 'Tonight we'll call you Katherine, and you can show me how it works with girls.'

Some of the dream-haze left her eyes, replaced by fear. That was all right with me. I had two hundred men and no secret door into the Castle Red. It seemed only right that somebody should be worried.

23

My book shifted again. I say 'my' book, but in truth it was stolen, filched from Father's library on the way out of the Tall Castle. The book lurched at me, threatening to snap shut on my nose.

'Lie still, damn you,' I said.

'Mmmgfll.' Sally gave a sleepy murmur and nestled her face in the pillow.

I settled the book back between her buttocks and nudged her legs slightly further apart with my elbows. Over the top of the page I could see the faint-knobbed ridge of Sally's spine tracing its path across her smooth back to be lost in the red curls around her neck. I wasn't convinced that the text before me was more interesting than what lay beneath it.

'It says here that there's a valley in Gelleth they call the Gorge of Leucrota,' I said. 'It's in the badlands down below the Castle Red.'

The morning light streamed through the open window. The air had a chill to it, but a good one, like the bite on ale.

'Mmmnnn.' Sally's voice came from the pillow.

I'd tired her out. You can wear even whores out when you're that young. The combination of a woman and time on my hands wasn't one I'd tried before. I found the mix to my liking. There's a lot to be said for not being in a queue, or not having to finish up before the flames take hold of the building. And the willingness! That was new too, albeit paid for. In the dark I could imagine it was free.

'Now if I know my ancient Greek, and I do, a leucrota is a monster that speaks with a human voice to lure its prey.' I bent my neck to bite at the back of her thigh. 'And in my experience, any monster that talks in a human voice, is human. Or was.'

My feet hung over the end of the bed. I wiggled my toes. Sometimes that helps.

I reached for the oldest of the three books I'd stolen. A Builder text on plasteek sheets, wrinkled by some ancient fire. Scholars in the east would pay a hundred in gold for Builder texts, but I hoped for more profit than that.

I'd been taught the Builder speech by Tutor Lundist. I learned it in a month and he'd gone bragging to anyone who'd listen, until Father shut his mouth with one of those dark looks he's famed for. Old Lundist said I knew the Builder speech as well as any in the Broken Empire, but I couldn't make sense of more than half the words in the little book I'd stolen.

I could read the 'Top Secret' at the head and foot of every page, but 'Neurotoxicology', 'Carcinogen',

'Mutagen'? Maybe they were old styles of hat. To this day I don't know. The words I did recognize were interesting enough though. 'Weapons', 'Stockpile', 'Mass Destruction'. The last but one page even had a shiny map, all contours and elevations. Tutor Lundist taught me a little geography as well. Enough to match that small map to the 'Views from Castle Red' painstakingly executed in the large but dull *A History of Gelleth* whose leather-bound spine nestled in the cleft of dear Sally's oh-so-biteable backside.

Even when I understood the Builder words, the sentences didn't make sense. 'Binary weapon leakage is now endemic. The lighter than air unary compounds show little toxic effect, though rosiosis is a common topological exposure symptom.'

Or, from the same page: 'Mutagenic effects are common downstream of binary spills.' I could stretch my Greek to guess the meaning, but it hardly seemed reasonable. Perhaps I'd stolen an old storybook?

'Jorg!' Makin hollered through the door. 'The escort's here to take you to the Forest Watch.'

Sally started up at that, but I pressed her down.

'Tell them to wait,' I called.

The Forest Watch weren't going to be much use to me. Not unless they had ten thousand friends that wanted to come along.

'Sweet Jesu I'm sore.' Sally tried to get up again. 'Oh! It's morning already. Sammeth will kill me.'

'I said still, damn it.' I found a coin from my purse on the table and tossed it up to her. 'That for your damn Sammeth.'

She slumped back with a comfortable protest.

'Binary weapon leakage…' As if speaking the words would add meaning.

'You're going to the Castle Red then?' Sally said. She stifled a yawn.

I raised a hand to slap her into silence. Of course she didn't see it and *A History of Gelleth* blocked the best target.

'Say hello to all those little red people for me,' she said.

Rosiosis.

I lowered my hand to her hip. 'Little red people?'

'Uh huh.'

I felt her wiggle under my palm. I gripped harder. 'Little red people?'

'Yes.' A whine of irritation tinged her voice. 'Why do you think they call it the Castle Red?'

I pulled myself to a sitting position. 'Makin! Get in here!' I shouted it loud enough for the whole inn to hear. He came in sharp enough, one hand on his sword. A smile found its way to his lips when he saw Sally sprawled out naked, but he kept his hand where it was.

'My prince?'

Sally really did try to get up at that. She almost made it to all fours and *A History* went flying.

'Prince? Nobody said nothing about a prince! He ain't no bleedin' prince!'

I pushed her down again.

'That conversation we had yesterday, Makin,' I said.

'Yes?'

'Anything you'd like to add to the description? Anything about those nine hundred veterans?' I asked.

For a moment he looked as blank as idiot Maical.

'Something about the colour scheme?' I gave him a prompt.

'Oh.' He grinned. 'The Blushers? Yes. They're red as a cooked lobster, every one of them. Something in the water they say. I thought everyone knew that.'

Rosiosis.

'I never knew it,' I said.

'Sounds like your father should have hanged Tutor Lundist then,' Makin said. 'Everyone knows that.'

Monsters down below.

'He's never a prince!' Sally sounded outraged.

'You've been royally fucked.' Makin gave her a little bow.

Castle Red and all its red soldiers up above.

I got off the bed.

Weapons stockpile.

Leakage.

'So,' Makin said. 'Are we ready to go?'

I reached for my trews. Sally rolled over as I laced them up, which didn't help at all. I watched her nakedness, highlights courtesy of the morning sun. I wondered – should I gamble the Forest Watch and the brothers both on some wild conjectures and blind guesses at what obscure words meant…

'Tell them an hour.' My fingers flipped from lacing to unlacing. 'I'll be ready in an hour.'

Sally lay back on the pillows and smiled. 'Prince, eh?'

Lying in seemed like a good idea all of a sudden.

24

'What ho! Captain Coddin!' I came down the stairs in remarkably good spirits shortly before noon.

The Captain gave me a stiff bow, his lips pressed into a tight line. In a far corner the younger brothers, Roddat, Jobe, and Sim nursed hangovers. I could see Burlow under a table, snoring.

'I'd have thought you'd be back at Chelny Ford, Captain, protecting our borders from the predations of villains and rogues,' I said, all cheery-like.

'There was some dissatisfaction with my performance in the role. Certain voices at court maintained that I'd let a sight too many villains and rogues past my garrison of late. I'm assigned to escort duty in Crath City.' He gestured to the street-door. 'If Prince Jorg is ready?'

I decided I liked the man. That surprised me. I'm not given to liking people as a rule. I blamed it on my mood. Nothing like a night of whoring to turn a man soft.

So Coddin and his four soldiers led us out through the West Gate. I had Makin with me of course, and Elban because old though he was, there weren't many among the brothers with more than half a brain. I brought the Nuban along too. Not sure why, but he'd been sat by the bar eating an apple, with that crossbow of his across his lap, and I thought I'd have him along.

We took the Old Road toward Rennat Forest, twelve miles or so as the crow flies, and of course the Old Road flies like a crow, following the line laid down by men of Rome an age upon an age ago.

Coddin rode at the fore, flanked by his boys, us behind enjoying the day. Makin nudged Firejump up alongside Gerrod and the two of them exchanged whatever threats pass between stallions.

'You should have left me to Sir Galen, Jorg,' Makin said.

'You think you could have taken him?' I asked.

'No. He knew his swordwork, that Teuton,' Makin said, and he wiped a hand across his mouth. 'I've never crossed blades with a better man.'

'He wasn't the better man,' I said.

A silence fell between us for a moment. Elban broke it.

'Makin found a man he couldn't beat? Sir Makin? I don't believe it.' His lisp made a wet 'Thur' of 'Sir'.

Makin turned in the saddle to face Elban. 'Believe it. The King's champion had me cold. Jorg beat him, though.' He nodded toward the Nuban. 'With a crossbow. You'd have been proud.'

179

The Nuban ran a soot-black hand over the iron-work of his bow, touching the faces of his pagan gods. 'There's no pride in this, Makin.'

I could never read the Nuban. One moment he'd seem as simple as Maical, the next, deeper than a deep well. Sometimes both at once.

'Maical,' I said, remembering. 'What happened to our pet idiot in the end? Did he die? I forgot to ask.'

'We left him in Norwood, Jorth. He should have been dead, with that gut-wound, but he just hung on, moaning all the time,' Elban said. He wiped the spittle from his chin.

'Too stupid to die,' Makin said. He grinned. 'We had to drag him off to a house at the edge of town. Little Rikey was all for finishing him off, just to shut him up.'

We had us a chuckle over that.

'Seriously though, Jorg, you should have left Galen to it,' Makin said. 'If you had, you'd be sitting pretty at court. You're still heir to the throne. You'd have got that saucy princess in time. The Castle Red is a death sentence for smashing that stupid tree. That and calling his wife a Scorron whore. Your father is not a forgiving man.'

'You'd be right in all that, Makin,' I said. 'If my ambition were limited to "sitting pretty", I'd have let the Teuton do his worst. Luckily for you, I want to win the Hundred War, reunite the Broken Empire, and be Emperor. And if I'm going to stand any chance of that, then taking the Castle Red with two hundred men will be a piece of cake.'

We had our lunch at a milestone on the margins of the forest. Mutton, swiped from the kitchens at The Falling Angel. We were still wiping the grease from our fingers when we rode in under the trees – big oaks and beeches in the main – blushing crimson with the kiss of autumn frost. Riding under those branches, with the crunch of hoof on leaves, and the breath of horses pluming before us, I felt it again, that sweet hook sinking beneath the skin. They say a man can travel a lifetime and not escape the spell of the Ancrath valleys.

I yawned, cracking my jaw. It hadn't been a night for sleeping. Warm in my cloak I let Gerrod's gentle gait rock me.

I found myself thinking of smooth limbs and softness. My lips spoke her name as if to taste it.

'Katherine?' Makin asked. I jerked my head up to find him watching me, with an eyebrow raised in that irritating way of his.

I looked away. To our left a long sprawl of hook-briar writhed around the boles of three elms. I'd learned a hard lesson among the hook-briar one stormy night. It wasn't just the beauty of the land that had its hooks in me.

Kill her.

I turned round in the saddle, but Makin had fallen back to joke with the Nuban.

Kill her, and you'll be free forever.

It seemed that the voice came from the darkness beneath the briar's coils. It spoke under the crunching of hooves in the dry leaf-fall.

Kill her. An ancient voice, desiccated, untouched by mercy. For a moment I saw Katherine, blood welling over her white teeth, her eyes round with surprise. I could feel the knife in my hand, hilt against her stomach, hot blood running over my fingers.

Poison would be quieter. A distant touch.

That last voice – it could have been mine, or the briar, they started to sound the same.

Strength requires sacrifice. All weakness carries its cost. Now that was me. We'd left the briar behind and the day had grown cold.

The Forest Watch found us quick enough, I'd have been worried if they hadn't. A six-man patrol, all in blacks and greens, came out of the trees and bade us state our business on the King's road.

I didn't let Coddin introduce me. 'I've come to see the Watch Master,' I said.

The watchmen exchanged glances. I'm sure we seemed a ragged bunch, only Makin with any courtly touch about him, having polished up to see Father Dear. I had my old road plate on, and Elban and the Nuban, well their looks would earn them a bandit's noose without the tedium of a trial.

Coddin spoke up then. 'This is Jorg, Prince of Ancrath, heir to the throne.'

His words, hard to swallow as they might be, had the weight of a uniform behind them. The watchmen looked dumbfounded.

'He's come to see the Watch Master,' Coddin said, by way of a prompt.

That got them moving and they led us into the deep forest along a series of deer-paths. We followed in single-file, riding until I got tired of being slapped in the face by every other branch, and dismounted. The watchmen kept up a stiff pace, showing little regard for royalty or heavy armour.

'Who is the Watch Master anyhow?' I asked, short of breath and clanking along loud enough to keep the bears from hibernation.

One of the watchmen glanced back, an old fellow, gnarled as the trees. 'Lord Vincent de Gren.' He spat into the bushes to show his regard for the man.

'Your father appointed him this spring,' Captain Coddin said from behind me. 'I gather it was a punishment of some sort.'

The Forest Watch made its headquarters by Rulow's Fall on the plain where the River Temus meandered before gathering its courage for the leap down a two-hundred-foot step in the bedrock. A dozen large cabins, wood-shingled and log-built, nestled among the trees. An abandoned mill house served as the Watch Master's keep, fashioned from granite blocks and perched at the head of the fall.

A few dozen watchmen came out to watch our column wind up to the keep. Not much entertainment in these parts I guessed.

The old watchman went in to announce us while we tied our steeds. He didn't hurry out, so we waited. A cold wind blew up, stirring the fallen leaves. The watchmen stood with us, black-green cloaks flapping. Most of the watch held shortbows. A longbow will get tangled in the trees and you'll never need great range in the forest. No Robin of Hood here, the watchmen weren't merry, and they were apt to kill you if you stepped out of line.

'Prince Jorg.' The keep door opened and a man clad in ermine stepped out, his fingers hooked in a belt of gold plates.

'Lord Vincent de Gren, I'm guessing.' I gave him my most insincere smile.

'So you're here to tell us we're all going to die over some stupid promise a boy made to impress his father!' he said, loud enough for the whole clearing to hear.

I had to hand it to Lord Vincent, he certainly cut straight to the chase. And I like that in a man, I really do, but I didn't like the way he said it. He had a screwed-up sort of face did Lord Vincent, as if the world tasted sour in his mouth, which was odd, because he had the sort of butterball shape that takes some serious eating to acquire and a few dozen extra stoats to cover in ermine. I took him to be about thirty, but it's hard to tell with fat people: they've no skin spare for wrinkles.

'News travels fast, I see.' I wondered if my father wanted me to fail even more than he wanted the Castle Red. In a way it would be a compliment, implying he felt I had a chance. But no, this had a woman's touch, maybe the touch of a woman still smarting over 'Scorron whore'. A woman used to teasing out post-coital secrets. A woman who might send riders to Rennat Forest. Even to Gelleth.

I strode across to the man. 'I wonder my Lord de Gren, would your men follow you to the death? I'm impressed that you've won their respect so rapidly. I hear that the Forest Watch are a hard lot, tougher than nails.' I put an arm around his shoulders. He didn't like it, but you can do things like that when you're a prince. 'Walk with me.'

I didn't give him a choice. I steered him downstream toward the glistening line where the River Temus vanished, replaced by a faint haze of mist. 'Follow on,' I shouted. 'This isn't a private meeting.'

So we came to stand on a shelf of wet stone, fifty yards down from the mill house, where the waters leapt white over the rocks, gathering for their plunge over Rulow's Fall.

'Prince Jorg, I don't…' Lord Vincent began.

'You, come here!' I took my arm from de Gren and pointed to the old watchman who'd spat out the Watch Master's name earlier. I had to shout above the voice of the river.

The old fellow came to join us by the edge.

'And who's this proud example of the watch, Watch Master?' I asked.

Fat people's faces are wonderful for emotion. Or at least Lord Vincent's was. I could see his thoughts twitching across his brow, quivering in his jowls, twisting in the rolls around his neck. 'I…'

'There's two hundred of the buggers. You can't be expected to know them all,' I said, all sympathy. 'What's your name, watchman?'

'Keppen, yer highness,' he said. He looked as if he'd rather be somewhere else, had his eyes open, looking for the out.

'Order him to jump, Watch Master,' I said.

'W— what?' Lord Vincent went very pale very quickly.

'Jump,' I said. 'Order him to jump over the fall.'

'What?' Lord Vincent seemed to be having difficulty hearing over the roar.

Keppen had his hand on his dagger-hilt. Sensible fellow.

'If your men are all going to die over some stupid promise a boy made his father, well, it's only sensible for the boy to make sure they'll follow your orders when it means certain death,' I said. 'And if you say "what" again, I'm going to have to slice you open here and now.'

'W— But, my prince … Prince Jorg…' He tried to laugh.

'Order him to jump, now!' I barked it in de Gren's face.

186

'J-jump!'

'Not like that! Put some conviction into it. He's not going to jump if you make it a suggestion.'

'Jump!' Lord Vincent reached for some lordly command.

'Better,' I said. 'Once more, with feeling.'

'Jump!' Lord Vincent screamed the word at old Keppen. The colour came back now, flushing him bright crimson. 'JUMP! Jump, damn you!'

'Buggered if I will!' Keppen shouted back. He pulled his knife, a wicked bit of steel, and backed off, wary like.

I shrugged. 'Not good enough, Lord Vincent. Just not good enough at all!' And with a hearty shove he went over. Never a wail from him. Didn't even hear a splash.

I moved quickly then. In two strides I had Keppen by the throat, with my other hand on his wrist, keeping that knife at bay. I took him by surprise and in another step I had him backed out over the edge, heels resting on air, and my grip on his neck all that kept him with us.

'So, Keppen,' I said. 'Will you die for the new Watch Master?' I gave him a smile, but I don't think he noticed. 'This is the bit where you say, "yes". And you'd better mean it, because there are a lot worse things than dying easy when given an order.'

He got a 'yes' out past my fingers.

'Coddin.' I pointed him out. 'You're the new Watch Master.'

I pulled Keppen back and walked back toward the keep. They all followed me.

'If I ask you to die for me, I expect you to ask when and where,' I said. 'But I'm not in any hurry to ask. It'd be a waste. The Forest Watch is the most dangerous two hundred soldiers Ancrath has, whether my father knows it or not.'

It wasn't all flattery. In the forest they were the best we had. With a good Watch Master they were the sharpest sword in the armoury, and too clever to jump when told.

'Watch Master Coddin here is taking you into Gelleth.' I saw a few lips curl at that. Lord Vincent's long jump or not, I was still a boy, and the Castle Red was still suicide. 'You'll get within twenty miles of the Castle Red, and no closer. You're to spend two weeks in the Otton forests, cutting wood for siege engines and killing any patrols that come in after you. Watch Master Coddin will tell you the rest when the time comes.'

I turned from them and pushed open the door to the keep. 'Coddin, Makin!'

They followed me in. The entrance hall gave onto a homely dining room where the table was set with cold goose, bread, and autumn apples. I took an apple.

'My thanks, Prince Jorg.' Coddin gave another of his stiff bows. 'Saved from escort duty in Crath City, I can enjoy my winter running around the woods in Gelleth now.' The faintest hint of a smile flickered at the corner of his mouth.

'I'm coming with you. In disguise. It's a closely guarded secret that you're to ensure leaks out,' I said.

'And where will we be really?' Makin asked.

'The Gorge of Leucrota,' I told him. 'Talking to monsters.'

25

We returned to the Tall Castle through the Old Town Gate, with the noonday sun hot across our necks. I carried the family sword across my saddle and none sought to bar our way.

We left the horses in the West Yard.

'See he's well shod. We have a road ahead of us.' I slapped Gerrod's ribs and let the stable lad lead him away.

'We've company.' Makin laid a hand upon my shoulder. 'Have a care.' He nodded across the yard. Sageous was descending the stair from the main keep, a small figure in white robes.

'I'm sure our little pagan can learn to love Prince Jorgy just like all the rest,' I said. 'He's a handy man to have in your pocket.'

Makin frowned. 'Better to put a scorpion in your pocket. I've been asking around. That glass tree you felled the other day. It wasn't a trinket. He grew it.'

'He'll forgive me.'

'He grew it from the stone, Jorg. From a green bead. It took two years. He watered it with blood.'

Behind us Rike sniggered, a childish sound, unsettling from such a giant.

'His blood,' Makin finished.

Another of the brothers snorted laughter at that. They'd all heard the story of Sir Galen and the glass tree.

Sageous stopped a yard in front of me and cast his gaze across the brothers, some still handing over their steeds, others pressed close at my side. His eyes flicked up to take in Rike's height.

'Why did you run, Jorg?' he asked.

'Prince. You'll call him Prince, you pagan dog.' Makin stepped forward, half-drawing. Sageous took him in with a mild look and Makin's hand fell limp at his side, the argument gone from him.

'Why did you run?'

'I don't run,' I said.

'Four years ago you ran from your father's house.' He kept his voice gentle, and the brothers watched him as though charmed by a spinning penny.

'I left for a reason,' I said. His line of attack unsettled me.

'What reason?'

'To kill someone.'

'Did you kill him?' Sageous asked.

'I killed a lot of people.'

'Did you kill him?'

'No.' The Count of Renar still lived and breathed.

'Why?'

Why hadn't I?

'Did you harm him? Did you hurt his interests?'

I hadn't. In fact if you looked at it, if you traced the random path of four years on the road, you might say I had furthered Renar's interests. The brothers and I had nipped at Baron Kennick's heels and kept him from his ambitions. In Mabberton we had torn the heart from what might have been rebellion…

'I killed his son. I stuck a knife in Marclos, Renar's flesh and heir.'

Sageous allowed himself a small smile. 'As you came closer to home you came under my protection, Jorg. The hand that steered you fell away.'

Was it true? I couldn't see the lie in him. My eyes followed the scriptures written across his face, the complex scrolls of an alien tongue. An open book, but I couldn't read him.

'I can help you, Jorg. I can give you back your self. I can give you your will.'

He held out his hand, palm open.

'Free will has to be taken,' I said. When in doubt reach for the wisdom of others. Nietzsche in this case. Some arguments require a knife if you're to cut to the quick, others require the breaking of heads with a philosopher's stone.

I reached out and took his hand in mine, from below, his knuckles to my palm.

'My choices have been my own, pagan,' I said. 'If someone sought to steer me, I would know it.'

'Would you?'

'And if I knew it… Oh if I knew it, I would teach such a lesson in pain that the Red Men of the East themselves would come to learn new tricks.' Even as they left me the words rang hollow. Childish.

'It is not I who has led you, Jorg,' Sageous said.

'Who then?' I squeezed his hand until I heard the bones creak.

He shrugged. 'Ask for your will and I shall give it to you.'

'If there were a glamour on me I would find the one that placed it and I would kill them.' I felt an echo of the old pain that plagued me on the roads, a pang from temple to temple, behind the eyes like a sliver of glass. 'But there is none, and my will is my own,' I said.

He shrugged again, and turned away. Looking down I saw that I held my left hand in my right, and blood ran between my fingers.

26

From my encounter with Sageous in the West Yard
I went straight to mass. Meeting the pagan had left
me wanting a touch of the church of Roma, a breath
of incense, and a heavy dose of dogma. If heathens
held such powers it seemed only right that the church
should have a little magic of its own to bestow upon the
worthy, and hopefully upon the unworthy who bothered to show up. Failing that, I had need of a priest in
any case.

We marched into the chapel to find Father Gomst
presiding. The choir song faltered before the clatter of
boots on polished marble. Nuns shrank into the shadows
beneath the brothers' leers, and, no doubt, the rankness
of our company. Gains and Sim took off their helms and
bowed their heads. Most of them just glanced around for
something worth stealing.

'Forgive the intrusion, Father.' I set a hand in the font
by the entrance and let the holy water lift the blood from
my skin. It stung.

'Prince!' He set his book upon the lectern and looked up, white-faced. 'These men … it is not proper.'

'Oh shush.' I walked the aisle, eyes on the painted marvel of the ceiling, turning slowly as I went, one hand raised and open, dripping. 'Aren't they all sons of God? Penitent children returned for forgiveness?'

I stopped before the altar and glanced back toward the brothers by the door. 'Put that back, Roddat, or you'll be leaving both thumbs in the alms box.'

Roddat drew a silver candlestick from the grey rot of his travel cloak.

'That one at the least.' Father Gomst pointed at the Nuban, a tremble in his finger. 'That one is not of God's flock.'

'Not even a black sheep?' I came to stand by Gomst. He flinched. 'Well maybe you can convert him on our journey.'

'My prince?'

'You're to accompany me to Gelleth, Father Gomst. A diplomatic mission. I'm surprised the King didn't tell you.' I wasn't so surprised in truth, since it was a lie. 'We leave immediately.'

'But—'

'Come!' I strode toward the door. A pause, and then he followed. I could hear the reluctance in his footsteps.

The brothers began to file out ahead of me, Rike trailing his hand along the walls, over reliquary and icon.

195

Having secured the priest I was keen to be off. I directed Makin to oversee a swift provisioning and led Gomst back to the West Yard.

'We should not take this Nuba-man on a mission of diplomacy, Prince. Or any other,' Gomst whispered as we walked. 'They drink the blood of Christian priests to work their spells, you know.'

'They do?' I think it was the first interesting thing I ever heard Gomst say. 'I could use a little magic myself.'

The priest paled behind his beard. 'A superstition, my prince.'

A few more paces and, 'Even so, were you to burn him, the Lord's blessing would be upon us and our journey.'

Within the hour, saddlebags bulging, we rode back out into the Old Town. Sageous was waiting for us. He stood alone by the side of the cobbled path. I drew up before him, still uneasy in my mind. He had driven a wedge of doubt into me. I had told myself I'd set Count Renar aside as an act of strength, a sacrifice to the iron will I needed to win the game of thrones. But sometimes, now for instance, I didn't quite believe it.

'You should accept my protection, Prince,' Sageous said.

'I've survived long enough without it.'

'But now you're going to Gelleth, bound on a path to strengthen your father's hand.'

'I am.' The brothers' horses snorted around me.

'If any had a mind that you might truly succeed, they would stop you,' Sageous said. 'The one who has played you these past years will seek to tighten the bonds you have loosened. Perhaps the priest will help you. His presence did before. He has value as a talisman, but past that he is empty robes.'

A horse pushed against Gerrod, the rider moving beside me.

I set my hand on my sword hilt. 'I don't like you, pagan.'

'What do you think scared the marsh-dead, Jorg?' No ripple in his calm watchfulness.

'I—' The boast sounded hollow before I spoke it.

'An angry boy?' Sageous shook his head. 'The dead saw a darker hand upon your heart.'

'I—'

'Accept my protection. There are grander dreams you can dream.'

I felt the soft weight of sleep upon me, the saddle unsure beneath me.

'Dream-witch.' A dark voice spoke at my shoulder.

'Dream-witch.' The Nuban held out his crossbow, black fist curled around the stock, muscle strained against the load. 'I carry your token, Dream-witch, your magics will not stain the boy.'

Sageous shrank back, the tattooed writings seeming to writhe across his face.

In an instant my eyes were wide. 'You're him.' The

clarity of it was blinding. 'You set my brothers in Father's dungeon. You sent your hunter to kill me.'

I set a hand upon the Nuban's bow, remembering how he took it from the man I killed in a barn one stormy night. The dream-witch's hunter.

'You sent your hunter to kill me.' The last tatters of Sageous' charm left me. 'And now it's my hunter who holds it.'

Sageous turned and made for the castle gate, half running.

'Pray I don't find you here on my return, pagan.' I said it quietly. If he heard it, he might follow my advice.

We left then, riding from the city without a backward look.

The rains first found us on the Ancrath Plains and dogged our passage north into the mountainous borders of Gelleth. I've been soaked on the road many a time, but the rains as we left my father's lands were a cold misery that reached deeper than our bones. Burlow's appetite remained undampened though, and Rike's temper too. Burlow ate as if the rations were a challenge, and Rike growled at every raindrop.

At my instruction, Gomst took confession from the men. After hearing Red Kent speak of his crimes, and learning how he earned his name, Gomst asked to be excused his duties. After listening to Liar's whispers, he begged.

Days passed. Long days and cold nights. I dreamed of Katherine, of her face and the fierceness of her eyes. Of an evening we ate Gains's mystery stews and Fat Burlow tended the beasts, checking hooves and fetlocks. Burlow always looked to the horses. Perhaps he felt guilty about weighing so heavy on them, but I put it down to a morbid fear of walking. We wound further up into the bleakness of the mountains. And at last the rains broke. We camped in a high pass and I sat with the Nuban to watch the sun fall. He held his bow, whispering old secrets to it in his home tongue.

For two days we walked the horses across slopes too steep and sharp with rock for any hooves save the mountain goats'.

A pillar marked the entrance to the Gorge of the Leucrota. It stood two yards wide and twice as tall, a stump shattered by some giant's whim. The remnants of the upper portion lay all around. Runes marked it, Latin I think, though so worn I could read almost nothing.

We rested at the pillar. I clambered up it to address the brothers from the top and take in the lie of the land.

I set the men to making camp. Gains set his fire and clanked his pots. The wind blew slight in the gorge, the oil-cloth tents barely flapping before it. The rain came again, but in a patter, soft and cold. Not enough to stir Rike lying on the rocks some five yards from the pillar, his snoring like a saw through wood.

199

I stood looking up at the cliff faces. There were caves up there. Many caves.

My hair swung behind me as I scanned the cliff. I'd let the Nuban weave it into a dozen long braids, a bronze charm at the end of each. He said it would ward off evil spirits. That just left me the good ones to worry about.

I stood with my hands on the Ancrath sword, resting its point before me. Waiting for something.

The men grew nervous, the animals too. I could tell it from their lack of complaint. They watched the slopes with me, toothless Elban as weatherbeaten as the rocks, young Roddat pale and pockmarked, Red Kent with his secrets, sly Row, Liar, Fat Burlow and the rest of my ragged bunch. The Nuban kept close by the pillar with Makin at his side. My band of brothers. All of them worried and not knowing why. Gomst looked set to run if he had a notion where to go. The brothers had a sense for trouble. I knew that well enough to understand that when they all worry together it's a bad thing coming. A very bad thing.

Transcript from the trial of Sir Makin of Trent:

Cardinal Helot, papal prosecution: *And do you deny razing the Cathedral of Wexten?*

Sir Makin: *I do not.*

Cardinal Helot: *Or the sack of Lower Merca?*

Sir Makin: *No, nor do I deny the sack of Upper Merca.*

Cardinal Helot: *Let the record show the accused finds amusement in the facts of his crime.*

Court recorder: *So noted.*

27

The monsters came when the light failed. Shadows swallowed the gorge and the silence thickened until the wind could barely stir it. Makin's hand fell on my shoulder. I flinched, edging the fear with momentary hatred, for my own weakness, and for Makin for showing it to me.

'Up there.' He nodded to my left.

One of the cave mouths had lit from within, a single eye watching us through the falling night.

'That's no fire,' I said. The light had nothing of warmth or flicker.

As we watched, the source of illumination moved, swinging harsh shadows out across the slopes.

'A lantern?' Fat Burlow stepped up beside me, puffing out his cheeks in consternation. The brothers gathered around us.

The strange lantern emerged onto the slope, and darkness erased the cave behind. It shone like a star, a cold light, reaching from the source in a thousand bright lines.

A single figure cut a wedge of shadow into the illumination; the lantern bearer.

We watched the unhurried descent. The wind sought my flesh with icy fingers and tugged for attention at my cloak.

'*Ave Maria, gratia plena, dominus tecum, benedicta tu in mulieribus.*' Somewhere in the night old Gomsty muttered his Ave Marias.

A slow horror eased itself among us.

'Mother of God!' Makin spat the oath out as if to rid himself of the fear. We all felt it, crawling over the unseen rocks.

The brothers might have run, but where was there to go?

'Torches, damn you. Now!' I broke the paralysis, shocked that I'd stood hypnotized by the approach for so long.

'Now!' I drew my sword. They moved at that. Scurrying to the embers of the fire, stumbling over the rough ground.

'Nuban, Row, Burlow, see there's nothing coming up along the river.' Even as I said it I knew we'd been flanked.

'There! There, behind that rise!' The Nuban motioned with his crossbow. He'd seen something, the Nuban wasn't one to spook at nothing. We'd watched the pretty light and they'd flanked us. Simple as a market play of kiss-and-dip. Distract your mark with a pretty face, and come up from behind to rob him blind.

The torches flared, men ran to their weapons.

The light drew closer and we saw it for what it was, a child whose very skin bled radiance. She walked an even pace, every inch a-glow, white like molten silver, making mere shadows of the rags she wore.

'*Ave Maria, gratia plena!*' Father Gomst's voice rose, lifting the prayer like a shield.

'Hail Mary,' I echoed him. 'Full of grace, indeed.'

The girl's eyes burned silver and the ghosts of flames chased across her skin. There was a fragile beauty to her that took my breath.

A monster walked behind her. In any other circumstance it would have been him that drew the eye. The monster had been built in parody of a man, sharing Adam's lines as a cow apes a horse. The light revealed the horror of his flesh, sparing no detail. The thing might have topped seven foot in height. It even had a few inches on Little Rikey.

Liar raised his bow, disgust on his pinched face. I took his arm as he sighted on the monster.

'No.' I wanted to hear them speak. Besides, it looked as if an arrow would just annoy our new friend.

Under a twisted red hide the monster's chest looked like a hundred-gallon barrel. A set of ribs pierced the flesh, reaching for each other above his heart.

The girl's light touched us with a cold kiss and I felt her in my mind. She spoke and her voice seemed to rise from the rocks. I heard her footsteps in the corridors of my memory.

There are places where children shouldn't wander. I met the girl's silver gaze, and for a moment shadows licked across her.

'Welcome to our camp,' I said.

I stepped forward to greet them, leaving the brothers and entering the brilliance of the child's aura. The monster smiled at me, a wide smile showing teeth stolen from the wolf. He'd the eyes of a cat, slitted against the light and throwing it back.

I passed beauty by and stood before the beast. We had us a moment of judging. I ran an eye over the muscle heaped on his bones, crossed over with pulsing veins and hard ridges of scar tissue. I could have eaten dinner off one of his hands. He had three fingers and a thumb on each, thick as the girl's arm. He could have taken my head in one hand and crushed it.

I snapped my neck forward, sudden-like, and jumped at him with a shout, thrusting my face at his. He flinched backward and stumbled on the loose rock. The laughter escaped me. I couldn't stop it.

'Why?' The girl looked puzzled. She tilted her head and the shadows ran.

'Because.' I gasped for my breath as the monster righted himself.

Why? For a moment I didn't know.

'Because … because, fuck him. Because he's such a big bastard.' I pushed the grin from my face. Because he had given me pause. Because he had made me feel small.

I looked down at her. 'I'm bigger than you. Are you going to let that scare you?'

'I do fear you,' the girl said. 'Not for your size, Jorg. For the threads that gather around you. For the lines that meet where I can't see them. For the weight, and the knife-edge on which it sits.' She spoke in a sing-song, high and sweet.

'You make a fine oracle, girl,' I said. 'You've got that mix of profound and empty just right.' I slammed my sword back into its sheath. 'So, you've my name. Shall we share? Do the leucrota have names?'

'Jane,' she said. 'And this is Gorgoth, a leader under the mountain.'

'Charmed.' I gave them a little bow. 'Perhaps your friends could come out from behind the rocks, and that way my brothers won't feel so tempted to shoot at shadows.'

Gorgoth set his cat's eyes on me, a narrow and feral stare.

'Up!' His voice rolled out even deeper than I'd imagined, and I'd imagined it pretty deep.

Other monsters rose around our camp, some of them shockingly close. Had every gargoyle and grotesque torn free from the great cathedrals and gathered to form an army, the leucrota would be that army made flesh. No two stood alike. All had been sketched on the frame of a man, but with a poor hand. None were as huge and hale as Gorgoth. Most leaked from sores, sported withered limbs, or laboured beneath growths of wart and tumour heaped in foul confusion.

'Jesu, Gorgoth! Your friends make Little Rikey look almost handsome,' I said.

Makin came to join me, eyes screwed up against Jane's light. He shaded his face with a hand and looked Gorgoth up and down.

'And this will be Sir Makin,' I said. 'Knight of the court of King Olidan, terror of—'

'A man to trust.' Jane's high voice cut across me. 'If he gives you his word.'

She turned those silver orbs of hers on me and I felt my yesterdays crowding at my shoulder. 'You want to go to the heart of the mountain,' she said.

'Yes.' I couldn't deny that.

'You bring death, Prince of Ancrath,' she said.

Gorgoth growled at that. It sounded like rocks grinding together. The child put a glowing hand to his wrist. 'Death if we agree, death if we resist.' She kept her eyes on me. 'What have you to offer for passage?'

I had to admit she was good at her game. It wouldn't go well for them if my plan worked, and it wouldn't go well for them if they tried to stop us.

'I did bring a gift,' I said. 'But if it proves not to your liking then I can make you some promises. I'll have Sir Makin promise you too, and he's a man of his word.' I smiled down at her. 'When I saw this place on a map…' I paused and remembered the circumstances with a certain fondness.

'Sally…' the girl whispered, remembering the tavern with me.

That shocked me for a moment. I didn't like the idea of this little girl in my head, opening doors, making childish judgment, shining her light in places that should be dark. Part of me wanted to cut her down, a large part of me.

I unclenched my jaw. 'When I saw this gorge on my map, I thought to myself "what a godforsaken spot". And that's when it occurred to me what to bring for barter. I brought you God.' I turned and pointed to Father Gomst. 'I've brought you salvation, the blessing of communion. I've brought you benediction, catechism … confession if you must. All the saving your ugly little souls can handle.'

Gomst let out a girlish scream and started to run. The Nuban caught a dark arm around his waist and hauled him up over one shoulder.

I expected Jane to answer, but Gorgoth made the deal.

'We will take the priest.' Something about his voice made my chest hurt. 'We will guide you to the Great Stair. The necromancers will find you, though. You will not return.'

Some said that Red Kent had a black heart, and that might be true, but anyone who had seen him take out a six-strong foot patrol with hatchet and knife would tell you the man had an artist's soul.

28

'Necromancers?' I trudged behind Jane with Gorgoth at my back. There had been nothing about necromancers in my books.

'They command the dead. Mages—'

'I know what they are.' I cut across Gorgoth. 'What are they doing in my way?'

'Mount Honas attracts them,' Jane said. 'There's death at the heart of the mountain. Old magics. It makes their work easier.'

Even the leucrotas' caves looked ugly. When I was seven, and William five, Tutor Lundist took us secretly to the caverns of Paderack. Unknown to any at court, the heirs of Ancrath slid and slipped into the blind depths, and came to a cathedral hall of such pillared wonder that it beggared the grace of God. I carry the glory of that place with me still. The chambers of the leucrota had none of that fluid elegance, no touch of the hidden artistry that lies in the deep places of the world. We walked through corridors of Builder-stone, poured and shaped using arts long forgotten. Jane's light showed us ancient vaults, cracked in places and scaled with lime. We wove a path around fallen blocks, larger than cart-horses, heading deeper all the time, like worms burrowing to the core, seeking the roots of the mountain.

'Shut your moaning, priest.' Row came up behind the Nuban and showed old Gomsty his knife, a wicked piece of ironwork to be sure.

Father Gomst let up his wailing at that, and I did miss it for the echoes had been quite haunting. I fell back for a word. That, and to make sure Row didn't decide to carve up our gift to the monsters before we'd handed it over proper-like.

'Peace now, Father,' I said.

I pushed Row's blade aside. He scowled at that, did Row, all pock-marks and squinting eyes.

'You'll just be changing flocks, Father,' I told Gomsty. 'Your new congregation might look a little fouler, but on the inside? Well I'm sure they'll be fairer than Row here.'

The Nuban grunted and shifted Father Gomst's weight on his shoulder.

'Set him down,' I said. 'He can walk. We're good and lost now, there'll be no running.'

The Nuban set old Gomsty on his feet. He looked at me, his face too black to read. 'It's wrong, Jorg. Trade in gold, not people. He's a holy man. He speaks for the white-Christ.'

Gomst looked at the Nuban with a hatred I'd never seen in him before, as if he'd just grown horns and called on Lucifer.

'Well now he can speak to Gorgoth for Christ,' I said.

The Nuban said nothing, his face a blank.

Something about the Nuban's silences always made me want to say a little more. As if I had to make it right with him. Makin scraped at me that same way, but not so bad.

'It's not like he can't leave,' I said. 'He's free to walk home if he really must. He'll just have to earn himself some food for the journey and a map is all.'

The Nuban gave me the white crescent of his smile.

I walked on, a cold voice inside me whispering, whispering of weakness, of the thin edge of a wedge, of a sharp knife cutting without tears, of a hot iron to cauterize a wound before infection spread. It doesn't do to love a brother.

Jane's light dimmed and flickered as I drew near. She recoiled slightly with an intake of breath. I curled my lip and imagined her falling from a cliff. It worked better than I'd hoped. She gave a squeal and covered her eyes.

Gorgoth stepped between us. 'Keep away from her, Dark Prince.'

So I walked in the shadows, and they led us on into the mountain. We followed wide tunnels that stretched for miles, level-floored with curved ceilings. Rust stains ran the length of the passages in parallel lines, though to what end men would lay iron in such a manner I can't say, unless these were the pipes through which the secret fire of the Builders ran.

We left Jane and all but two of her kindred at the shores of a lake so wide even her silver light could not reach across the waters. The Builders had made this place too. Stone gave away to water with a single sharp step, the ceiling stretched flat and without adornment. Jane's folk moved away toward shelters of wood and skins huddled at the water's edge. Gorgoth led them, one hand enveloping Father Gomst's shoulders.

Jane paused, her gaze moving between the two grotesques who remained to guard us. She said nothing but I could feel the undercurrent of unvoiced speech as she instructed them.

'No final words for me, little one?' I asked. I went on one knee before her. A fierce humour gripped me. 'No predictions? No pearls to throw before this swine? Come, share a glimpse with me. Blind me with the future.'

She met my gaze and the light dazzled, but I wouldn't look away.

'Your choices are keys to doors I cannot see beyond.'

I felt anger rise in me and pushed it down with a snarl. 'There's more than that.'

'You have a dark hand on your shoulder. A hole in your mind. A hole. In your memories. A hole – a hole – pulling me in – pulling—'

I seized her hand. That was a mistake, for it burned the skin and froze the bone in equal measure. I'd have set it down if I could, but the strength left me. For a moment I could see only the child's eyes.

'When you meet her, run. Just run. Nothing else.' It felt as though I were speaking the words, though I could hear Jane's voice frame them. Then I fell.

I woke to the light of torches.

'He's up.'

I found myself face to face with Rike.

'Jesu, Rike, you been gargling rat piss again?' I pushed his brutal jaw to one side and used his shoulder to lever myself up. The brothers began to rise around me, hefting their packs. Makin came from the water's edge, Gorgoth looming behind him.

'Don't go touching the Prophetess of the Leucrota!' He used a mock-scold. I could see the relief hidden in his eyes.

'I'll bear it in mind,' I said.

Gorgoth paused to scowl at me, then led the way, holding a pitch-torch the size of a small tree.

Our path angled up now, the tunnel thick with dust that tasted of bitter almonds. We walked for less than a thousand yards before the way broadened into a wide gallery crossed by stone trenches of obscure purpose, yards across, and as deep as a man is tall. At the mouth of the gallery a wooden pen hugged the wall, the stays bound with rope. Two children huddled together in the middle of the bare cage. Two leucrota. Gorgoth hauled the door open.

'Out.'

They were neither of them past seven summers, if summers were a proper count for the dark halls of the leucrota. They came out naked, two skinny boys, brothers to look at them, the younger one perhaps five. Of all the leucrota I'd seen they looked the least monstrous. A black-and-red stippling marked their skin, colouring them like the tigers of Indus. Dark barbs of horn jutted from their elbows, mirrored in the talons on their fingers. The elder of the two shot me a glance, his eyes utterly black, no white, iris, or pupil.

'We don't want your children,' Makin said. He reached into his pocket and tossed a twist of dry-meat to the brothers. 'Put them back.'

The meat twist skittered to a halt at the elder child's feet. He kept his eyes on Gorgoth. The littlest watched the dry-meat intently, but made no move. Their skin stretched so tight over the bone I could count every rib.

'These are for the necromancers, don't waste your food on them.' Gorgoth's rumble came so low it hurt to hear it.

'A sacrifice?' the Nuban asked.

'They're dead already,' Gorgoth said. 'The strength of the leucrota isn't in them.'

'They look hearty enough to me,' I said. 'With a meal or two in 'em. Sure you're not just jealous because they're not as ugly as the rest of you?' I didn't much care what Gorgoth did with the runts, but I took a pleasure in taunting him.

Gorgoth flexed his hands and six giant knuckles popped like logs on the fire.

'Eat.'

The two boys fell on Makin's food, snarling like dogs.

'The leucrota are pure-born, we gain our gifts as we grow. It is a slow change.' He gestured to the boys licking the last fragments of dry-meat from the stone. 'These two have the changes of a leucrota twice their age. The gifts will come faster now, faster and stronger. None can bear such changes. I have seen it before. Such gifts will turn a man inside out.' Something in those cat's eyes of his told me he meant it, told me he'd seen it. 'Better they serve us as payment to keep the necromancers from our caves. Better the dead-ones take these than search for victims who could have lived. They will find a quick death and a long peace.'

'If you say it, then it is so.' I shrugged. 'Let's be moving on. I'm keen to meet these necromancers of yours.'

We followed Gorgoth through the gallery. The brothers scampered around us, and I saw the Nuban slip them dried apricots from the woollen depths of his tunic.

'So what's your plan?' Makin sidled close to me, voice low.

'Hmmm?' I watched the younger child skip away from Liar's well-aimed boot.

'These necromancers – what's your plan?' Makin kept to a hiss.

I didn't have a plan, but that was just one more obstacle to overcome. 'There was a time when the dead stayed dead,' I said. 'I've read it in Father's library. For the longest time the dead only walked in stories. Even Plato had the dead comfortably far away, over the river Styx.'

'That's what you get for all that reading,' Makin said. 'I remember the marsh road. Those ghosts hadn't read your books.'

'Nuban!' I called him over. 'Nuban, come tell Sir Makin why the dead don't rest easy any more.'

He joined us, crossbow over one shoulder, oil of cloves in the air around him. 'The wise-men of Nuba tell it that the door stands ajar.' He paused and ran a very pink tongue over very white teeth. 'There's a door to death, a veil between the worlds, and we push through when we die. But on the Day of a Thousand Suns so many people had to push through at once, they broke the door. The veils are thin now. It just takes a whisper and the right promise, and you can call the dead back.'

'There you have it, Makin,' I said.

Makin furrowed his brow at that, then rubbed his lips. 'And the plan?'

'Ah,' I said.

'The plan?' He could be annoyingly persistent could Makin.

'Same as normal. We just keep killing them until they stay down.'

Brother Row you could trust to make a long shot with a short bow. You could trust him to come out of a knife fight with somebody else's blood on his shirt. You could trust him to lie, to cheat, to steal, and to watch your back. You couldn't trust his eyes though. He had kind eyes, and you couldn't trust them.

29

The Builders had an aversion to stairs it seems. Gorgoth led us up through the mountain by treacherous paths cut into the walls of endless vertical shafts. Perhaps the Builders grew wings, or like the far-seers of Indus they could levitate through force of will. In any case, the picks of later men had chewed a stair into the poured stone of the shaft walls, narrow and crudely hewn. We climbed with care, our arms tight before us, keeping narrow for fear of pitching ourselves into a fall with an inadvertent shrug of the shoulders. If the depths had been lit I don't doubt but some of the brothers would have needed the point of a sword to help them up, but darkness hides all sins, and we could fool ourselves a floor lay unseen twenty feet below.

Strange how the deeper a hole the stronger it draws a man. The fascination that lives on the keenest edge, and sparkles on the sharpest point, also gathers in depths of a fall. I felt the pull of it every moment of that climb.

Gorgoth seemed least well crafted for such an ascent,

but he made it look easy. The two leucrota children danced in front of me, skipping up the steps with a disregard that made me want to shove them into space.

'Why don't they run off?' I called ahead to Gorgoth. He didn't answer. I guessed the boys' disdain for the fall had to be set against the fate that awaited them if they made it safely to the top.

'You're taking them to die. Why do they follow you?' I called the words at the broad expanse of his back.

'Ask them.' Gorgoth's voice rumbled like distant thunder in the shaft.

I caught the elder brother by the neck and held him out over the fall. There was almost no weight to him and I needed a rest. I could feel the tally of all those steps fuelling a fire in my leg muscles.

'What's your name, little monster?' I asked him.

He looked at me with eyes that seemed darker and wider than the drop to my right.

'Name? No name,' he said, high and sweet.

'That's no good. I'll give you a name,' I said. 'I'm a prince, I'm allowed to do things like that. You'll be Gog, and your brother can be Magog.'

I glanced around at Red Kent who stood behind me, puffing, not the slightest flicker of comprehension on his peasant face.

'Gog, Magog... Jesu, where's a priest when I need someone to get a biblical joke!' I said. 'I never thought to miss Father Gomst!'

I turned back to young Gog. 'What're you so happy about? Old Gorgy-goth up there, he's taking you to be eaten by the dead.'

'Can fight 'em,' Gog said, quiet-like. 'Law says so.' If he felt uncomfortable being held up by the neck, he didn't show it.

'What about little Magog?' I nodded to his brother squatting on the step above us. 'He going to fight too?' I grinned at the notion of these two doing battle with death mages.

'I'll protect him,' Gog said, and he started to twist in my hand, so hard and fast that I had to set him down, or else pitch over the edge with him.

He scampered to his brother's side and set striped hand to striped shoulder. They watched me with those black eyes, quieter than mice.

'May be some sport in this,' Kent said behind me.

'I bet the littlest one lasts longest,' Rike shouted, and he bellowed with laughter as if he'd said something funny. He almost slipped off then, and that shut up his laughing quick enough.

'You want to win this game, Gog, you leave little Magog to look after himself.' As I spoke the words a chill set the hairs standing on my neck. 'Show me you've the strength to look after yourself, and maybe I'll find something those necromancers want more than they want your scrawny soul.'

Gorgoth started up again, and the brothers followed without a word.

I walked on, rubbing the scars on my forearms where the hook-briar had started to itch at me again.

I counted a thousand steps, and I only started out of boredom, so I missed the first ten minutes of the climb. My legs turned to jelly, my armour felt as though it were made from inch-thick lead, and my feet got too clumsy to find the stairs. Brother Gains convinced Gorgoth to call a rest halt by stumbling into space, and wailing for a good ten seconds before the unseen floor convinced him to shut up.

'All these stairs so we can reach "The Great Stair"!' I spat a mess of phlegm after dear departed Brother Gains.

Makin flashed me a grin and wiped the sweaty curls from his eyes. 'Maybe the necromancers will carry us up.'

'Going to need a new cook.' Red Kent spat after Gains.

'Can't anyone be worse than Gainsy.' Fat Burlow moved only his lips. The rest of him slumped lifeless, hugging the wall. I thought it a rather poor eulogy for Gains, since Burlow seemed to put away more of the man's culinary efforts than the rest of us put together.

'Rike would be worse,' I said. 'I see him tackling an evening meal the way he approaches burning a village.'

Gains was all right. He'd carved me a bone flute once, when I first came to the brothers. On the road, we talk away our dead with a curse and a joke. If we'd not liked Gains, nobody would have made comment. I felt a little stupid for letting Gorgoth walk us so hard. I took the bitter taste of that and set an edge on it, to save for the necromancers if they wanted to test our mettle.

We found the top of the stair without losing any more brothers. Gorgoth took us through a series of many-pillared halls, echoingly empty, the ceilings so low that Rike could reach up to touch them. Wide curving ramps stepped us up from one hall to the next, each the same as the one before, dusty and empty.

The smell crept up around us, so slowly that there wasn't a point where I could say I noticed it. The stink of death comes in many flavours, but I like to think I recognize the Reaper in all his guises.

The dust became thicker as we made our way, an inch deep in places. Here and there the occasional bone lay half-covered. Then more bones, then a skull, then three. Where the Builder-stone cracked and the waters oozed, the dust became a grey mud and flowed in miniature deltas. I pulled a skull from one such swamp. It came free with a satisfying squelch and mud poured from its sockets like syrup.

'So where are these necromancers of yours, Gorgoth?' I asked.

'We make for The Great Stair. They will find us,' he said.

'They've found you.' She slid around the pillar closest to me, a woman from the night of my imagination. She moved her body over the rough stone as if it were sheerest silk. Her voice fell on the ear like velvet, dark and rich.

Not one sword left its scabbard. The Nuban lifted his crossbow and heaved the loading lever back, bunching the heavy muscle in his arm into a black ball. The necromancer ignored him. She let the pillar go with a lover's reluctance and turned to face me. I heard Makin suck in his breath at my side. The woman mixed supple strength with a succulence that young princes doodle into the margins of their studies. She wore only paints and ribbons, the patterns swirled across her in Celtic knots of grey on black.

When you meet her, run.

'Well met, my lady.' I sketched her a court bow.

Just run.

'Gorgoth, you bring us guests as well as tribute!' Her laughter set a tingling in my groin.

Nothing else. Just run.

She offered her hand. For a moment I hesitated.

'And you would be?' Her eyes, that had held only the reflection of fire, now stole the green I remembered from a distant throne-room.

'Prince Honorous Jorg Ancrath.' I took her hand, cool and heavy, and kissed it. 'At your service.' And I was.

'Chella.' A dark fire ran in my veins. She smiled and I felt the same smile cross my face. She stepped closer. My skin sang with the thrill of her. I breathed her in, the bitter scent of old tombs, cut with the hot tang of blood.

'The little one first, Gorgoth,' she said, without taking her eyes from mine.

From the corner of my eye I saw Gorgoth take Gog in the hugeness of his hand.

The air became suddenly icy. The sound came of rock grinding on rock, setting my teeth on edge. The hall itself seemed to let forth a sigh of release, and with that exhalation mists swirled up among us, wraiths finding momentary form in the pale coils. I felt my finger freeze in the muck within the skull that dangled in my grasp.

The scraping ceased as bones found their partners. First one skeleton rose in a complex ballet of inter-articulation, then the next. The mists bound each bone in a spectral mockery of flesh.

I saw Gog explode into a fit of thrashing and writhing within Gorgoth's implacable grip. Little Magog stood his ground as the first skeleton advanced on him. Gog was too far gone in his rage to demand release. The roar that came from him sounded comical, so high-pitched and thick with fury.

The necromancer slipped her arm around me. I can't tell you how it felt. We turned to watch Magog fight.

The leucrota child reached up to the skeleton's knee, no higher. He saw his moment, or rather, thought he did, and threw himself forward. You can't expect much from a five year-old. The undead caught him in bony fingers and threw him carelessly against a pillar. Magog hit hard, leaving it bloody. He didn't cry though. He struggled to

225

get up as the second skeleton stepped toward him. A flap of the child's pretty skin hung away from the red flesh of his shoulder.

I looked away. Even with Chella's softness pressed to me, this sport tasted sour in ways I didn't understand. My eyes found Gog, still fighting in Gorgoth's fists. Gorgoth had both hands on the child now, though I doubted even I could fight out of his single grip. I hadn't imagined strength like that could lie in so small a thing.

The skeleton had Magog in one hand, two bone fingers of the other hand ready to drive through his eyes.

It seemed to me that a storm rose, though maybe it rose just in me, a storm lashing a moonless night and showing the world in lightning slices. A child's voice howled in my head and would not quiet though I cursed it to silence. Every fibre of me strained to move – and no part of me so much as twitched. Hooks held me. There in the cradle of the necromancer's arms I watched the skeletal fingers plunge toward the black pools of the leucrota's eyes.

When the hand exploded I was as surprised as anyone. A big crossbow bolt will do that to a hand. The Nuban turned his face toward me, away from the sights of his bow. I saw the white crescent of his smile and my limbs were free. I swung my arm up, sharp and hard. The skull in my hand hit the necromancer's face with a most satisfying crunch.

Whoever made the Nuban must have fashioned him from bedrock. I never knew a man more solid. He held his words close. Few among the brothers sought his counsel, men upon the road have little use for conscience, and although he never judged, the Nuban carried judgement with him.

30

I cleared scabbard and followed the arc of my family blade to face the necromancer. It's one of those swords they say can make the wind bleed. Appropriately the edge found only empty air, which hissed as if cut.

The necromancer fell back too swiftly for me to reach. The skull had taken her by surprise, but I didn't think I'd catch her again so easily.

I guess the skull hit her in the bridge of the nose, because that's where the mess was. No blood, but a dark stain and a writhing of the flesh as though a hundred worms wriggled, one over another.

For the most part the brothers still stood in the daze that had held me. The Nuban worked to load another bolt into his crossbow. Makin half-drew his sword. Gorgoth let go of Gog.

The necromancer took a breath, like a rasp drawn over ironwork, rattling in her throat. 'That,' she said, 'was a mistake.'

'So sorry!' I kept my voice cheerful and lunged at her.

She slipped around the pillar, leaving me to skewer the stonework.

Gog hurled himself bodily at Magog, and tore his little brother from the skeleton's one-handed grip. I caught a glimpse of pale finger-marks on the child's neck.

I moved around the pillar with a little caution, only to find the necromancer had somehow slipped back to a further pillar, five yards off.

'I'm very particular about who I allow to place spells on me,' I said, turning and aiming a swift kick at Rike. He's hard to miss. 'Come on, Rikey! Up and at 'em!'

Rike came to with a wordless howl of complaint, somewhere between disturbed walrus and bear-prodded-out-of-hibernation. Just in front of him the two skeletons bent to reach for the leucrota brothers, still a tangle of limbs on the dusty floor. Rike loomed over both of the undead, and took a skull in each hand. He wrenched them together in a clap that reduced the pair to shards.

Roaring unintelligibly, he shook his hands. 'Cold!' He graduated to words. 'Fecking freezing!'

I turned to the necromancer, some witticism ready on my tongue. The taunt died where it sat. Her whole face writhed now. The flesh lay shrunken on her limbs, pulsing sporadically. The body that seduced my eyes now held all the allure of a famine-corpse. She held me with a dark gaze, glittering in rotting slaughter. She laughed and her laughter came as the sound of wet rags flapping at the wind.

The brothers stood with me now. Gorgoth made no move, keeping his place. The little leucrotas crouched together in the shadows.

'We're many, and you're one, my lady. And a damned ugly one at that. So you'd best step aside and let us past,' I said. Somehow I didn't think she was going to, but nothing ventured nothing gained, as they say.

That worm-flesh of hers crawled into a smile so wide I could see her jawbones past the hinge-point. For a second her face rippled and we saw Gains there, screaming as he fell.

'The dead are many, child,' she said. 'I'll let you pass – into their realm.'

The temperature fell, and kept falling, like there was no bottom for it to hit. It went from uncomfortable, to painful, to plain stupid in no time at all. And the noise. The awful grinding as the skeletons built themselves from pieces and wrapped themselves in the spirit-mist that rose around us. A sound to make you want to pull your teeth out. The torch in Makin's hand gave up its struggle against the cold and guttered out.

The mist hid all but our nearest neighbours. The skeletons came at us slowly, as if in a dream. If not for the fire of Gorgoth's torch we'd have been left in utter darkness.

I swung my sword at the first attacker. The hilt felt frozen onto my hand, but I wasn't inclined to drop it in any case. I needed the exercise to keep warm. The skeleton disintegrated into a shower of brittle bone. I had no time to cheer before the next came lurching out of the fog.

We fell to the fight, and time left us. We hung in a freezing limbo where only the shattering of bone and the rise and fall of swords held meaning. Every time I cut ghost-flesh it seemed that the cold bit a little deeper into me. The sword grew heavy in my hand until it felt as if they'd fashioned it from lead.

I saw Roddat die. A skeleton caught him with his guard down. Bony fingers found either side of his head and a whiteness spread from them; the living flesh dying where the ghost flesh touched. He was a weasel, was Roddat, but I took a pleasure in cutting in half the dead thing that killed him. Behind me someone screamed. Sounded like Brother Jobe. It wasn't the kind of scream you get up from.

Makin found his way to my side, frost on his breast-plate, blue in his lips. 'They just keep coming.'

I could hear a roaring behind us. The mist seemed to swallow sound, but the roaring ripped on through.

'Rike?' I had to shout to be heard above it.

'Gorgoth! You want to see him fight. He's a monster!' Makin shouted.

I had to smile at that.

They just kept coming. More and more, rank by rank, out of the dark. Somebody died beside me. I couldn't tell you who.

We must have smashed two hundred of the bastards and still they kept coming.

My sword got caught in the ribs of the skeleton I'd swung at. Not enough force in the blow. Makin shattered its neck with a flat swing.

'Thanks.' The word came out blunt, through numb lips.

I'm not going to die here. I kept running the thought through my head. It held less conviction each time. *I'm not going to die here.* I felt too cold to think. *Not going to die here. Swing low to cut off those reaching hands. These bastards don't even feel it. The bitch felt it though, when I broke her face.*

The bitch.

When in doubt, let your hate lead you. Normally I'd reject that advice. It makes a man predictable. But there, in that miserable hall of bones, I was past caring. Hate was all I had to keep me warm. I cut a skeleton down and lunged past.

'Jorg!' I heard Makin's startled shout behind me, then the darkness took my sight and the mist threw a thick blanket over the crash of battle.

Oh it was black out there. So dark as to reach inside you and rip out all memory of colour. I swung my sword a few times, broke some bones, carved air for a while, then hit a pillar which shook the damn thing out of my frozen grip. I hunted my sword frantically, with hands too numb to find my face. Gradually it came to me that I was free of the skeletons. No bone fingers sought me in the night. Without sword or direction I stumbled on.

The bitch. She'd be somewhere near. Surely. Waiting to trap our souls as we died. Waiting to feed.

I stopped and stood as still as my shivering would let me. The necromancer had lifted the veil. Just like the Nuban said, she had lifted the veil between the worlds and the dead were coming through. If I stopped her, they'd stop coming. I listened, listened deep, to a silence as velvet as the dark. I held more still, straining for her, tight and focused.

'Cloves.' My lips formed the word. I wrinkled my nose. Oil of cloves? The scent drew me on. It hung fainter than faint but, with nothing to fight against, it held me. I let it carry me forward, swaying, turning, seeking the source.

My hands found a narrow doorway and I stepped through into a chamber lit by the flickers of a dropped torch.

I understood the scent. The Nuban's crossbow lay a foot from the torch, dropped carelessly, the cable drawn but the bolt spilled to the stones. He'd broken from the brothers to hunt her. Beaten me to the chase.

'Necromancer,' I said.

She stood at the mouth of one of the Builders' shafts. The square maw filled the rear of the chamber behind her and the feeble light could not plumb its depths. She held the Nuban before her, holding his head to one side and her mouth to the straining cables of his neck. I could see the tension in his thick arms, but his fingers curled useless by his sides and his broadsword lay at his feet, hilt jutting into space over the edge of the shaft.

The necromancer lifted her face from the Nuban's neck. Blood dripped from her teeth. Whatever strength she gleaned from it had restored her looks. The blood ran over full lips and down a perfect throat.

'You sent such a fresh one to hunt me down, Prince Jorg,' she said. 'Mmmm, flavoured with heathen spices. I thank you.'

I knelt and picked up the Nuban's bow. The weight of it always surprised me. I set the bolt in place. She moved to use him as a shield, her heels to the pit.

'You're cold, my prince,' she said. The sudden music of her voice caught me off guard. It ran deep, rich with complexity. 'I could warm you.'

My tired body thrilled with the dark melody of her. It took the memory of Gains's face crawling across her worm-flesh to stop me rising to her call. I lifted the bow. I knew I couldn't hold it for long.

'It's grave-cold that's in you.' Her voice became an angry hiss. 'It will kill you.'

She smiled at me over the Nuban's shoulder, enjoying his helplessness. 'You're trembling, Jorg. Put the bow down. You probably couldn't even hit your friend here, let alone me.'

It felt so tempting. Put the bow down.

'He's not my friend,' I said.

She shook her head. 'He'd die for you. I can taste it in his blood.'

'You're playing the wrong game with me, dead-thing.'
I raised the bow and sighted it. The tremor in my arms
kept the aim-point jumping. Any worse and the bolt
would have shaken from its groove.

She laughed at me. 'I can see the ties that bind the
living. You only have two friends, Prince Jorg. You're as
bound to this sweet-blooded man as any son to his father.'

Sacrifice.

She set her fingers to the red holes in the Nuban's
neck. 'Let me have the others. Let me take their life-juice,
and you and him, you can stay with me. You can help
me harvest the leucrota. There are several tribes, some
of them quite fractious. There are other necromancers
against whom a living ally, one as sharp as you, would be
most useful.'

Play the game.

She smiled, and that dark fire lit in me again. 'I like
you, Prince. We can rule under the mountain, together.'
Sex dripped off her words. Not that pallid roll in the
sheets that Sally surrendered, but something potent,
unseen, and consuming. She offered me a draw. Life,
power, and command. But in her service.

Play to win.

The Nuban's eyes were on mine. For the first time
ever, I could read what he held there. I could have taken
anything else. I could have taken hatred, or fear, or plead-
ing. But he forgave me.

ChooOom!

235

The bolt hit the Nuban square in the chest. It put a hole through both of them and took them off the edge. Neither of them screamed, and it took forever before they hit the bottom.

Most men have at least one redeeming feature. Finding one for Brother Rike requires a stretch. Is 'big' a redeeming feature?

31

I came back to find the brothers nursing their wounds among drifts of broken bone. Roddat, Jobe, Els, and Frenk lay stretched out, apart from the group. Death makes lepers of even the most popular men. I didn't bother with them: any loot would be long gone.

'Thought you'd left us, Brother Jorg.' Red Kent spared me a glance from beneath lowered brows and returned to the business of whetstone and sword.

That 'brother' held a note of reproach. A note at the least, perhaps a whole symphony. No 'prince' for the runaway.

Makin watched me with dark speculation, sprawled on the floor, too spent to prop himself against a pillar.

Rike hefted himself to his feet. He came toward me slowly, polishing a ring against the leather padding of his breastplate. I recognized it as Roddat's luck-ring, a nice piece of yellow gold.

'Thought you'd left us, Brother Jorgy,' he said. He loomed over me, a broad and brooding form.

There's some, like Liar, that aren't much to look at, and it's a surprise for folks when they find out what a truly nasty bastard they're dealing with. Rike never surprised anyone that way. The menace of him, the sheer brutality, his love of other people's pain, well Mother Nature wrote it in every line of him just to warn us.

'The Nuban is dead.' I ignored Rike and looked to Makin. I pulled the Nuban's crossbow off my back and showed it. No doubt after that. The man was dead.

'Good,' said Rike. 'Serves him right for running. Never did like that weasel coward.'

I hit Rike as hard as I could. In the throat. I made no conscious decision. If I'd given it the smallest moment's consideration I'd have held my blow. I might have stood a chance against him with a sword, but never with bare hands.

Actually 'bare hands' is going too far. I had my gauntlets on, riveted iron. I stood six foot tall at fourteen, lean, but hard with muscle from swinging a sword and carting my armour around. I knew how to punch too. I put my whole weight behind that blow, and every ounce of my strength.

Iron knuckles crunched into Rike's bull-throat. I may not have been thinking with my head, but thankfully some part of me hadn't abandoned all sense. Punching Rike's blunt face would have probably broken my fist and just tickled him a little.

He gave a kind of grunt and stood there, looking slightly bewildered. I supposed the idea that I'd just committed suicide in such grand style took some getting used to.

Somewhere in the back of my mind it dawned on me that I'd made a very big mistake. The rest of me didn't much care. I think blind rage, and the pure enjoyment of using Rike as a punch-bag, figured in equal measure.

Since I'd been offered a second free blow, I took two. An iron-clad knee driven accurately into the groin will give pause for thought even to a seven foot maniac who's twice your weight. Rike folded up obligingly and I brought both fists down together on the back of his neck.

I studied the fighting arts of the Nippon with Tutor Lundist. He brought a book on the subject with him from the Utter East. Page upon rice-paper page of fighting stances, kata moves, and anatomical diagrams to show the pressure points. I'm sure I hit the two stun points on the back of Rike's neck, and I know I hit hard.

I blame him for being too stupid to know how they work.

Rike swung at me. A lucky thing, because if he'd grappled me he'd have twisted my head off in no time. His vambrace caught my ribcage. I guess if I'd not been wearing that breastplate all my ribs would have broken, rather than just the two. The force took me off my feet and sent me sliding among the bones. I fetched up against one of those pillars with a painful little clang.

I could have drawn my sword then. It would have been the only sensible decision. Against all the unwritten rules, of course. I started it with a punch and that was the way the thing should have ended. But when you weigh a loss of face with the brothers against having Rike actually rip your face off, well it's not a hard decision.

I picked myself up. 'Come here, you fat bastard.'

The words emerged without a by-your-leave. The anger spoke for me. Anger at having lost control, more that now than anger at him calling the Nuban a coward. The Nuban didn't need Rike beaten bloody to prove his courage. Angry at being angry – there's a worm that will eat its tail and no mistake. I should have Oroborus on my family crest.

Rike rushed me with that wordless howl of his. He reached a fair clip. Not many castle doors would stop Little Rikey at that speed. Pretty scary, unless you know he can't turn corners.

I stepped aside nice and sharp, cursing at my ribs. Rike hit the pillar and bounced off. To his credit several bits of stone came loose. I picked up a good stout thigh-bone and smacked him around the head with it as he tried to get up. The thing cracked almost in two, so I finished the job and had myself two knob-ended clubs.

The single most depressing thing about fighting Rike would have to be the way he'd never stay down. He came at me, a bit woozy now, but snarling dire threats and meaning every one of them.

'Gonna feed you your own eyeballs, boy.' He spat out a tooth.

I danced back and hit him in the face with the longer of my two clubs. He spat out another tooth at that. I had to laugh. The anger left me and it felt good.

So Rike lumbered after me, and I kept my distance, clouting him a good one when I could. The closest thing I can think of is bear-baiting. *Whack! Growl. Clang! Snarl!* I had the giggles, which was a bad thing, because one slip and he really would have me. If he got just one of those paws of his on me and got a grip … well I *would* be eating my own eyeballs. He did things like that.

The brothers started to lay bets and clap the sport.

'I'll pull your guts out.' Rike seemed to have an endless supply of threats.

Unfortunately he seemed to have an endless supply of energy too, and my dancing days were coming to an end, my footwork getting a little clumsy.

'Break every little bone in that pretty face o' yours, Jorgy.'

Our circle took us back to where I threw the first blow.

'Pull those skinny arms out of their sockets.' He looked an evil sight with blood spilling down his chin.

I saw my chance. I ran straight at him, taking him by surprise yet again. In the long run it promised to be a pushing contest as unequal as Rike against the pillar, but he gave a step. A step gave me all I'd hoped for. He hit Makin's legs, stumbled and went over backward. I scooped up the Nuban's bow, and before Rike could get

242

up I was over him. I had the snout of the bow, a heavy iron falcon, poised above Rike's face.

'What's it going to be, Little Rikey?' I asked. 'I think I can crush your skull like an egg before you get your hands on me. Should we try it and see? Or do you want to take that back?'

He gave me a blank look.

'About the Nuban,' I said. Rike had genuinely forgotten what he'd said.

'Uh.' Doubt crinkled his brow. He tried to focus on the bow. 'I take it back.'

'Christ bleeding!' I sagged, exhausted, clothed in sweat. The brothers surged round us then, a new life in them, paying their bets, reliving the moment when Rike charged the pillar. I made note of who backed me, Burlow, Liar, Grumlow, Kent, the older men who could look past youth. Makin even went so far as to get up off the floor. He clapped a hand to my shoulder. 'You and the Nuban, you caught her?'

I nodded.

'I hope she went to Hell screaming,' Makin said.

'She died hard,' I said. An easy lie.

'The Nuban...' Makin had to hunt for the words. 'He was better than the rest of us.'

I didn't have to hunt. 'Yes.'

Gorgoth hadn't stirred while I fought Rike. He sat on the cold stone, legs crossed under him. Here and there the ghost-flesh of skeletal fingers had marked his hide with dead spots, little white fingerprints where the flesh had died. He didn't move, but he watched me with those cat's eyes of his.

A yard or two from Gorgoth I could make out a small dark huddle, Gog and Magog clutched one to another.

'A fine fight, lad,' I called to Gog. 'You were as good as your word.'

Gog lifted his face to me. Magog's head flopped back, rolling on a neck scored by white lines, dead white lines across his tiger stripes.

I found myself kneeling beside them. Gog snarled when I touched his brother, but he didn't stop me. Magog felt so light in my hands, a curious mix of bony starvation and child softness.

'Your brother,' I said. For the longest moment I had nothing else to say, as though my throat closed away all my words. 'So little.' I remembered him scampering up those endless stairs. In the end I had to press on my broken ribs to let the pain sharpen me and chase out the stupidity.

I set the dead child down, and stood. 'You fought for him, Gog. Stupid, but maybe you'll find comfort in it.' Maybe his reproach won't follow you the length of your days.

'We have a new mascot!' I announced to the brothers. 'Gog here is now part of our merry band.'

Gorgoth started up at that. 'The necromancers—'

I stepped in before he rose to his feet, the iron face of the Nuban's crossbow three inches from his ridged forehead. 'What's it going to be, Gorgoth?' I asked. He sat himself back down.

I turned away. 'We burn the dead. I'm not having them come back to say hello.'

'Burn 'em with what?' Red Kent wanted to know.

'Bones is poor kindling, Jorth.' Elban hawked a wad of phlegm into the nearest pile as if to prove his point.

'We'll have us a bone-fire even so,' I said. 'I saw a tar drip on my way back.'

So we took the bones to where the black stuff leaked slow and stinking from a crack in the Builder-stone and daubed them one by one. We made a heap for Roddat and the others, and a little pyre for the leucrota. Elban built it like the ones they fashion for kings in the Teuton lands.

I set the fire with Makin's torch. 'Goodnight, lads,' I said. 'Thieves and road-scum the lot of you. Tell the Devil I said to take good care of you.'

I gave the torch to Gog. 'Light it up, you don't want the necromancers playing with his bones.' A heat came off the boy, as if a fire banked inside him had woken. Any hotter and he might light the pyre without the torch.

He set the flame and we backed off before the billowing smoke. Tar never burns clean, but I wasn't sorry for the veil it gave us. Gog gave me the torch back. The inky pools of his eyes held their secrets even tighter than the

Nuban's did, but I could see something in there. A kind of pride.

We made our way on. I let Burlow carry the Nuban's bow. A prince must exercise some privilege after all. We walked with our tar-bone torches smoking, and Gorgoth at the fore to find the path.

He showed us mile after mile of dull box-chamber, square corridor, and low gallery. I guess when the Builders bought their hell-fire from Lucifer they must have paid for it with their imaginations.

The Great Stair took me by surprise.

'Here.' Gorgoth halted at a spot where a natural tunnel undercut the passage.

The Great Stair proved to be less grand than I had imagined. No more than ten yards across in any place I could see, and a squeeze at the entrance. At least it was natural though. My eyes had ached for a curved line, and here I could rest them. Some ancient stream had carved a path down a fault-line, stepping by leaps and bounds into the deep places. The waters, long since reduced to a trickle, dripped in a rocky gullet as steep and twisting as a man could hope for.

'Seems we have a climb ahead of us,' I said.

'These stairs are not for the living.' A necromancer insinuated himself into the narrow entrance, pulling himself from the shadows as though they clung like webs. He could have been a twin to the bitch that took the Nuban.

'For Christ's sake!' I drew my sword and swung on a rising arc in the same motion. His head came off clean. I let the momentum carry me round, and brought the blade down with all my strength, overhand on the pulsing stump of his neck. The blow caught him before he could fall and cut deep, splitting his sternum.

'I'm not interested!' I shouted the words at his corpse as I let its weight pull me to the ground. As with so many things in life the bringing of death is simply a matter of timing. I made the mistake of giving Chella a moment and she took it. Jane should have told me just to attack her, nothing else, just attack her. Forget running. I had in mind that if my reply to Chella's first words had been a well judged sword blow, the Nuban might yet be standing with me.

A savage twist on my sword hilt opened the necromancer's chest. I keep a little dagger in my boot, wicked sharp. I took it out, and whilst the brothers watched in silence I cut out the necromancer's heart. The thing pulsed in my hand, warmish, lacking the heat of the living or the cold of the dead. His blood lacked a certain vitality too. When cutting out a heart, and I speak from experience here, expect to be crimson head to toe. The necromancer's blood looked purple in the torchlight and barely reached past my elbows.

'If any more of you bastards want to waste my time with stupid melodrama, please form an orderly queue.' I let my voice echo down the corridors.

The Nuban once told me about a tribe in Nuba that ate the heart and the brains of their enemies. They thought it gave them their foes' strength and cunning. I never saw the Nuban do it, but he didn't dismiss the idea.

I held the heart up to my mouth.

'Prince!' Makin stepped toward me. 'That's evil meat.'

'There is no evil, Makin,' I said. 'There's the love of things, power, comfort, sex, and there's what men are willing to do to satisfy those lusts.' I kicked the ruin of the necromancer's corpse. 'You think these sad creatures are evil? You think we should fear them?'

I took a bite, as big as I could manage. Raw flesh is chewy, but the necromancer's heart had some give in it, like a game bird hung until it's ready to drop off the hook. The bitter gall of the blood scoured my throat. I swallowed my mouthful and it slid down, slow and sour.

I think for the first time Burlow watched me eat without the green eyes of jealousy. I threw the rest of it down. The brothers stood mute, eyes watering from the torch-smoke. That's the problem with tar-torches, you have to keep moving. I felt a touch odd. I had the feeling you get when you know you really should be somewhere else, as if you'd promised a duel that morning or some such but couldn't quite remember what it was. Chills ran up my back and along my arms, as if ghosts trailed their fingers over me.

I opened my mouth, then closed it, interrupted by a whisper. I looked around. Whispers came from every

248

corner, just at that maddening level where you can hear the words but not understand them. The brothers started to look around too, nervous.

'Do you hear it?' I asked.

'Hear what?' Makin said.

The voices came louder, angry but indistinct, louder, a multitude advancing, louder. A faint breeze disturbed the air.

'Time to climb, gentlemen.' I wiped my hand across my mouth, scraping away purple muck on the back of my gauntlet. 'Let's see how fast we can do this.'

I picked the necromancer's head from the floor, half expecting the eyes to roll down and fix me with a glare. 'I think our heartless foe has friends coming,' I said. 'Lots of friends.'

Everyone likes to eat. One man marches on his stomach as much as an army does. Only Fat Burlow didn't much take to marching, and took too much to munching. And some of the brothers were apt to hold that against a man. Still, I had more time for old Burlow than I did for most of my road-kin. Of all of them, save Makin, he was the only one who owned to reading. Of course he bore watching for that. There's a saying on the road, 'Never trust a lettered man'.

32

We ascended the Great Stair with the screams of ghosts rising beneath us. They say fear lends a man wings. None of the brothers flew up the Stair, but the way they scrambled over the slickness of that rocky throat would teach a lizard plenty about climbing.

I let them lead the way. It was as good a means as any to test the footing. Grumlow first, then Liar and young Sim. Gog scrambled behind them, followed by Gorgoth. I guessed the leucrotas' accord with the necromancers might be somewhat broken.

Makin was the last of them. He could feel the dead coming. I saw it in the pallor of his skin. He looked like a dead thing himself.

'Jorg! Get up here! Climb!' He grabbed at my arm as he passed.

I shook him off. I could see ghosts boiling along the tunnel toward us, others stepping from the walls.

'Jorg!' Makin took my shoulders and pulled me toward the Stair.

He couldn't see them. I knew from the wild sweep of his gaze. His eyes never touched them. The closest of them looked to me like chalk drawings half-erased, hanging in the air. Sketches of corpses, some naked, some clad in rags, or pieces of broken armour. A coldness came from them, reaching for my flesh, stealing warmth with invisible fingers.

I laughed at them. Not because I thought they had no power to harm me, but because they had. I laughed to show them what I cared for their threat. I laughed to hurt them. And they suffered for it. The taste of dead heart-meat lingered at the back of my throat, and a dark power ran through me.

'Die!' I shouted at them, spitting away the laughter. 'A man should at least know how to stay dead!'

And they did. I think. As if my words held them to obey. Makin had me dragged away, nearly round the corner, but I saw the spirits stop. I saw pale flames light upon their limbs, the ghost of fire. And, oh, the screaming. Even Makin heard it, like the scrape of nails on slate, cold wind on a migraine. We both ran then, close enough to flying.

It was hours before we stopped, a thousand feet or more up the Stair. The downward tumble of the long-vanished river paused here to scour out a bowl, set about with smaller sinkholes and decorated with the frozen tracery of stone that graces the deep places of the world.

'Fuckit.' Fat Burlow collapsed in a boneless heap and lay motionless.

Red Kent sat back against a stalagmite, his face coloured to match his name.

Close by, Elban spat into a sinkhole pool then turned, wiping mucus from his wizened lips. 'Heh! You looks like one o' them Blushers, Kent.'

Kent just gave him mean eyes.

'So.' Makin hauled in a huge breath and tried again. 'So, Prince, we're climbing up. Well and good. But if we keep on up we're just going to reach the Castle Red.' Another breath. A long climb in armour will do that for you. 'We might surprise the hell out of them, coming up out of their vaults, but we're still twice a dozen men against nine hundred.'

I smiled. 'It's a dilemma ain't it, Brother Makin? Can Jorg work the magic one more time?'

The brothers all had an eye on me now. All save Burlow, after that climb he wouldn't turn his head for anything less than the Second Coming.

I pulled myself to my feet and gave a little bow. 'That Jorg, that Prince Jorg, he's got a madness in him. A stranger to reason, a little in love with death perhaps?'

Makin had a frown on him, worried, wanting me to shut up.

I strode around them. 'Young Jorg, he's apt to throw it all away on a whim, gamble the brotherhood on wild chance … but somehow, just somehow, it keeps turning out a-right!'

I clapped a hand to Rike's greasy head and he gave me a bruise-faced scowl.

'Is it luck?' I asked. 'Or some sort of royal magic?'

'Nine hundred o' them Blushers up there in the Castle Red, Jorth.' Elban gestured at the ceiling with his thumb. 'No way we can turn them out of there. Not if we were ten times the number.'

'The wisdom of age!' And I crossed to Elban and threw an arm around his shoulders. 'Oh my brothers! I may have given our priest away, but it sorrows me that your faith departs so swiftly on his heels.'

I steered Elban to the Stair. I felt the tension in him as we neared the point where the floor fell away. He remembered the Watch Master.

I pointed up the stepped river course. 'That's where our path lies, Old Father.'

I let him go and he drew in a sigh. Then I turned to face the brothers once again. Gorgoth watched me with his cat's eyes, Gog with strange fascination from behind a pillar of rock.

'Now I'm thinking that I'll find what I'm looking for before we reach the under-vaults of the Castle Red.' I put a little iron in my voice. 'But if it turns out we have to murder us a quiet path to Duke Merl's bedchamber, and I have to plant him on my sword like a puppet on a stick to get him to sign the place over to me…' I swept my gaze across them, and even Burlow managed to look up. 'Then…' I let my voice fill the chamber and it echoed marvellously. 'Then that is what you will fecking well do, and the first brother that doubts my fecking luck, will be the first to leave this little family of ours.' I left them in no doubt that such a parting would be ungentle.

So we climbed again, and in time we left the Great Stair behind us, finding once more the box-halls of the Builders. Gorgoth's knowledge reached only to the Stair's foot so I led the way. Lines danced in my mind. Rectangles, squares, precise corridors, all etched into scorched plasteek. A turn there, a chamber on the left. And with sudden certainty, like one of Lundist's potions turning to crystal at the addition of the smallest grain, I knew where we were.

I pictured the map and followed it. The Builders' book sat in my pack, and I'd returned to its pages many times on our journey from The Falling Angel. No need to dig it out now. Let the brothers have their magic show.

We came to a five-way intersection. I put one hand to my forehead and let the other wander the air as if seeking our path. 'This way! We're close.'

An opening on the left, edged by the ancient rust-stain of a long vanished door.

I paused and lit a new torch of tar and bone from the blackened stick of my old one.

'And here we are!'

With my best courtly flourish I pointed the way, then stepped through.

We entered an ante-chamber to the vault I sought from my map. The door that blocked the way from our chamber into the vault stood maybe ten foot tall, a huge circular valve of gleaming steel, set about with rivets thick as my arm. Damned if I know what Builder spells kept it from rusting away like the rest, but there it was, big shiny and implacably in my way.

'So how're you going to open that?' Rike's words came out mumbled. I'd mashed his lips up pretty good.

I hadn't the slightest idea.

'I thought we could try knocking it down with your head.'

I named him Liar the day I put a knife through his hand. The knife came out, but the name stuck. He was a mean bit of gristle wrapped round bone. Truth might burn his tongue but his looks didn't lie.

33

'Looks pretty solid to me,' Makin said.

I couldn't argue. I'd never seen anything more solid than that door. I could hardly even scratch it with my sword.

'So what's the plan?' Red Kent stood with both hands on the hilts of his short-swords.

I held the gleaming wheel at the centre of the door and leaned back. The door loomed above me. It looked like silver, a king's ransom in silver.

'We could dig through,' I said.

'Builder-stone?' Makin raised an eyebrow.

'Try anyway.' I released the wheel and pointed to Burlow then Rike. 'You two. Start over there.'

They moved forward with shrugs. Rike reached the spot and kicked the wall. Burlow held his hands out before him and studied them with a speculative pout.

I had picked them for strength, not initiative. 'Makin, give them your flail. Row, let's put that war-hammer of yours to good work.'

Rike took the hammer in one hand and set to pounding on the wall. Burlow took a swing with the flail and nearly got both the spiked iron balls in his face as they bounced back.

'My money's on the wall,' Makin said.

After five minutes I could see we'd be there a while. The wall fell away not in chunks but in scatters of pulverized stone. Even Rike's furious attack left only shallow scars.

The brothers began to settle, leaning back against their packs. Liar set to cleaning his nails with a small knife. Row put down his lantern, Grumlow took out cards, and they hunkered down to play a hand. Lost most of their loot that way, Row and Grumlow, and practice never made them better. Makin pulled out a stick of dried meat and set to chewing. 'We've a week's rations at most, Jorg.' He got the words out between swallows.

I paced the room. I knew we weren't going to dig through. I'd given them make-work to keep them quiet. Or at least as quiet as men wielding hammers can be.

Perhaps there's no way through. The thought gnawed at me, an unscratchable itch, refusing to let me rest.

The hammering made the room ring. The noise struck at my ears. I walked the perimeter, trailing the point of my sword along the wall, deep in thought. *No way through.* Gog crouched in a corner and watched me with dark eyes. Where the brothers lay, I stepped over them as though they were logs. As I passed by Liar I felt a change in the texture of the wall. It looked the same, but beneath my blade it felt like neither stone nor metal.

'Gorgoth, I need your strength here, if you please.' I didn't look to see if he got up.

I sheathed my sword and pulled the knife from my belt. Moving in close, I scratched at the strange patch and managed to score a line across the surface. It left me little wiser. Not wood.

'What?' The torches threw Gorgoth's shadow over me.

'I hoped you could tell me,' I said. 'Or at least open it.' I struck my fist on the panel. It gave the faintest hint at some hollow behind.

Gorgoth pushed past and felt out the edges. It was about a yard by half a yard. He struck it a blow that would have caved in an oak door. The panel hardly shook, but the edge on the left lifted ever so slightly. He set the three thick fingers of each hand to the edge, digging in with dark red talons. Beneath his scarred hide the muscles seemed to fight each other, one surging over the next in a furious game of King of the Mountain. For the longest time nothing happened. I watched him strain, then realized I'd forgotten to breathe. As I released my breath, something gave inside the wall. With a snap and then a tortured groan the panel came free. The empty cupboard behind it proved to be somewhat of an anti-climax.

'Jorg!' The hammering had stopped.

I turned to see Rike wiping sweat and dust from his face, and Burlow beckoning me over.

I crossed the room slowly, though half of me wanted to run, and the other half not to go at all.

'Doesn't look like you're through yet, Burlow.' I shook my head in mock disappointment.

'Not going to be neither.' Rike spat on the floor.

Burlow brushed the dust from the shallow hole their labour had forged. Two twisted metal bars showed through, bedded in the Builder-stone. 'Reckon these run through the whole wall,' he said.

My eyes strayed to the knife I held clenched in one fist. I have, on occasion, punished the messenger. There are few things more satisfying than taking out your frustrations upon the bearer of bad tidings.

'Reckon they might at that.' I pushed the words through gritted teeth.

Quickly, before Fat Burlow could open his mouth again and earn himself the name Dead Burlow, I turned and went back to the secret compartment. Just enough space to hold a folded corpse. Empty save for dust. I drew my sword and reached in to check the back of the compartment. As I did a strange chime sounded.

'External sensors malfunctioning. Biometrics offline.' The voice came from the empty cupboard, the tone calm and reasonable.

I looked to either side, then back to the space before me. The brothers looked up and started to get to their feet.

'What language is that?' Makin asked. The others were looking for ghosts, but Makin always asked good questions.

'Damned if I know.' I knew a few languages, six fluent enough for conversation and another six well enough to recognize when spoken.

'Password?' The voice came again.

I recognized that. 'So you can speak Empire Tongue, spirit.' I kept my sword raised, looking all around to find the speaker. 'Show yourself.'

'State your name and password.'

Beneath the dust on the back wall of the compartment I could see lights moving, like bright green worms.

'Can you open that door?' I asked.

'That information is classified. Do you have clearance?'

'Yes.' Four foot of edged steel is clearance enough in my book.

'State your name and password.'

'How long have you been trapped in there, spirit?' I asked.

The brothers gathered around me, peering into the compartment. Makin made the sign of the cross, Red Kent fingered his charms, Liar pulled his self-collected reliquary from beneath his mail shirt.

A long moment passed while the green worms marched down the back wall, a flood of light beneath the dust. 'One thousand one hundred and eleven years.'

'What's it going to take for you to open that door? Gold? Blood?'

'Your name and password.'

'My name is Honorus Jorg Ancrath, my password is divine right. Now open the fecking door.'

'I don't recognize you.' Something about the spirit's calmness infuriated me. If it had been visible I'd have run it through right there and then.

'You haven't recognized anything but the back of this panel for eleven hundred years.' I kicked the panel in question for emphasis and sent it skittering across the room.

'You are not authorized for chamber twelve.'

I looked to the brothers for inspiration. A more blank sea of faces is hard to imagine.

'Eleven hundred years is a long time,' I said. 'Wasn't it lonely there in the dark, all those long years?'

'I was alone.'

'You were alone. And you could be again. We could wall you up so you'd never be found.'

'No.' The tone remained calm, but there was something frenzied in the pattern of lights.

'...or, we could set you free.' I lowered my sword.

'There is no freedom.'

'What do you want then?'

No reply. I leaned into the compartment, far enough that I could set my fingers to the far wall. The surface beneath the dust felt glassy and cool.

'You were alone,' I said. 'Trammelled in the thousand-year dark with only memories for company.'

What had it witnessed, this ancient spirit, trapped by the Builders? It had lived through the Day of A Thousand Suns, it had seen the end of the greatest empire, heard the scream of millions.

'My creator gave me awareness, for a "flexible and robust response to unforeseen situations",' the spirit said. 'Awareness has proved to be a weakness in periods of pro-longed isolation. Memory limitations become significant.'

'Memories are dangerous things. You turn them over and over, until you know every touch and corner, but still you'll find an edge to cut you.' I looked into my own darkness. I knew what it was to be trapped, and to watch ruination. 'Each day the memories weigh a little heav-ier. Each day they drag you down that bit further. You wind them around you, a single thread at a time, and you weave your own shroud, you build a cocoon, and in it madness grows.' The lights pulsed beneath my fingers, ebbing and flowing to the beat of my voice. 'You sit here with your yesterdays queuing at your shoulder. You listen to their reproach and curse those that gave you life.'

Veins of light spread through the glass beneath my palm, miniature lightning reaching across the wall. My hand tingled. I felt a moment of kinship.

'I know what you want,' I said. 'You want an end.'

'Yes.'

'Open the door.'

'The EM-bolts failed over six hundred years ago. The door is not locked.'

I drove my sword into the panel. The glass shattered and a brilliant flash lit the compartment. I pushed on, through a softness yielding like flesh, and things that crunched and gave like the bones of birds. Something hit me in the chest and I staggered back, caught by Makin. When I'd shaken the after-images from my eyes I could see my sword standing from the rear wall, smoking and blackened.

'Open the damn door!' I shook Makin off.

'But—' Burlow started. I cut through his objection.

'It's not locked. Gorgoth, Rike, give it a decent pull. Burlow, get in there and make that lard work for us for once.'

They did as I said, setting their bulk to the task, well over a thousand pounds of dumb muscle between them. For a moment nothing happened. Another moment, and then, without the slightest whisper from the hinges, the massive door stole into motion.

The road may go ever on, but we don't: we wear out, we break. Age makes different things of different men. It will harden some, sharpen them, to a point. Brother Elban has that toughness, like old leather. But in the end the weakness comes and the rot. Perhaps that's the fear behind his eyes. Like the salmon, he's been swimming upstream all his life, and he knows there's no shallows waiting for him, no still waters. Sometimes I think it would be kindness to make a swift end for Elban, before the fear eats up the man he was.

34

'What is this place?' Makin stood at the entrance with me.

The vault stretched beyond sight. On the ceiling ghost lights flickered into life, some obedient to the opening of the door, others struggling into wakefulness, tardy children late for the day's lesson. I could see little of the floor past the crush of treasures. No Hollander grain-master owns a warehouse so well packed. To describe it fully would require all the vocabulary of shape and solid so kindly furnished by Euclid and by Plato. Cylinders longer and wider than a man, and cubes a yard on each side, lay stacked to scrape the Builder-stone above, and against the wall-cones and spheres in wire cradles, all skinned with dust. Row upon row, stack upon stack, marching beyond sight.

'It's an armoury,' I said.

'Where are the weapons?' Rike came to join us from his struggles with the door. He wiped the sweat from his brow, and spat into the dust.

'Inside the boxes.' Makin rolled his eyes.

'Let's get 'em open then!' Burlow said. He pulled a small crowbar from his belt. It never took much encouragement to set the brothers to looting.

'Surely.' I waved him in. 'But open one at the back please. They're all filled with poison.'

Burlow took a few steps into the vault before that sunk in. 'Poison?' He turned round slow-like.

'The best the Builders could make. Enough to poison the whole world,' I said.

'And this will help us how?' Makin asked. 'We sneak into the Castle Red's kitchens and slip some in their soup? That's a plan for children's games, Jorg.'

I let that slide. It was a fair question, and I didn't feel like falling out with Makin.

'These poisons can kill by a touch. They can kill through the air,' I said.

Makin put a hand to his face and drew it down in a slow motion, pulling at his cheeks and lips. 'How do you know this, Jorg? I looked at that old book of yours, there was nothing about this in there.'

I stabbed a finger toward the piled weapons. 'These are the poisons of the Builders.' I pulled the Builders' book from my belt. 'This is the map. And that,' I pointed to Gorgoth, 'is the evidence of their potency. Him and the Blushers of the Castle Red.'

I crossed to where Gorgoth leaned against the silvery mass of the door.

'If you were to search the depths of this vault, and I don't advise that you do, you'll find fissures where underground waters have found their way in and out. And where do these waters run?'

For a moment I expected an answer, then I remembered who my audience were. 'Where does any water run?' Still dumb looks and silence. 'Down!'

I put a hand to the deformed rib-bones that reached out of Gorgoth's chest. He made a growl that would put a grizzly bear to shame, and the vibration of his ribs undercut it.

'Down to the valley where, in the tiniest of doses, it makes monsters of men. And where did the water run from?' I asked.

'Up?' Makin at least was game to try.

'Up,' I said. 'So our poison wafts up, and what hint escapes into the Castle Red paints the folk that live there, the Blushers, an attractive lobster red. Which, my brothers, is what it says the stuff does in this here book handed down through some thousand years to your own sweet Jorgy.'

I spun away from Gorgoth, caught up in my display, and mindful of his fists. 'And these poisons, in their interesting boxes, can do all this when what we have is an ancient spill, washed over for a thousand years. So all in all, Brother Burlow, it would be best not to open one with your crowbar, just yet.'

'So what will we do with them, Jorth?' Elban came to lisp at my elbow. 'Sounds like dirty work, no?'

'The dirtiest, old man.' I clapped a hand to his shoulder. 'We're going to build a slow fire, bank it well, and run for our lives. The heat will crack open these marvellous toys, and the smoke will make a charnel house of the Castle Red.'

'Will it stop there?' Makin shot me a sharp glance.

'Maybe.' I looked around at the brothers. 'Liar, Row, and Burlow, see to finding some fuel for our fire. Bones and tar if you must.'

'Jorg, you said "enough to poison the world",' Makin said.

'The world is already poisoned, Sir Makin,' I said.

Makin pursed his lips. 'But this could spread. It could spill out over Gelleth.'

Burlow and the others stopped by the door and turned to watch us.

'My father asked for Gelleth,' I said. 'He did not specify the nature of its delivery. If I hand him a smoking ruin he will thank me for it, by God he will. Do you think there is a crime he would not countenance to secure his borders? Even one crime? Any single sin?'

Makin frowned. 'And if the fumes roll into Ancrath?'

'That,' I said, 'is a risk that I am prepared to accept.'

Makin turned from me, his hand on his sword hilt.

'What?' I questioned his back, and my voice echoed in the Builders' dusty vault. I spread my arms. 'What? And don't you dare speak to me of innocents. It is late in the day for Sir Makin of Trent to champion maids and babes in arms.' My anger sprang from more than Makin's doubt. 'There are no innocents. There is success, and there is failure. Who are you to tell me what can be risked? We weren't dealt a hand to win with in this game, but I will win though it beggar heaven!'

The tirade left me breathless.

'But it'd be so many, Jorth,' Elban said.

You'd think seeing me knife Brother Gemt not so many weeks earlier, over a far smaller dispute, would have taught them sense, but no.

'One life, or ten thousand, I can't see the difference. It's a currency I don't understand.' I set my sword to Elban's neck, drawing too quick for him to react. 'If I take your head once, is that less bad than taking it again, and then again?'

But I had no appetite for it. Somehow losing the Nuban had made what brothers I had left seem more worth keeping, scum though they were.

I put the blade away. 'Brothers,' I said. 'You know it's not like me to lose my temper. I'm out of sorts. Too long without sight of the sun perhaps, or maybe something I ate...' Rike smirked at the reference to the necromancer's heart. 'You're right, Makin, to destroy more than the Castle Red would be ... wasteful.'

Makin turned to face me, hands together now. 'As you say, Prince Jorg.'

'Little Rikey, get you just one of those wonderful toys. That one, like a giant's gonad, if you please.' I pointed

271

out the closest of the spheres. 'Don't drop it mind, and have Gorgoth help out if it's as heavy as it looks. We'll take it up a little higher and set it cooking for the castle's breakfast. One should be enough.'

And we did.

With hindsight, if all the detail were known, Makin's stand there in the Builders' vault should be sufficient to wash the blood from his hands, to erase all his crimes, the cathedral at Wexten notwithstanding, and make of him a hero fit to stand beside any that may be found in legend. Given the swathe of death downwind of the Castle Red, it's clear that the drastic scaling-down of my original plan saved the world from a rather unpleasant death. Or at least delayed it.

35

'We should have seen something by now,' Makin said.

I looked back over my shoulder. The ugly bulk of Mount Honas made a black fist against the sky, the Castle Red cradled in its grip. Behind us the brothers straggled, a line of vagabonds labouring down the slope.

'This death walks softly, Makin,' I said. 'An invisible hand with fatal fingers.' I gave him a grin.

'Finding every baby in its crib?' Distaste thinned Makin's thick lips.

'Would you rather it were Rike that found them, or Row?' I asked. I set a hand to his shoulder, gauntlet to breastplate, both smeared with the grey mud from our escape tunnel. He had it in his hair too, drying on black curls.

'You seem troubled of late, old friend,' I said. 'The past sins weigh so heavy that you're afraid to add more?'

I noticed that we stood nearly of a height, though Makin was a tall man. Another year's growth and he'd be tilting his head to meet my gaze.

'Sometimes you almost fool me, you're that good, Jorg.' He sounded weary. I could see the web of fine lines around the corners of his eyes. 'We're not old friends. A little over three years ago you were ten. Ten! Maybe we're friends, I can't tell, but "old"? No.'

'And what is it that I'm so good at?' I asked.

He shrugged. 'Playing a role. Filling in for lost years with that intuition of yours. Replacing experience with genius.'

'You think I have to be old to think with an old head?' I asked.

'I think you need to have lived more to truly know a man's heart. You need to have made more transactions in life to know the worth of the coin you spend so freely.' Makin turned to watch the column close on us.

Rike came into view at the rear of the line, cresting a ridge, black against a dawn-pale sky. Behind him the clouds ran out in ribbons, the dirty purple of a fresh bruise, reaching for the west. Bandages on his upper arm, and around his brow, flapped in the breeze.

Something tickled at me, the ghosts of whispers, colder than the wind.

Makin turned to go.

'Wait—'

Screams now. The terror of those already dead.

No sound came, but Mount Honas lifted, like a giant drawing breath. A light woke beneath the rock, bleeding incandescence through spreading fissures. In one moment, the mountain vanished, thrown at heaven in a spiralling inferno. And, somewhere within that gyre, every stone of the Castle Red, from deepest vault to tower high.

A brilliance took all glory from the morning, making a pale wash of the land. Rike became a flicker of shadow against the blinding sky. I felt the hot kiss of that distant fury, like sunburn on my cheeks.

What burns so bright cannot endure. The light failed, leaving us in shadow, the kind of darkness that precedes a squall. I saw the storm's outriders, newborn ghosts, driven before the rage. I watched them sweep out across the land, like the ripple from a pond-thrown stone, a grey ring where rock became dust, racing fast as thought. The sky rippled too, the ribbon-cloud now whips for the cracking.

'Dear Jesu.' Makin left his mouth open, though he had no more words.

'Run!' Burlow's shout sounded oddly mute.

'Why?' I spread my arms to welcome the destruction. We had nowhere to run.

I watched the brothers fall. Time ran slow and the blood pulsed cold in my veins. Between two beats of my heart, the blast cut them all down, Rike first, lost beneath the grey maelstrom, a child before an ocean breaker. The hot wind took my feet. I felt the dead flow through me, and tasted the bitter gall of necromancer blood once more.

For a time I floated, like smoke above the slaughter.

I lay in nothing. I knew nothing. A peace deeper than sleep, until…

'Oh! Bravo!' The voice cut into me, too close, and somehow familiar. 'Now is the winter of our Hundred War made fearsome summer by this prodigal son.' His words flowed like rhyme, and carried strange accents.

'You maul Shakespeare worse than you abuse his mother tongue, Saracen.' This a woman, velvet and rich.

Just run.

'He has woken a Builders' Sun, and you make jokes?' A child spoke, a girl.

'You're not dead yet, child? With the mountain levelled into the valley?' The woman sounded disappointed.

'Forget the girl, Chella. Tell me who stands behind this boy. Has Corion grown weary of Count Renar and taken a new piece to the board? Or has the Silent Sister shown her hand at last?'

Sageous! I knew him.

'She thinks to win the game with this half-grown child?' The woman laughed.

And I knew her too. The necromancer.

'I sent you to Hell, with the Nuban's bolt through your heart, bitch,' I said.

'What in Kali's n—'

'He hears us?' She cut across him, Chella, I knew her voice, the only corpse ever to make me rise.

I hunted for them, there in the smoke.

'No, it's not possible,' Sageous said. 'Who stands behind you, boy?'

I could find nothing in the swirl of blindness enfolding me.

'Jorg?' A whisper at my ear. The girl again. The monsters' glowing child.

'Jane?' I whispered back, or thought I did, I couldn't feel my lips or any other part of me.

'The ether doesn't hide us,' she said. 'We are the ether.'

I thought on that for a moment. 'Let me see you.'

I willed it. I reached for them. 'Let me see you.' Louder this time. And I painted their image on the smoke.

Chella appeared first, lean and sensual as I first met her, the coils of her body-art spiralled from etheric wisps. Sageous next. He watched me with those mild eyes of his, wider and more still than mill-pools, as I cut his form from nothing. Jane stepped out beside him, her glow faint now, a mere glimmer beneath the skin. There were others, shapes in the mist, one darker than the rest, his shape half-known, familiar. I tried to see him, poured my will into it. The Nuban came to mind, the Nuban, the glimpse of my hand on a door, and the sensation of falling into space. *Déjà vu.* 'Who lends you this power, Jorg?' Chella smiled seduction at me. She stepped around me, a panther at play.

'I took it.'

'No,' Sageous shook his head. 'This game has played out too long for trickery. All the players are known. The watchers too.' He nodded toward Jane.

I ignored him, and kept my eyes on Chella. 'I brought the mountain down on you.'

'And I am buried. What of it?' An edge of her true age crept into her voice.

'Pray I never dig you out,' I said.

I looked to Jane. 'So you're buried too?'

For a moment her glow flickered, and I saw another Jane in her place, this one a broken thing. A rag-doll held between shards of rock in some dark place where she alone gave light. Bones stood from her hip and shoulder, very white, traced with blood, black in the faint illumination. She turned her head a fraction, and those silver eyes met mine. She flickered again, whole once more, standing before me, free and unharmed.

'I don't understand.' But I did.

'Poor sweet Jane.' Chella circled the girl, never coming too close.

'She'll die clean,' I said. 'She's not afraid to go. She'll take that path you fear so much. Cling to carrion flesh and rot in the bowels of the earth if that's where cowardice keeps you.'

Chella hissed, venom on her face, the wet flap of decay in her lungs. The smoke began to take her again, writhing around her in serpent coils.

'Kill this one slow, Saracen.' She threw Sageous a hard look. And she was gone.

I felt Jane at my side. The light had left her. Her skin held the colour of fine ash when the fire has taken all there is to give. She spoke in a whisper. 'Look after Gog for me, and Gorgoth. They're the last of the leucrota.'

The thought of Gorgoth needing a guardian brought sharp words to the tip of my tongue, but I swallowed them. 'I will.' Maybe I even meant it.

She took my hand. 'You can win the victories you seek, Jorg. But only if you find better reasons to want them.' I felt a tingle of her power through my fingers. 'Look to the lost years, Jorg. Look to the hand upon your shoulder. The strings that lead you…'

Her grip fell away, and smoke coiled where she had been.

'Don't come home again, Prince Jorg.' Sageous made his threat sound like fatherly advice.

'If you start running now,' I said. 'I might not catch you.'

'Corion?' He looked into the coiling ether behind me. 'Don't send this boy against me. It would go ill.'

I reached for my sword, but he'd gone before I cleared scabbard. The smoke became bitter, catching at my throat, and I found myself coughing.

'He's coming round.' I heard Makin's voice as if from a great distance.

'Give him more water.' I recognized Elban's lisp.

I struggled up, choking and spitting water. 'God's whore!'

A vast cloud, like the anvil of a thunderhead, stood where Mount Honas had been.

I blinked and let Makin haul me to my feet. 'You're not the only one to take a hard knock.' He nodded across to where Gorgoth crouched a few yards off, with his back to us.

I stumbled over, stopping when I noticed the heat – the heat and a glow that made a silhouette of Gorgoth despite the daylight, as if he were huddled over a fierce campfire. I edged around and to the side. Gog lay coiled like a babe in the womb, every inch of him white hot, as if the light of the Builders' Sun were bleeding through him. Even Gorgoth had to shuffle back.

As I watched, the boy's skin shaded down through colours seen in iron in the forge, hot orange, then the duller reds. I took a step toward him and he opened his eyes, white holes into the centre of a sun. He gasped, the inside of his mouth molten, then curled more tightly. At times fire danced across his back, running along his arms, then guttering out. It took ten minutes for Gog to cool so that his old colours returned and a man could stand beside him.

At last he lifted his head and grinned. 'More!'

'You've had enough, lad,' I said. I didn't know what the Builders' Sun had woken as it echoed through him, but from what I'd seen, better it went back to sleep.

I looked back at the cloud still rising above Mount Honas and the countryside burning for miles around.

'I think it's time to go home, lads.'

36

Four years earlier

It can't be done,' said the Nuban.

'Few things worth having can be got easily', I said.

'It can't be done,' he said. 'Not by anyone who expects to live five minutes past the act.'

'If a suicidal assassin were all it took, then the Hundred would be the Dozen by now.' My own father had survived several attempts in which the would-be killer had no interest in escape. 'No one with a claim to the empire throne is that easy to bring to an end.'

The Nuban turned in the saddle to frown at me. He'd given up asking how a child knew such things. I wondered how long before he gave up telling me it couldn't be done.

I nudged my horse on. The towers of the Count's castle hadn't seemed to get any closer over the last half hour.

'We need to find the Count's strongest defence,' I said. 'The protection that he most relies upon. The one upon which his faith rests.'

The Nuban frowned again. 'Seek out your enemy's weakness,' he said. 'Then take your shot.' He patted the heavy crossbow strapped across his saddlebags.

'But you've already told me it can't be done,' I said. 'Repeatedly.' I pulled my cloak tight against the evening wind. The man I had taken it from had been a tall one, and it hung loose about me. 'So you're just planning the most sensible way to lose.'

The Nuban shrugged. He never argued for the sake of being right. I liked that in him.

'The weakest spot in a good defence is designed to fail. It falls, but in falling it summons the next defence and so on. It's all about layers. At the end of it all you'll find yourself facing the thing you sought to avoid all along, only now you're weaker, and it's forewarned.'

The Nuban said nothing, the blackness of his face impenetrable in the dying light.

'Surprise is our only real weapon here. We sidestep that process of escalation. We cut straight to the heart of the matter.'

And the heart is what we want to cut.

We rode on, and at length the towers grew closer, and taller, and loomed until the castle gates yawned before us. A sprawl of buildings pooled before them like vomit – taverns and tanneries, hovels and whorehouses.

'Renar's shield is a man named Corion.' The Nuban twitched his nose at the stench as the horses threaded a path to the gates. 'A magician from the Horse Coast, they

282

say. Certainly a good councillor. He has the Count guarded by mercenaries from his homeland. Men with no families to threaten, and an honour code that keeps them true.'

'So, what could get us an invitation to see this Corion, I wonder?'

The queue at the gates moved in fits and starts, but never above a snail's pace. Ten yards ahead of us a peasant with an ox in tow argued with a guard in the Count's livery.

'Is he really a magician, do you think?' I watched the Nuban for his answer.

'The Horse Coast is the place for them.'

The peasant seemed to have won his case, and moved on with his ox, into the outer yard where the market stalls would still be set out.

By the time we reached the gate a light rain had started to fall. The guard's plume drooped somewhat in the drizzle, but there was nothing tired about the look he gave us.

'What's your business in the castle?'

'Supplies.' The Nuban patted his saddlebags.

'Out there.' The guard nodded to the sprawl before the gates. 'You'll find all you want out there.'

The Nuban pursed his lips. The castle market would have the best goods, but that line wasn't going to carry us far. We'd need a better reason before the Count's man was going to let a road-worn Nuban mercenary across his master's threshold.

'Give me your bow,' I said to the Nuban.

He frowned. 'You're going to shoot him?'

The guard laughed, but there wasn't an ounce of humour in the Nuban. He was getting to know me.

I held out my hand. The Nuban shrugged and hauled his crossbow up from where it hung behind his saddle. The weight of it nearly took me to the ground. I had to grab the bow in both hands and cling to my mount with my legs but I managed the feat without too great a loss of dignity.

I offered it to the guard.

'Take this to Corion,' I said. 'Tell him we're interested in selling.'

Irritation, scorn, amusement, I could see them all fighting to put the next words on his tongue, but he raised a hand for the weapon even so.

I pulled the bow back as the guard reached up. 'Be careful, half the weight is enchantments.' That lifted his brow an inch. He took it gingerly, eyeing the iron faces of Nuban gods. Something he saw there seemed to set aside his objections.

'Watch these two,' he said, calling another man from the shadows of the gatehouse. And off he went, holding the Nuban's crossbow before him as if it might bite given half a chance.

The drizzle thickened into a steady downpour. We sat on our horses, letting it all soak in.

I thought about vengeance. About how it wouldn't give me back what had been taken. About how I didn't care. Hold to a thing long enough, a secret, a desire, maybe a lie, and it will shape you. The need lay in me, it could not be set aside. But the Count's blood might wash it out.

The night came, the guards lit lanterns in the gatehouse, and in niches along the wall of the entry way. I could see the teeth of two portcullises waiting to drop if some foe should storm the entrance whilst the gates stood wide. I wondered how many of Father's soldiers would have died here if he had sent his armies to avenge my mother. Perhaps it was better this way. Better that I come calling. More personal. She was my mother after all. Father's soldiers had their own mothers to be worrying about.

The rain dripped from my nose, ran cold down my neck, but I felt warm enough, I had a fire inside me.

'He'll see you.' The guard had returned. He held a lantern up. His plume lay plastered to the back of his helm now, and he looked as tired himself. 'Jake, get their horses. Nadar, you can walk these boys in with me.'

And so we entered Count Renar's castle on foot, as wet as if we'd swum a moat to get there.

Corion had his chambers in the West Tower, adjacent to the main keep where the Count held court. We followed a winding stair, gritty with dirt. The whole place had an air of neglect.

'Should we give up our weapons?' I asked.

I caught the whites of the Nuban's eyes as he shot me a glance. Our guard just laughed. The man behind me tapped the knife at my hip. 'Going to jab Corion with this little pig-sticker are you, boy?'

I didn't have to answer. Our guard pulled up before a large oak door, studded with iron bolts. Somebody had burned a complex symbol into the wood, a pictogram of sorts. It made my eyes crawl.

The guard rapped on the door, two quick hits.

'Wait here.' He thrust his lantern into my hands. He gave me a brief look, pursed his lips, then pushed past the Nuban to head back down the stairs. 'Nadar, with me.'

Both men were out of sight, behind the curve of the stair, before we heard the sound of a latch being raised. Then nothing. The Nuban set his hand to the hilt of his sword. I flicked it away. Shaking my head I knocked again on the door.

'Come.'

I thought I'd faced down all my fears, but here was a voice that could melt my resolve with one word. The Nuban felt it too. I could see it in every line of him, poised to flee.

'Come, Prince of Thorns, come out of your hiding, come out into the storm.'

The door fell away, eaten by darkness. I heard screaming, awful screaming, the sort you get from prey with a broken back as it crawls to escape the hunter's claws. Maybe it was me, maybe the Nuban.

And then I saw him.

37

The Castle Red left no ruins to gaze upon. All we had were the ruins of the mountain on which it had stood. We beat the most hasty of retreats and made thanks that the wind blew against us not chasing us to share the smoke and taint of Gelleth. That night we slept cold and none amongst us had an appetite, not even Burlow.

The road from the Castle Red to the Tall Castle is a long one, longer in the coming back than in the going. For one thing, on the way out we rode – on the way back we had to walk. And most of those miles back pointed down. Given the choice I'd rather climb a mountain than come down one. The down-slope puts a different kind of hurting in your legs, and the gradient pulls on you every step, as if it's steering you, as if it's calling the shots. Going up you're fighting the mountain.

'Damn but I miss that horse,' I said.

'A fine piece of horse-flesh.' Makin nodded and spat from dusty lips. 'Have the King's stable-master train you another. I'm sure there's not a paddock in Ancrath without it has at least one of Gerrod's bastards.'

'He was a lustful one, I'll give you that.' I hawked and spat. My armour chafed, and the metal held the heat of the late afternoon sun, sweat trickling underneath.

'It doesn't feel right though,' Makin said. 'The most convincing victory in memory and all we have to show for it is a lack of horses.'

'I've had more loot from a peasant hut!' Rike called out from back down the line.

'Christ bleeding! Don't start Little Rikey off,' I said. 'We're rich in the coin that counts the most, my brothers. We return laden in victory.' There indeed was a currency I could spend at court. Everything is for sale at the right price. A king's favour, a succession, even a father's respect.

And that's another thing that made those returning miles longer than the going ones. Not only did I have to carry myself, my armour, my rations, but I had a new burden. It's hard to carry a weight of news with none to tell and days ahead before you can release it. Good news weighs just as heavy as bad. I could imagine myself back at court, boasting of my victory, rubbing noses in it, a certain stepmother's nose in particular. What would not paint itself on the canvas of my imagination was my father's reaction. I tried to see him shake his head in disbelief. I tried to see him smile and stand and put his hand on my shoulder. I tried to hear him thank me, praise me, call me son. But my eyes went blind and the words I heard were too faint and deep for distinction.

The brothers had little to say on the return journey, feeling the holes left in our ranks, haunted by the space where the Nuban should be. Gog on the other hand bubbled over with energy, running ahead, chasing rabbits, asking question after question.

'Why is the roof blue, Brother Jorg?' he asked. He seemed to think the outside world was just a bigger cave. Some philosophers agree with him.

There were other changes too. The red marks on Gog's hide had shaded to a fiercer red, and the nightly campfires fascinated him. He would stare into the flames, entranced, edging closer moment by moment. Gorgoth discouraged the interest, flicking the child into the shadows, as if the attraction worried him.

The roads became more familiar, the inclines gentle, the fields rich. I walked the paths of my childhood, a golden time, easy days without care, scored by my mother's music and her song, with no sour note until my sixth year. My father had taught me the first of the hard lessons then, lessons in pain and loss and sacrifice. Gelleth had been the sum of that teaching. Victory without compromise, without mercy or hesitation. I would thank King Olidan for his instruction and tell him how his enemies had fared at my hands. And he would approve.

I thought of Katherine too, as we drew nearer. My idle moments filled with her image, with the moments I had spent close enough to touch her. I saw again how the light caught her, how it found the bones of her face, the softness of her lips.

We came footsore and road-weary to the heartlands of Ancrath, too deep in our own thoughts even to steal the horses that would ease the last of our journey. I had but to close my eyes and I would see the new sun rise over Gelleth, rise through Gelleth, and hear the screams of her ghosts.

We saw the Tall Castle's battlements from the Osten Ridge, with seven miles still before us to the gates. The sun descended in the west, crimson, racing us to the city.

'We'll be heroeth, Jorth?' Elban asked. He sounded uncertain as if all his years had yet to teach him that the end justifies the means.

'Heroes?' I shrugged. 'We will be victors. And that's what counts.'

We walked the last mile in dusk. The guards at the gates of the Low City had no questions for me. Perhaps they recognized their prince, or perhaps they read my look and some instinct for self preservation kicked in. We walked through unopposed.

'Brother Kent, why don't you lead the way to the Low Town and find the lads somewhere to drink? The Falling Angel, maybe.' Sir Makin and I would go to court. The remainder of my brothers would find no welcome in the Tall Castle.

With Makin at my side I set off for the High City

and at last we came to the castle itself. I put fatigue aside when we entered by the Triple Gate. We crossed the Lectern Courtyard in the deepest shadows, thrown by a failing sun.

By the time we passed the table knights at Father's doors I had a spring in my step. I looked first for Sageous, seeking him at the King's side, then amongst the glitter of the crowd. I let the herald finish our introduction, and still I sought the heathen. I found Katherine beside the Queen, one hand on her sister's shoulder, hard eyes for poor Jorg. I let the silence stretch a moment longer.

'Where have you hidden your painted savage, Father-dear? I did so want to meet the old poisoner of dreams again.'

I slid my gaze across the sea of faces one more time.

'Sageous's services to the Crown have taken him from our borders.' Father held his face impassive, but I saw the quick glance exchanged between his queen and her sister.

'I'll be sure to look for his return.' So, the heathen had run before me…

'I'm told that you limped back without the Forest Watch.' Queen Sareth spoke from Father's side, her hands upon the greatness of her belly. 'Are we to assume your losses were total?' A smile escaped the tight line of her mouth. An exceptionally pretty mouth, it has to be noted.

I spared her a small bow. A bow for my half-brother,

struggling to claw his way from her womb. 'Lady, there were losses among the Forest Watch, I cannot deny it.'

Father inclined his head, as if the crown weighed heavy upon him. Pale eyes watched me from the shadow of his brow. 'We will have an account of this rout.'

'Lord Vincent de Gren…' I counted him off on my index finger.

An intake of breath hissed through the aristocracy.

'Even the Watch Master!' Queen Sareth struggled to her feet. 'He has even lost the Watch Master! And this boy seeks our throne?'

'Lord Vincent de Gren,' I resumed my count. 'I had to push him over the Temus Falls. He vexed me. Coddin is the Watch Master now, low born but a sound fellow.'

'Jed Willox.' I counted a second finger. 'Killed in a knife fight over a game of cards, two days' march past the Gelleth border.'

'Mattus of Lee.' I counted a third finger. 'Apparently he urinated on a bear by mistake. It seems that the legendary woodcraft of the Forest Watch maybe somewhat overstated. And… that's it.'

I held the three fingers at arm's length above my head and turned left, then right, to survey my audience.

'The losses among my own picked men were similarly grievous, but in our defence you must consider that the razing of a castle defended by nine hundred Gellethian veterans is a dangerous undertaking. With two hundred and fifty lightly-armed forest rangers, there is a limit to what can be achieved without casualties.'

'The coward never reached Castle Red!' The Queen pointed at me – as if anyone would mistake her target – and her voice became a shriek.

I smiled and held my peace. Women are apt to lose perspective when fat with child. I saw Katherine try to press Sareth back into her throne.

'I ordered you to assault the Castle Red.' Father's words held no hint of anger, and carried all the more threat for it.

'Indeed.' I advanced on the throne, leaving Sir Makin in my wake. 'Bring me Gelleth, you said.'

A yard separated us, no more, before the first palace guard thought to raise his crossbow. Father lifted a finger, and we paused, me and the guard sweating in his hauberk.

'Bring me Gelleth, you said. And you were good enough to grant me the Forest Watch to do it with.'

I reached into the road-sack at my hip, ignoring the crossbows held on me, and the fingers ever tighter on their triggers.

'Here is Merl Gellethar, Lord of Gelleth, master of the Castle Red.' I opened my hand and dust trickled through my fingers. 'And here,' I drew out a chunk of rock no bigger than a walnut. 'Here is the largest stone that remains of the Castle Red.'

I let the stone fall, dropped into silence. Neither dust nor stone were what I purported, of course, but the truth lay there on the throne-room floor. Merl Gellethar was dust on the wind, and his castle rubble.

'We killed them all. Every man in that fortress is dead.' I looked to the Queen. 'Every woman. Lady, scullion, drudge, and whore.' My eyes fell to her belly. 'Every child, every babe in cradle.' I raised my voice. 'Every horse and dog, every hawk and every dove. Each rat, and down to the last flea. Nothing lives there. Victory does not come in half measures.'

Father lurched to his feet.

In one pace I stood almost nose to nose with him. I couldn't read what his eyes held, but the old fear had left me, as if it too had trickled from my hands.

'Give me my birth right.' I kept all colour from the words, though my jaw ached from the strain of it. 'Let me lead our armies, and I will take the Empire, and make it whole once more. Set aside the heathen. And his plans.' I glanced toward the new queen at that.

I should have kept my eyes on him, should have remembered where I got my mean streak.

I felt a sharp pain under my heart. It made me bite off my sentence, nearly my tongue too. I tasted blood, hot and copper. One step back, two, staggering now. I saw the blade, exposed in Father's hand when I slipped from it.

Is this a dagger I see before me? The quotation bubbled up, and laughter too, breaking out of me, crimson with spittle. I wanted to speak, but for once words escaped me, leaking away with my life's blood.

The throne-room swam before me, its architecture

no longer certain in the face of such betrayal. Every eye watched my retreat toward the great doors. Their stares lanced me, lords and ladies, Princess, Queen, and King. The legs that had borne me league upon league from Gelleth now turned traitor, as if each mile from the ruin of the Castle Red settled upon my shoulders and left me drunk with weariness.

He stabbed me!

There was a time when I loved my father. A time remembered, in dreams, or in rare waking moments, like the shadow of a high cloud crossing my mind. There's a laughing face from a year I no longer own, from a season when I was too young to see the distance between us. The face is bearded, fierce, but without threat.

Is this a dagger I see before me? My mouth wouldn't frame the joke. The laugh burst from me, and I fell, as if the knife had cut my strings.

For an eternity I lay before them, my cheek to the cold marble. I heard Makin roar. I heard the clatter as he went down beneath too many guards. The slow thud of a heartbeat filled me.

When I fell I saw the blackness of my father's hair, darker than night, with the faintest sheen of emerald like a magpie's wing.

'Take this away.' He sounded weary. The slightest hint of human weakness at the last.

'Will he lie by his mother's tomb?' A new voice. The words drew out to fill an age, but somewhere in me they echoed and I saw their owner, Old Lord Nossar who bore us on his shoulders, Will and I, a lifetime ago. Old Nossar, come to carry me one last time. I heard the answer, too faint and deep for distinction. My eyes went blind. I felt the floor scrape between my cheek, and then no more.

38

I swallowed darkness, and darkness swallowed me.

Without light, without the beat of a heart to count the time, you learn that eternity is nothing to fear. In fact, if they'd just leave you to it, an eternity alone in the dark can be a welcome alternative to the business of living.

Then the angel came.

The first glimmers felt like paper-cuts on my eyes. The illumination built from a distant pin-point, splinters of light lodging in the back of my mind. A dawn came, and in an instant, or an age, darkness fled, leaving no hint of shadow to record its passage.

'Jorg.'

Her voice flowed through the octaves, an echo of every kind word and every promise fulfilled.

'Hello.' My voice sounded like a cracked reed. *Hello?* But what do you say to heaven when you meet her? Two syllables, weakness and doubt underwriting both.

She opened her arms. 'Come to me.'

I crouched, naked on a floor too white for any shadow to dare. I could see the dirt on my limbs, like veins, and blood, blood from the wound that killed me, dried and black as sin.

'Come.'

I tried to look at her. No point in her held constant. As if definition were a thing for mortals, a reduction that her essence would not allow. She wore pale, in shades. She had the eyes of everyone who ever cared. And wings – she had those too, but not in white and feathers, rather in the surety of flight. The potential of sky wrapped her. Sometimes her skin seemed to be clouds, moving one across the other. I looked away.

I crouched there, a knot of flesh and bone, with only dirt and old blood to define me beneath the scrutiny of her brilliance.

'Come to me.' Arms open. A mother's arms, a lover's, father's, friend's.

I looked away, but she drew me still. I felt her breathing. I felt the promise of redemption. I had but to lift my eyes and she would forgive me.

'No.'

Her surprise fluttered between us, a palpitation of the light. I felt tension in the muscles of my jaw, and the bitter taste of anger, hot at the back of my throat. Here at last were things familiar to me.

'Put aside your pain, Jorg. Let the blood of the Lamb wash your sins away.' Nothing false in her. She stood transparent in her concern. The angel held her gifts in open hands, compassion, love, … pity.

One gift too many. The old smile twisted on my lips. I stood, nice and slow, head bowed still. 'The Lamb doesn't have enough blood for my sins. May as well hang a sheep for me as a lamb.'

'No sin is too great to repent,' she said. 'There's no evil that cannot be put aside.'

She meant it too. No lie could pass those lips. That truth, at least, was self-evident.

I met her eyes then, and the wash of her love, so deep and so without condition, nearly carried me away. I dug deep and fought her. I manufactured my smile once again, cursing myself for a slack-jawed fool.

'I left few sins untasted.' I took a step toward her. 'I cursed … in church. I coveted my neighbour's ox. I stole it too, roasted it whole, and finished it off with gluttony, a deadly sin, the first of the Seven, learned at my mother's breast.'

The hurt in her eyes hurt me, but I'd lived a life striking blows that cut two ways.

I moved around the angel, and my feet stained the floor, leaving bruises that faded in my wake.

'I coveted my neighbour's wife. And I had her. Murder too. Oh yes, murder and more murder. So few sins untasted … If I'd not died so young I'm sure I'd have met you with a full list.' Anger closed my jaw. Any tighter and my teeth would have exploded. 'If I'd lived but five minutes longer you could have put patricide at the head of the tally.'

'It can be forgiven.'

'I don't require your forgiveness.' Veins of darkness reached across the floor, growing outward from where I stood.

'Let it go, Child.' A warmth and a humour ran through her words, so strong it nearly carried me with it. Her eyes stood as windows to a world of things made whole. A place built of tomorrows. It could all be made right. I could taste it, smell it. If she weren't so sure of her success, she'd have had me, there and then.

I held to my anger, drank from my well of poison. These things are not good things, but at least they're mine.

'I could go with you, Lady. I could take what you offer. But who would I be then? Who would I be if I let go the wrongs that have shaped me?'

'You would be happy,' she said.

'Someone else would be happy. A new Jorg, a Jorg without pride. I won't be anyone's puppy. Not yours, not even His.'

The night crept back like mist rising from the mire.

'Pride is a sin too, Jorg. Deadliest of the Seven. You have to let it go.' At last, a hint of challenge in her words. All I needed to give me strength.

'Have to?' Darkness swirled around us.

She held out her hands. The dark grew and her light quailed.

'Pride?' I said, my smile dancing now. 'I *am* pride! Let the meek have their inheritance – I'd rather have eternity in shadows than divine bliss at the price you ask.' It wasn't true, but to speak otherwise, to take her hand rather than to bite it, would leave nothing of me, nothing but pieces.

Glimmers held her now, glimmers against the velvet blackness. 'Lucifer spoke thus. Pride took him from heaven, though he sat at God's right hand.' Her voice grew faint, the hint of a whisper. 'In the end pride is the only evil, the root of all sins.'

'Pride is all I have.'

I swallowed the night, and the night swallowed me.

39

'He's not dead yet?' A woman's voice, Teuton accent with a creak of age in it.

'No.' A younger woman, familiar, also Teuton.

'It's not natural to linger so long,' the older woman said. 'And so white. He looks dead to me.'

'There was a lot of blood. I didn't know men had so much blood in them.'

Katherine! Her face came to me in my darkness. Green eyes, and the sculpted angles of her cheekbones.

'White and cold,' she said, her fingers on my wrist. 'But there's mist on the mirror when I hold it to his lips.'

'Put a pillow over his face and be done with it, I say.' I imagined my hands around the crone's neck. That brought a hint of warmth.

'I did want to see him die,' Katherine said. 'After what he did to Galen. I would have watched him die on the steps of the throne, with all that blood running down, one step after the next, and been glad.'

'The King should have slit his throat. Finished the job there and then.' The old woman again. She had a servant's tone about her. Voicing her opinion in the security of a private place, opinions held back too long and grown bitter in the silence.

'It's a cruel man who will take a knife to his only son, Hanna.'

'Not his only son. Sareth carries your nephew. The child will be born to his due inheritance now.'

'Will they keep him here, do you think?' Katherine said. 'Will they lay him in his mother's casket, beside his brother?'

'Lay the whelps with the bitch and seal the room, I say.'

'Hanna!' I heard Katherine move away from me.

They'd taken me to my mother's tomb, a small chamber in the vaults. The last time I'd visited the dust had lain thick, unmarked by footprints.

'She was a queen, Hanna,' Katherine said. I heard her brush at something. 'You can see the strength in her.'

Mother's likeness had been carved into her coffer's marble lid, as if she lay there at rest, her hands together in devotion.

'Sareth is prettier,' Hanna said.

Katherine returned to my side. 'Strength makes a queen.' I felt her fingers on my forehead.

Four years ago. Four years ago I'd touched that marble cheek, and vowed never to return. That was my last tear.

I wondered if Katherine had touched her face, wondered if she'd stroked the same stone.

'Let me end this, my princess. It would be a kindness to the boy. They'll lay him with his mother and the little prince.' Hanna honeyed her voice. She set her hand to my throat, fingers coarse like sharkskin.

'No.'

'You said yourself that you wanted to see him die,' Hanna said. She had strength in that old hand. She'd throttled a chicken or three in her time, had Hanna. Maybe a baby once or twice. The pressure built, slow but sure.

'On the steps I did, while his blood was hot,' Katherine said. 'But I've watched him cling to life for so long, with such a slight hold, it's become a habit. Let him fall when he's ready. It's not a wound that can be survived. Let him choose his own time.'

The pressure built a little more.

'Hanna!'

The hand withdrew.

40

We wrap up our violent and mysterious world in a pretence of understanding. We paper over the voids in our comprehension with science or religion, and make believe that order has been imposed. And, for the most of it, the fiction works. We skim across surfaces, heedless of the depths below. Dragonflies flitting over a lake, miles deep, pursuing erratic paths to pointless ends. Until that moment when something from the cold unknown reaches up to take us.

The biggest lies we save for ourselves. We play a game in which we are gods, in which we make choices, and the current follows in our wake. We pretend a separation from the wild. Pretend that a man's control runs deep, that civilization is more than a veneer, that reason will be our companion in dark places.

I learned these lessons in my tenth year, although little of them stayed with me. It took Corion only moments to teach me, the heartbeats in which my will guttered like a candle flame in the wind, and then blew out utterly.

I lay with the Nuban, boneless on the stairs. Only my eyes would move, and they followed the old man. He could have looked kindly in a different light. He had something of Tutor Lundist about him, though more gaunt, more hungry. The horror wasn't in his face, or even his eyes, just in the knowing that these were mere skins, stretched taut across all the emptiness in the world.

The sight of him, just an old man in a dirty robe, put the kind of fear into me that shame erases from our memories. The fear the rabbit has when the eagle strikes. The kind of fright that makes a nothing of you. The kind of fear that'd make you sacrifice mother, brother, everything and anything you've ever loved, just for the chance to run.

Corion shuffled closer, and stooped to take my wrist. In one instant the touch silenced the raw terror that had so unmanned me. As completely as if he'd turned the spigot on a wine-barrel, the flow stopped. Without a word he hauled me into his room. I felt the flagstones scrape my cheek.

The chamber held nothing, save for the Nuban's crossbow, propped against the far wall. I imagined Corion closeted here in his empty chamber, a place to leave his old flesh whilst he stared into eternity.

'So, Sageous's hunter finally tracked down something with more bite than him, eh?'

I tried to speak, but my lips didn't as much as twitch. He knew about the dream-witch and his hunter. He'd called me the Thorn Prince. What else did he know?

'I know it all, child. The things you know, the secrets you hold. Even the secrets you've forgotten.'

He could read my mind!

'Like an open scroll.' Corion nodded. He turned my head with his boot, so that I could see the Nuban's bow once more.

'You intrigue me, Honorous Jorg Ancrath,' he said. He moved to stand beside the bow. 'You're wondering why a man with such power isn't emperor over all the lands.'

I was too.

'It has to be one of the Hundred. Nations won't follow monsters like me. They'll follow a lineage, divine right, the spawn of kings. So we who have taken our power from the places where others fear to reach … we play the game of thrones with pieces like Count Renar, pieces like your father. Pieces like you, perhaps.'

He reached out to touch the bow. The air around it shimmered as if the mouth of a furnace had opened.

'Yes. I rather like that idea. Let Sageous have King Olidan, let him work to bend your father to his will, and I will have the firstborn son.'

The fear had sunk low enough to let my anger rise. I pictured the old man dying on a blade, my hand on the hilt.

'Let the wilds temper you, and if you weather it, in time the prodigal will return, a viper to his father's bosom. Pawn takes king.' He mimed the chess-board gesture. 'You might become something, Thorn Prince. A piece to win the game.'

Corion took the bow as if it weighed nothing. Raising it to his lips, he whispered a word, too soft for hearing. Five paces took him to the door and he set the bow on the steps by the Nuban's head. 'A black knight to guard my pawn.'

'And you, boy. You will forget the Count of Renar.'

Like hell I will.

'Turn your vengeance anywhere you choose, share it with the world, spill some blood; but never return to these lands. Set no foot upon these paths. Your mind will not wander here.'

I could only watch him. He came closer. He knelt beside me, took my collar and drew my face to his. I met his blank eyes. I could feel the horror rising, a flood that would carry me away. And worse, I felt his fingers cold inside my skull, erasing memories, turning aside purpose.

'Forget Renar. Take your vengeance to the world.'

Renar will die. 'By … my … hand…' Somehow my lips spoke the words.

But already he'd taken the conviction from me. I could no longer say how I'd reached the tower, or even name him.

The old man smiled. He bent to whisper in my ear. I remember his breath on my neck, and the smell of rot.

Then I heard his words and all reason left me.

Worms writhed behind my eyes. Nothing remained of him in my thoughts, just a hole where I couldn't look.

Renar became a name without weight, and my hatred a gift for anyone and everyone.

I fell, through darkness, deafened by my own howling. Unknown hands locked around my throat, and in the darkness my own hands found a neck to throttle. The grip tightened, and tightened again. The screams died to a hiss, a rattle, and then silence. I squeezed. My hands became iron hooks. If I could have squeezed harder my finger-bones would have snapped like dry twigs.

I fell through darkness, through silence, only the hands on my throat, and the throat in my hands, and the hunger for air, my heart beating sledgehammer blows.

I fell through years. I've been falling through my life...

I hit the ground. Hard. My eyes opened. I lay on a stone floor. A purple face stared at me, eyes distended, tongue protruding. Daylight streamed in from a high window. My heart hammered at my breastbone, wanting out. Everything hurt. I saw hands on the neck below that face. My hands. With great effort I unlocked them. The white fingers had little inclination to obey.

Still the pain swelled in me. I needed something, but couldn't name it. My vision pulsed red, dimming from one moment to the next. I touched a stiff-fingered hand to my neck and found hands there.

I didn't recognize the face. A woman?

The world grew distant, the pain less.

Renar… The name rose through me, and with it a whisper of strength. The hands that prised the strangler's fingers from my neck didn't feel like mine. *Renar!* My first breath whistled into me, as if sucked through a reed.

Air! I needed air.

I choked, heaved but nothing came, hauled in breaths through a throat grown too narrow for the task.

Renar.

The purple face belonged to a woman with grey hair. I didn't understand.

Renar. And Corion.

Oh Jesu! I remembered. I remembered the horror, but it burned pale against the cold fury that ate me now.

'Corion.' For the first time in the four years since that night in the tower, I spoke his name. I remembered. I recalled what had been taken, and for the first time in forever, I felt whole.

I found the strength to lift myself up on my arms.

I was in a chamber in a castle. Beside a bed … I'd fallen out of bed. Whilst an old woman tried to throttle me.

The door shook. Somebody rattled at the latch. 'Hanna! Hanna!' A woman's voice.

Somehow I stood before the door opened.

'Katherine.' My voice escaped a bruised throat as a squeak.

There she was. Beautiful in disarray. Mouth half open, green eyes wide.

310

'Katherine.' I could only get her name out as a whisper, but I wanted to shout, I wanted to scream so many things at once.

I understood. I understood the game. I understood the players. I knew what had to be done.

'Murderer!' she said. She took a knife from her sash, a sharp bodkin long enough to run a man through. 'Your father knew best.'

I tried to tell her, but no words would come now. I tried to raise my arms, but I had no strength.

'I'll finish what he started,' she said.

And all I could do was marvel at the beauty of her.

41

In a duel, man to man, sword against sword, it can be a lack of skill that gets you killed. Often as not, though, it'll be a matter of luck, or if it goes on too long then it'll be the man who tires first that tends to die.

In the end it's about staying power. They should put that on headstones, 'Got tired', maybe not tired of life, but at least too tired to hold on to it.

In a real fight, and most fights are real, not the artifice of a formal duel, it's fatigue that's the big killer. A sword is a heavy chunk of iron. You swing that around for a few minutes and your arms start to get ideas of their own about what they can and can't do. Even when your life depends on it.

I've known times when to lift my sword was the equal of any labour of Hercules, but never before I faced Katherine's knife had I felt so drained.

'Bastard!'

The fire in her eyes looked fierce enough to burn until the deed was done.

I looked for the will to stop her, and came up empty.

A knife is a scary thing right enough, held to your throat, sharp and cool. The thought echoed back to me from that night when the dead came up out of their bog-pools around the Lichway.

The glitter along that knife edge as she came at me, the thought of it slicing my flesh, piercing an eye maybe, these are all the sort of thing that might give a man pause. Until you realize what they are. They're just ways to lose the game. You lose the game, and what have you lost? You've lost the game. Corion had told me about the game. How many of my thoughts were his? How much of my philosophy was filth from that old man's fingers?

I'd swum in the darkness too long. The game didn't seem so important any more.

With the embers of my strength I raised both arms. I stretched them wide, to receive the blow. And I smiled.

Something reached out and held her arm. I saw it in her face, twisting there on that perfect brow, wrestling with the rage.

'Father didn't quite reach the heart, it seems.' I managed a hoarse whisper. 'Perhaps, Aunt, you have a better hand?'

The knife shook. I wondered if she'd cut live meat before.

'You … you killed her.'

The fingers of my right hand closed around something, a heavy smooth something, on the shelf beside my bed.

313

Her eyes dropped to the old woman's face.

I hit her. Not hard, I didn't have the strength, but hard enough to break the vase I'd found. She collapsed without a murmur.

She lay in the sapphire pool of her dress, sprawled across the flagstones. Life flowed in my arms once more. It seemed as if my strength began to return the moment she fell. As if a spell were broken.

Kill her and you'll be free forever. A familiar voice, dry like paper. Mine, or his?

Her hair hid her face, auburn on sapphire.

She's your weakness. Cut the heart from her.

I knew it to be true.

Choke her.

I saw my hands, pale on a neck shading into crimson.

Have her. The voice of the briar. The hooks slipped beneath my skin, and drew me down to kneel beside her. *Have her. Take what might never be given.* I knew the creed.

Kill her, and you'll be free.

I heard the echo of a distant storm.

Katherine's hair ran like silk between my fingers. 'She's my weakness.' My voice now, my lips. One little step, one more death, and nothing would ever touch me again. One little step and the door on that wild night would close forever. The game would truly be a game. And I would be the player to win it.

Choke her. Have her. The voice of the briar. A crackle in the mind. A hollow sound. An emptiness.

Empty.

Her neck felt warm. Her pulse beat under my fingertips.

'Kill her, Briar Prince.'

I saw the words on thin lips, spoken in an empty chamber.

'Kill her.'

I saw the lips move again. I saw the blank eyes, fixed on eternity. 'Kill her.'

'Corion!'

For a moment my hands tightened around Katherine's neck.

'I'm coming for you, you old bastard.' I released my grip.

A smile twisted those thin lips, a fierce twist. I saw it as the vision faded, those blank eyes, and that twist of a smile. My smile.

He had played me. I'd wandered for years with no recollection of him, thinking it my own idea to turn from Renar, thinking the choice a symbol of my strength and purpose, to put aside empty vengeance in favour of the true path to power. And now, on the edge of death, I had recovered what was taken. Recovered or been given. I glanced at Katherine. I recalled an angel in a dark place. The memory left me with a shiver.

I took Katherine's dagger from the floor, and stood. I left her where she lay, beside the crone I'd throttled. The door opened onto a corridor, one I recognized.

The West Corner, I knew where I was. I raised the knife to my lips and kissed the blade. Count Renar, and the puppet master who pulled so many strings, one sharp edge would be enough for them all.

Brother Roddat stabbed three men in the back for each one he faced. Roddat taught me all I know about running and about hiding. Cowards should be treated with respect. Cowards best know how to hurt. Corner one at your peril.

42

'Get out of my way.'

'Who the hell—'

'Please Jesu! You're the same old wart-bag that tried to stop me last time!' And he was. The stink that jumped me when he opened the door brought it all back. 'I'm surprised my father let you live.'

'Who—'

'Who the hell am I? You don't recognize me? You didn't last time either. I was shorter then, yay high.' I held out a hand to show him. 'It seems like a while ago to me, but you're an old man, and what're three or four years to the old?' I sketched a bow. 'Prince Jorg at your service, or rather you at mine. Last time I walked out of here with a band of outlaws. This time I just need one knight, if you please. Sir Makin of Trent.'

'I should call the guards on you,' he said, without conviction.

'Why? The King has issued no orders about me.' That was a guess, but Father thought he'd struck a mortal blow, so I was probably correct. 'Besides, it'd only get you killed. And if you're thinking of that big fellow with the pike, I rammed his head into the wall not three minutes ago.'

The jailer stepped back and let me pass, just as he had the time Lundist escorted me when I was a boy. On this occasion, I hit him as I went by. Once in the stomach, and a second blow to the back of the neck as he doubled up. For a moment I considered finishing the job with Katherine's knife, but it's good insurance to let ineffective jailers live.

I took his keys and moved on down the corridor, knife at the ready. I'd rather have had my sword. I felt half-dressed without it. My mind kept returning to the fact of its absence, to the weightless sensation around my hip, like a tongue returning to an empty socket in constant overestimation of the loss.

Makin put that sword in my hand on the day he found me. As captain of the guard in search of the heir, he had the right to bear it. I'd kept it close ever since, the family blade, Builder-steel.

I found my way to the torture chamber where I'd first met the Nuban. The table at the centre lay empty. There were no faces at the cell door windows. I made a slow circuit, directing the beam of my lantern into each cell in turn. The first held a corpse, or someone so near death as to be mere bones in a bag of skin. The next three were bare. The fifth held Sir Makin. He sat back against the far wall, bearded and smeared with filth, a hand lifting to shield his eyes from the light. He made no move to rise. I felt a hurt in the back of my throat. I don't know why, but I did. Anger in my stomach, and an acid pain in my throat.

'Makin, oh my brother.' Soft.

'Wha—?' A croak, the sound of something broken.

'I'm to the road again, Brother Makin. I have business to the south.'

I set the key in the lock. A slight tremble, a little rattle.

'Jorg?' A wet sob, half gurgle. 'He killed you, Prince. Your own father.'

'I'll die when I'm ready.'

The key turned, the door opened without resistance. The stink grew worse.

'Jorg?' Makin let his hand fall. They'd made a mess of his face. 'No! You're dead. I saw you fall.'

'All right, I'm dead and you're dreaming. Now get on your feckin' feet before I kick out whatever shit they left you. And that ain't too much by the smell of it.'

That got to him. He tried to rise, one hand scraping across the wall.

I hadn't thought what kind of state he might be in. To me it seemed I'd taken Father's knife only yesterday. Makin's beard said weeks at the least.

He got halfway to his feet, and his leg failed.

I took two steps toward him.

The Count's castle stood well over a hundred hard miles ahead of me, through the garden lands of Ancrath and into the Renar highlands. He'd never make it.

Makin slid to the floor with a groan. 'You're dead anyway.' The one good eye shone bright with tears.

Play the game. Sacrifice knight, take castle. That old dry voice again. I'd listened to it so long I couldn't tell if it were mine or Corion's. Either way, I should leave him.

'You've got one chance here, Makin. That's two more than most bastards get in life.' The lantern beam swung from wall to wall. 'Dead or not, I'll leave you if you can't stand and follow me. I left a man here to die before. A man I should have loved. I'll leave you in a heartbeat.'

He kicked out, fierce with fear or something else, but his arm buckled and his foot just skittered across the muck.

I turned and walked away. Two yards past the door I stopped.

'Lundist died here.' I was speaking too loud for safety, wasting breath on foolishness. 'On this spot.' I stamped on it. 'I left him to bleed.'

Nothing from the darkness of the cell.

I'd been soft with Katherine, but at no real cost. This was different. They'd broken Makin, he could do nothing but slow me at a time when I most needed speed.

I started for the exit.

'No...'

Don't let him beg.

'No … he didn't die there.' Makin's voice came a little stronger now.

'What?'

'He got a bad knock.'

Sounds of movement in the dark.

'A knock's all. Nothing but a bruise to show for it the next day.'

'Lundist is alive?'

'Your father had him executed, Jorg.' Makin came into the light, clutching the doorframe. 'For failing to protect you, he said.' He spat a black mess onto the floor. 'More likely he just didn't have any use for a tutor once his son had run off. That's been the King's way all these years. When a thing's no use any more – throw it away.'

Makin managed a grin. 'Damn but it's good to see you, lad.'

I watched him for a moment. I saw his smile die, and an uncertainty replace it, mirroring my own.

I should leave him. In truth, I should kill him. No loose ends.

I didn't look at my knife. You never take your eyes off your mark, not when it's a man like Makin, not even in his current state. But I knew the knife was there. In my mind's eye I could see the gleam where it cut the lantern's light from the air. Makin didn't look at it either. He knew better than to offer weakness to the viper. Nothing decides a man's mind better than opportunity.

Father would leave him. Dead.

The creature into which Corion had chosen to forge me, that tool, that piece in a game of thrones, he'd never even have come close enough to savour the dungeon stink.

But what about Jorg?

'I'm my father's son, Makin.'

'I know.' He didn't plead. I admired that in him. I chose my pieces well.

The knife felt like hot iron in my fist. I hated myself for what I was going to do, and just as much for hesitating. I hated myself for the weakness in me.

For a moment I saw the Nuban, just the white line of his teeth, and the darkness of his eyes, watching me as he'd watched since the day we met.

Makin took that moment. A swift kick snatched my legs from under me. He followed down with what weight remained to him, and sandwiched my head between the flagstones and his fist. We neither of us were in great shape. One punch was all it took to send me back to wherever it was I'd escaped from in Katherine's room.

Shakespeare had it that clothes maketh the man. The right clothes could take Brother Sim from a boy too young to shave to a man too old to be allowed to. He makes a fine girl also, though that was a dangerous business in road company and reserved for targets that just couldn't be killed any other way. Young Sim is forgettable. When he's gone, I forget how he looks. Sometimes I think of all my brothers it's Sim that's the most dangerous.

43

'Explain it to me again.' Makin leaned forward in the saddle to be heard above the rain. 'Your father stabs you, but it's to Count Renar's castle we're going so you can cut yourself some revenge?'

'Yes.'

'And it's not even the Count we're after. Not him that sent your sainted mother on her way, but some old charm seller?'

'Right.'

'Who had you and the Nuban at his mercy when you first ran from home. And let you go without so much as a beating?'

'I think he put a spell on the Nuban's crossbow,' I said.

'Well if he did, it must have been to prevent it missing. The Nuban could stop an army with that thing. Given the right spot.'

'There wasn't much that the Nuban missed, true enough,' I said.

'So?'

'So?'

'So, I don't understand why we're out here in the pissing rain on stolen nags, riding into the worst kind of danger.'

I rubbed my jaw where he'd hit me. It felt sore. The coldness of the rain did little to ease it.

'What's the world about, Makin?'

He looked at me, eyes narrowed against the wetness of the wind.

'I never had time for those philosophers of yours, Jorg. I'm a soldier, and that's the end of it.'

'So you're a soldier. What's the world about?'

'War.' He set a hand to the hilt of his sword, unconscious of the action. 'The Hundred War.'

'And what's that about, soldier?' I asked.

'A hundred noble-born fighting across as many lands for the Empire throne.'

'That's what I always thought,' I said.

The rain came down harder, bouncing off the backs of my hands with a sting as if it carried ice. Ahead, at a place where the road forked, I could see a glow, three of them in fact, three patches of warm light.

'Tavern up ahead.' I spat water.

'So aren't we fighting for the Empire then?' Makin kept pace, though his horse slipped in the mud torrent at the roadside.

'I killed Price here,' I said. 'Outside this inn. They called it The Three Frogs back then.'

'Price?'

'Little Rikey's big brother,' I said. 'You never met him. Made Rike look like a gentleman.'

'Oh right, I remember the story. The brothers told it around the fire once or twice when Rikey was off on some private whoring.'

We reached the inn. They still called it The Three Frogs if the sign was anything to go by.

'I'll bet they didn't tell you the whole story.'

'Brained him with a rock, didn't you? Now you mention it, none of them was too keen to talk about it.'

'Me and the Nuban had come down out of the highlands. We didn't speak the whole time. I had Corion in my head, or the touch of him, like a black hole behind my eyes.

'We didn't expect to see the brothers. We'd arranged to meet a week earlier on the other side of Ancrath. But I'd called the Nuban on his debt, and off we'd gone.

'Anyhow, there they were. A score of horses on the road, the flame just starting to lick the thatch. Burlow over by that tree, there, with a keg of ale all to his-self. Young Sim, axe on high, chasing a pig. And out comes Price, bending low to fit through the door, smoke billowing around him as if he was the devil himself, and dragging the landlord, one hand round the man's neck, not choking him, mind: Price could get his mitts all the way round a man's neck without so much as pinching.

'Price sees me and it's like something explodes inside him. He knocks the landlord against the doorframe, and there's brains everywhere. Keeps his stare nailed to me the whole time.

'"You little bastard. I'm going to open you up."

'He didn't shout it, but there wasn't one of the brothers who didn't hear him. Me and the Nuban were thirty yards off still, and it was like he'd hissed it into my ear.

'"With a big crossbow like that, I bet you could hit him between the eyes from here," I told the Nuban.

'"No", he said. Didn't sound like the Nuban though. Sounded like a dry voice I'd heard before. "They have to see you do it."

'Price came on at a stroll. I didn't have any illusions that I could stop him, but running wasn't an option, so I thought I might as well have a go.

'I picked up a stone. A smooth one. Fit my hand like it was made for me.

'"David had a sling," Price said. He had an ugly smile on him.

'"Goliath was worth one."

'He was only strolling, but thirty yards never seemed to vanish so fast.

'"What's got you so riled anyhow? You missed the Nuban that much?" I thought I might as well find out what I was going to die for.

'"I…" He seemed foxed at that. Had a distant look, like he was trying to see something I couldn't.

'I took the moment to let fly. With a stone like that you can't miss. It hit him in the right eye. Really hard. Even a monster like Price notices that sort of thing. He made an awful howling. You'd have shat yourself if you heard it, Makin, if you'd known he was after you.

'So, I crouched down, and my hands just found another couple of stones, each as perfect as the first one.

'Price is still hopping about, with a hand pressed to his eye and a goo leaking past his fingers.

'"Hey, Goliath!"

'That got his attention. I crack my arm out and let go a second stone. Hits him in the good eye. He roars like a mad beast and charges. I put that last stone through his front teeth and down the back of his throat.

'I tell you, Makin, they were all impossible throws. Not lucky, impossible. I've never thrown like that since.

'Anyhow, I step out of his way, and he blunders on for ten yards before going down, choking. I'd put that third one right into his windpipe.

'I pick up the biggest rock I can from that drystone wall over there, and I follow him. He'd probably have choked to death by himself. He had that hanged-man purple look by the time I got there. But I don't like to leave things to chance.

'He's half crawling, blind. And the stink of him, soiled most every way there is. I almost felt sorry for the bastard.

'I didn't think his skull would break first time. But it did.'

Makin, stepped off his horse, ankle-deep into mud. 'We could go inside.'

I didn't feel the weather any more. I felt the heat of the day I killed Price. The smoothness of the small stones, the coarse weight of the rock I'd used to end it.

'It was Corion that guided my hand. And I think it was Sageous who set Price on me. Father reckons the dream-witch serves him, but that's not the way of it. Sageous saw that Corion had sunk his hooks into me, he saw he'd lost his new pawn's heir, so he infected Price's dreams and fanned the hatred there just a little bit. It wouldn't have taken much.

'They play us, Makin. We're pieces on their board.'

He had a smile at that, through torn lips. 'We're all pieces on someone's board, Jorg.' He went to the tavern door. 'You've played me often enough.'

I followed him through into the warm reek of the main room. The hearth held a single log, sizzling and giving out more smoke than heat. The small bar held a dozen or so. Locals by the look of them.

'Ah! The smell of wet peasants.' I threw my sodden cloak over the nearest table. 'Nothing beats it.'

'Ale!' Makin pulled up a stool. A space began to clear around us.

'Meat too,' I said. 'Cow. Last time I came here we ate roast dog, and the landlord died.' It was true enough, though not in that order.

'So,' Makin said. 'This Corion just had to click his

fingers on your first meeting, and you and the Nuban keeled over. What's to stop him doing it again?'

'Maybe nothing.'

'Even a gambler likes to stand a chance, Prince.' Makin took two glazed jugs from the serving wench, both over-running with foam.

'I've grown a bit since we last met,' I said. 'Sageous didn't find me so easy.'

Makin drank deep.

'But there's more. I took something from that necro-mancer.' I could taste his heart, bitter on my tongue. I swigged from my jug. 'Bit off something to chew on. I've got a pinch of magic in me, Makin. Whatever runs in the veins of that dead bitch who did for the Nuban, that little girl too, who ran with the monsters, whatever kept her glowing, well I've got a spark of it now.'

Makin wiped the foam from his dungeon-grown moustache. He managed to convey his disbelief with the slightest arching of a brow. I hauled up my shirt. Well not *my* shirt, but something Katherine must have selected for me. Where Father's knife had found me, a thin black line ran across my hairless chest. Black veins ran from the wound, reaching out over my ribs, up for my throat.

'Whatever my father is, he isn't inept,' I said. 'I should have died.'

44

They call the castle 'The Haunt'. When you ride up the valley of an evening, with the sun going down behind the towers, you can see why. The place has that classic brooding malice about it. The high windows are dark, the town below the gates lies in shadow, the flags hang lifeless. It brings to mind an empty skull. Without the cheery grin.

'So the plan is?' Makin asked.

I gave him a smile. We nosed the horses up the road, past a wagon creaking beneath a load of barrels.

'We seem to have arrived in time for tourney,' Makin said. 'Is that a good thing, or a bad thing?'

'Well, we've come for a test of strength haven't we?' I'd been trying to make out the pennants on the pavilions lining the east side of the tourney field. 'Better to keep incognito for now though.'

'So about this plan—' The scattered thunder of approaching hooves cut him off.

We looked back over our shoulders. A tight knot of

horsemen was closing fast, half a dozen, the leader in full plate armour, long shadows thrown behind them.

'Nice bit of tourney plate.' I turned my nag in the road.

'Jorg—' It was Makin's day for getting cut off.

'Make way!' The lead horseman bellowed loud enough, but I chose not to hear him.

'Make way, peasants!' He pulled up rather than go around. Five riders drew alongside him, house-troops in chainmail, their horses lathered.

'Peasants?' I knew we looked down-at-heel, but we hardly counted as peasants. My fingers found the empty space where my sword should hang. 'Who might we be clearing a path for, now?' I recognized their colours, but asked by way of insult.

The man on the knight's left spoke up. 'Sir Alain Kennick, heir to the county of Kennick, knight of the long—'

'Yes, yes.' I held up a hand. The man fell silent, fixing me with a pale eye from beneath the rim of his iron helm. 'Heir to the Barony of Kennick. Son of the notoriously blubbery Baron Kennick.' I rubbed at my chin hoping that the grime there might pass as stubble in the half-light. 'But these are Renar lands. I thought the men of Kennick weren't welcome here.'

Alain drew his steel at that, four foot of Builder-steel cutting a bloody edge from the sunset.

'I'll not be debated in the road by some peasant boy!'

His voice held a whine to it. He lifted his face-plate then took the reins.

'I heard that the Baron and Count Renar made up their differences after Marclos got himself killed,' Makin said. I knew he'd have his hand on the flail we inherited with the horses. 'Baron Kennick withdrew his accusations that Renar was behind the burning of Mabberton.'

'Actually it was me that burned Mabberton,' I said. I had to wonder, though. I might have been the one to put torch to thatch. It had seemed like a good idea at the time. But whose good idea was it? Corion's perhaps.

'You?' Alain snorted.

'I had a hand in Marclos's death too,' I said. I kept his eyes and edged my horse closer. Without weapon or armour I didn't present much of a threat.

'I heard that the Prince of Ancrath turned Marclos's column with a dozen men,' Makin added.

'Did we have a full dozen, Sir Makin?' I asked in my best court voice. I kept my eyes on Alain and ignored his men. 'Perhaps we did. Well, no matter, I like these odds better.'

'What are—' Alain glanced to either side where the hedgerow seethed with possibilities.

'You're worried about an ambush, Alain?' I asked. 'You think Prince Honorous Jorg Ancrath and the captain of his father's guard can't take six Kennick dogs in the road?'

Whatever Alain might think, I could tell his men had heard their fill of Norwood stories. They'd heard of the Mad Prince and his road hounds. They'd heard how ragged warriors burst from the ruins, stood their ground, and broke a force ten times their number.

Something grunted in the gloom to our right. If Alain's men had any doubt that they were already targeted by bandits in the shadows, the grunt of a small forager hunting grubs was enough to convince them otherwise.

'Now! Attack!' I yelled it for the benefit of my non-existent ambush party, and flung myself from my saddle, dragging Alain off his horse.

The fight went out of Alain as soon as we hit the sod, which was good because the fall knocked all the wind out of me, and a clash of heads set me seeing stars.

I heard the whack of Makin's flail and the thump of retreating hooves. With a heave and a clatter I disentangled myself from Alain.

'Best get out of here quick, Jorg.' Makin was heading back after the briefest of pursuits. 'Won't take them long to work out we're alone.'

I found Alain's sword. 'They won't be back.'

Makin frowned at me. 'Head-butting a helmed knight scrambled your brains?'

I rubbed at the sore spot, fingers coming away bloody.

'We've got Alain. A hostage or a corpse. They don't know which.'

'He looks dead to me,' Makin said.

'Broke his neck, I think. But that's not the point. The point is that they know they're not getting him back in one piece, so they'll be looking to their own escape. There's no going back to Kennick for those lads now. No welcome in the Haunt either. They'll know Renar won't want any part of this.'

'So what now?'

'We get him off the road. That beer wagon is going to come by here in a few minutes.' I threw a look down the road. 'Hitch him to his horse. We'll drag him into the wheat field.'

We took the armour off him in the gloom, amongst the wheat still wet from the day's rain. It stunk a bit – Alain had soiled himself in death – but it was a good fit for me, if a bit roomy around the waist.

'What do you think?' I stepped back for Makin to admire me.

'Can't see a damn thing.'

'I look good, trust me.' I half-drew Alain's sword, then slammed it back into its scabbard. 'I think I'll give the jousts a miss.'

'Very wise.'

'The Grand Mêlée is more me. And the winner gets his prize from Count Renar himself!'

'That's not a plan. That's a way to get a death so famously stupid that they'll be laughing about it in ale-houses for a hundred years to come,' Makin said.

I started to clank back toward the road, leading Alain's horse.

'You're right, Makin, but I'm running out of options here.'

'We could hit the road again. Get a little gold together, get some more, enough to make lives somewhere they've never heard of Ancrath.' I could see a longing in his eyes. Part of him really meant it.

I grinned. 'I may be running out of options, but running out isn't an option. Not for me.'

We rode toward The Haunt. Slowly. I didn't want to visit the tourney field yet. We had no tent to pitch, and the Kennick colours would inevitably draw me deeper into the charade than my acting skills could support.

As we came out of the farmland into the sprawl of houses reaching from the castle walls, a hedge-knight caught up with us and pulled up.

'Well met, sir…?' He sounded out of breath.

'Alain of Kennick,' I supplied.

'Kennick? I thought…'

'We have an alliance now, Renar and Kennick are the best of friends these days.'

'Good to hear. A man needs friends in times like these,' the knight said. 'Sir Keldon, by the way. I'm here for the lists. Count Renar places generous purses where a good lance can reach them.'

'So I hear,' I said.

Sir Keldon fell in beside us. 'I'm pleased to be off the plains,' he said. 'They're lousy with Ancrath scouts.'

'Ancrath?' Makin failed to keep the alarm from his voice.

'You haven't heard?' Sir Keldon glanced back into the night. 'They say King Olidan is massing his armies. Nobody's sure where he'll strike, but he's sent the Forest Watch into action. Most of them are back there if I know anything!' He stabbed a gauntleted finger over his shoulder. 'And you know what that meant for Gelleth!' He drew the finger across his throat.

We reached the crossroads at the town centre. Sir Keldon turned his horse to the left. 'You're to the Field?'

'No, we've to pay our respects.' I nodded toward The Haunt. 'Good luck on the morrow.'

'My thanks.'

We watched him go.

I turned Alain's horse back toward the plains.

'I thought we were going to pay our respects?' Makin asked.

'We are,' I said.

I kicked my steed into a trot. 'To Watch Master Coddin.'

45

I like mountains, always have done. Big obstinate bits of rock sticking up where they're not wanted and getting in folk's way. Great. Climbing them is a different matter altogether though. I hate that.

'What in feck's name was the point of stealing a horse if I have to drag the damn thing up the slightest incline we meet?'

'To be fair, Prince, this is more by way of a cliff,' Makin said.

'I blame Sir Alain for owning a deficient horse. I should have kept the nag I came in on.'

Nothing but the labour of Makin's breath.

'I'm going to have to see Baron Kennick about that boy of his one day,' I said.

At that point a stone turned under my foot and I fell in a clatter of what little armour I'd kept on.

'Easy now, you've three bows on each of you.' The voice came from further up the slope where the moonlight made little sense of the jumbled rock.

Makin straightened up slow and easy, leaving me to find my own way to my feet.

'Sounds like a good Ancrath man to me,' I said, loud enough for any on the slopes. 'If you're going to shoot anyone, might I suggest this horse here, he's a better target and a lazy bastard to boot.'

'Lay your swords down.'

'We've only got one between us,' I said. 'And I'm not inclined to lose it. So let's forget about that now and you can take us to see the Watch Master.'

'Lay down—'

'Yes, yes, so you said. Look.' I stood up straight and turned to try and catch the moonlight. 'Prince Jorg. That's me. Pushed the last Watch Master over the falls. Now take me to Coddin before I lose my famously good temper.'

We reached an understanding and before long I had two of them leading Alain's horse, and another lighting the way for us with a hooded lantern.

They took us to an encampment a couple of miles further on, fifty men huddled in a hollow just below the saddle of a hill. Brot Hill, according to the leader of the band taking us in. Nice to know somebody had a clue.

The watch brought us in with whistled signals to the guards. The camp lay dark, which was sensible enough given they weren't ten miles from The Haunt.

We stumbled in amongst sleeping watchmen, tripping over the guys of various tents set up for command.

'Let's have some light!' I made enough noise to wake the sleepers. A prince deserves a little fanfare even if he has to make it himself. 'Light! Renar doesn't even know you've crossed the borders yet, he's holding a tourney in the shadow of his walls for Jesu's sake!'

'See to it.' I recognized the voice.

'Coddin! You came!'

Lanterns began to be lit. Fireflies waking in the night.

'Your father insisted on it, Prince Jorg.' The Watch Master ducked out of his tent, his face without humour. 'I'm to bring your head back, but not the rest of you.'

'I volunteer to do the cutting!' Rike stepped into the lantern glow, bigger than remembered, as always.

Men stepped aside, and Gorgoth came out of the gloom, huger than Rike, his rib-bones reaching from his chest like a clawed hand. 'Dark Prince, a reckoning is due.'

'My head?' I put a hand to my throat. 'I think I'll keep it.' I turned to see Fat Burlow arrive, a loaf in each hand.

'I believe my days of pleasing King Olidan are over,' I said. 'In fact I'm even tired of waiting for him to die. The next victory I take will be for me. The next treasure I seize will stay in these hands, and the hands of those that serve me.'

Gorgoth looked on, impassive, little Gog watching from his shadow. Elban and Liar elbowed their way through the growing ring of watchmen.

'And what treasure would that be, Jorth?' Elban asked.

'You'll see it when the sun rises, old man,' I said. 'I'm taking the Renar Highlands.'

'I say we take him in.' Rike loomed behind me. 'There'll be a price on his head. A princely price!' He laughed at his own joke, coughing on that fishbone again, the old *'hur! hur! hur!'*

'Funny you should mention Price, Brother.' I kept my back to him. 'I was reminiscing with Makin down at the Three Frogs just the other day.'

That stopped his laughing.

'I won't lie to you, it's not going to be easy.' I turned nice and slow to address the whole circle of faces. 'I'm going to take the county from Renar, and make it my kingdom. The men that help make that happen will be knights of my table.'

I found Coddin in the crowd. He'd brought the brothers to me on the strength of my message, but how much further he'd follow me was another matter: he was a hard man to predict.

'What say you, Watch Master? Will the Forest Watch follow their prince once more? Will you draw blood in the name of vengeance? Will you seek an accounting for my royal mother? For my brother who would have sat upon the throne of Ancrath had I fallen?'

The only motion in the man lay in the flicker of lamplight along the line of his cheekbone. After too long a wait, he spoke. 'I saw Gelleth. I saw the Castle Red, and a sun brought to the mountains to burn the rock itself. Mighty works.'

Around the circle men nodded, feet stamped approval. Coddin held up a hand.

'But the mark of a king is to be seen in those closest to him. A king needs be a prophet in his homeland,' he said.

I didn't like where we were going.

'The watch will serve if these … road-brothers stay true, once you have told them of their task,' he said, eyes on me all the while, steady and calm.

I made another half circle, until Rike filled my vision, my eyes level with his chest. He smelled foul.

'Christ Jesu, Rike, you stink like a dung heap that's gone bad.'

'Wh—' He furrowed his brow and jabbed a blunt finger toward Coddin. 'He said you had to win the brothers to the cause. And that's me that is! The brothers do what I say now.' He grinned at that, showing the gaps where I'd knocked out teeth under Mount Honas.

'I said I wouldn't lie to you.' I spread my hands. 'I'm done with lying. You men are my brothers. What I would ask of you would leave most in the grave.' I pursed my lips as if considering. 'No, I won't ask it.'

Rike's frown deepened. 'What won't you ask, you little weasel?'

I touched two fingers to my chest. 'My own father

stabbed me, Little Rikey. Here. A thing like that will reach any man.

'You take the brothers to the road. Break a few heads, empty a few barrels, and may whatever angel is set to watch over vagabonds fill your hands with silver.'

'You want us to go?' He spoke the words slowly.

'I'd make for the Horse Coast,' I said. 'It's that way.' I pointed.

'And what'll you be doing?' Rike asked.

'I'll go with Watch Master Coddin here. Perhaps I can make peace with my father.'

'My arse you will!' Rike hit Burlow in the arm, no malice in it, just an over-boiling of his natural violence. 'You've got it all planned out, you little bastard. Always playing the odds, always with the aces hidden away. We'll be slogging through dust and mud to the Horse Coast, and you'll be lording it here with a gold cup in your hand and silk to wipe your shit. I'm staying right where I can see you, until I get what's mine.'

'I'm telling you as a brother, you big ugly sack of dung, leave now while you've a chance,' I said.

'Stuff it.' Rike allowed himself a triumphant grin.

I gave up on him.

'Coddin's men can't get near that tourney. Men such as us though, we drift into every muster, we lurk at the edges of any place where there's blood and coin and woman-flesh. The brothers could slip into tourney crowds unseen.

344

'When I make my move I need you to hold until the watch can reach us. I need you to hold The Haunt's gates. For minutes only, but make no mistake, they'll be the reddest minutes you've seen.'

'We'll hold,' Rike said.

'We will hold.' Makin raised his flail.

'We'll hold!' Elban, Burlow, Liar, Row, Red Kent, and the dozen brothers left to me.

I faced Coddin once again.

'I guess they'll hold,' I said.

46

'Sir Alain, heir to the Kennick baronetcy.'

And there I was, riding onto the tourney field to take my place, accompanied by a scatter of half-hearted applause.

'Sir Arkle, third son of Lord Merk.' The announcer's voice rang out again.

Sir Arkle followed me onto the field, a horseman's mace in hand. Most of the entrants for the Grand Mêlée had can-openers of one sort or another. The axe, the mace, the flail, tools to open armour, or to break the bones closeted within. When you fight a man in full plate, it's normally a matter of bludgeoning him to a point at which he's so crippled you can deliver the coup de grâce with a knife slipped between gorget and breastplate, or through an eye-slot.

I had my sword. Well, I had Alain's. If he had a weapon more suited to the Mêlée, then it left with his guards when they rode off.

'Sir James of Hay.'

A big man in battered plate, heavy axe at the ready, an armour-piercing spike on the reverse.

'William of Brond.' Tall, a crimson boar on his shield, spiked flail.

They kept coming. A baker's dozen. At last we were all arrayed upon the field. A lucky thirteen. Knights of many realms, caparisoned for war. Silent save for the gentle nicker of horses.

At the far end of the field, in the shadow of the castle walls, five tiers of seating, and in the centre, a high-backed chair draped in the purple of empire. Count Renar rose to his feet. Beside him on the common bench, Corion, an unremarkable figure that drew on the eye as the lodestone pulls iron.

At two hundred paces I could see nothing of Renar's face save the glint of eyes beneath a gold circlet and a dark fall of hair.

'Fight!' Renar lifted his arm, and let it drop.

A knight spurred his horse toward mine. I'd not taken his name to heart. I only listened to the introductions after mine.

All around us men fell to battling. I saw William of Brond take a man from the saddle with a swing of his flail.

My attacker had a flanged mace, clutched tight, the steel of his gauntlet polished to dazzling silver. He shouted a war-cry as he came at me, trailing the mace for an overhead swing.

I stood in my stirrups and leaned toward him, arm fully extended. Alain's sword found its way through the perforated grille of the knight's helm.

'Yield?'

He wouldn't say, so I let him slip from his horse.

Another knight came my way, sidestepping his horse skilfully away from Sir William's frenzy. He wasn't even looking at me.

Around the back of the breastplate there's a gap just below the kidneys. A decent suit of plate will have chainmail to cover whatever vitals are exposed between breastplate and saddle. And his did. But Builder-steel with a little muscle behind it will cut through chain. The man fell with a vague expression of surprise, and left me facing William.

'Alain!' He sounded as if all his Christmases had come at once.

'I know, I hate him too.' I flipped my visor.

The thing about flails is you've got to keep them moving. An important point that Sir William forgot when he found himself staring into an unfamiliar face. I took the opportunity to urge Alain's horse forward, and to its credit the beast was fast enough to let me put four foot of razor-edged sword past Sir William's guard.

It's not the done thing to set to bloody slaughter at tourney. There's rarely a Grand Mêlée in which somebody doesn't die, but it's normally a day later under the knives of the chirurgeons. The foe is generally unhorsed, or stunned in the saddle. A few fractures and a lot of bruising are the normal consolation prizes distributed among the entrants who don't win. When a knight gets too thirsty for blood, he often finds himself meeting his opponent's friends and family in unpleasant circumstances shortly after.

I of course had a rather different view of things. The fewer armed men left able-bodied after the tourney, the better. Besides, a broadsword isn't the weapon to batter out submissions. It's for killing, pure and simple.

Sir Arkle charged me, galloping nearly the full length of the field, a felled knight in his wake. As he closed the gap, he set to swinging his mace in a tight pattern just out of kilter with his horse's gait. It looked worryingly well-practised.

If the sight of a heavy warhorse thundering toward you doesn't make at least part of you want to up and run, then you're a corpse. There's no stopping a thing like that. A thousand pounds of muscle and bone, sweating and panting as it hurtles your way.

I rolled out of the saddle as Sir Arkle arrived. I didn't just duck. He was ready for that. I fell. And yes it hurt. But not so much that it stopped me sticking old Alain's sword into that blur of thrashing legs as Arkle hurtled past.

That's another thing that isn't done in tourney. You go for the man, not the horse. A trained warhorse is frighteningly expensive, and be assured that when you break one, the owner is going to come after you for the price of a replacement.

I levered myself up, cursing, splattered with horse blood.

Sir Arkle lay under his steed, deathly quiet and still, in contrast to the horse's screaming and thrashing.

A lot of animals will suffer horrific injury in silence, but when they decide to complain, there's no holds barred. If you've heard the screams of rabbits as they're put to the knife you'll know what racket even such small creatures can make. It took two swings to fully silence Arkle's horse. Another two for good measure to take its head off.

By the time I'd finished, I'd become the archetypal Red Knight, my armour bright with arterial blood. I had the stink of battle in my nose now, blood and shit, the taste of it on my lips, salt with sweat.

There weren't many of us left standing in the tourney ring. Sir James stood amid a scatter of fallen knights at the far end, battling a man in fire-bronzed armour. Closer to hand an unhorsed knight with a war-hammer had just laid out his opponent. And that was it.

The hammer-man limped toward me, the iron plates around his knee buckled and grating.

'Yield.' I didn't move. Didn't so much as raise my sword.

A moment of silence. Nothing but the distant clash of weapons as Sir James of Hay put down his man.

Nothing but the faint pitter-pat of blood dripping from my platemail.

Hammer-man let his hammer fall. 'You're not Alain Kennick.' He turned and limped toward the white tent where the healers waited.

Half of me wanted the fight. More than half of me wondered if a hammer between the eyes wasn't a whole lot more appetizing than meeting with Corion again. It seemed impossible that he didn't already know I was here, that those empty eyes hadn't seen through Alain's armour at the first moment. I glanced toward the stands, closer now. He watched me, they all did, but this was the man who'd given me the power to fell Brother Price, the man who whispered from the hook-briar, who poisoned my every move, pulling the strings toward hidden ends. Had he drawn me here, to this moment, tugging on his puppet lines?

Sir James of Hay put an end to my speculation. He dismounted, presumably having noted my lack of respect for horseflesh, and advanced with purpose in his stride. The sunlight coaxed few glimmers from the scarred plates of his armour. His heavy axe had done good work today. I saw blood on the armour spike.

'You're a scary one,' I said.

He came on, stepping around Arkle's horse.

'Not a talker?' I asked.

'Yield, boy,' he said. 'One chance.'

'I'm not sure we even have choices, James, let alone chances. You should read—'

He charged, dragging that axe of his through the air in a blur. I managed a block, but my sword flew free, leaving my right hand numb to the wrist. He reverse-swung, his strength tremendous, and nearly took my head. I swayed aside, clear by half an inch, and staggered back.

Sir James readied himself. I knew then how the cow feels before the slaughterman. I may have been guilty of fine words about fear and the edges of knives, but empty-handed before a competent butcher like Sir James I found a sudden and healthy terror. I didn't want it all to end here, broken apart before a cheering crowd, cut down before strangers who didn't even know my name.

'Wait!'

But of course he didn't. He came on apace, swinging for me. If I hadn't tripped as I backed, I'd have been cut in two, or as near as makes no difference. The fall left me flat on my back with the air knocked out and Sir James carried two strides past me by his momentum. My right hand, grasping for purchase, found the haft of the discarded war-hammer. The old luck hadn't deserted me.

I swung and made contact with the back of Sir James' knee. It made a satisfying crunch, and he went down, discovering his voice on the way. Unfortunately the brute hadn't the grace to know he was supposed to be beaten. He twisted onto his good knee and raised his axe over my head. I could see it black against the blue sky. At least the sun was out. A blank visor hid his face, but I could hear the rattle of his breath behind it, see the flecks of foam around the perforations.

'Time to die.'

He was right. There's not much to be done with a war-hammer at close quarters. Especially when you're spread-eagled on your back.

ChooOm!

Sir James' head jerked from my field of view leaving nothing but blue heaven.

'Gods but you've got to love that crossbow!' I said.

I sat up. Sir James lay beside me, a neat hole punched through his faceplate, and blood pooling behind his head.

I couldn't see who had taken the shot. Probably Makin, having regained the Nuban's crossbow from one of the brothers. He must have loosed his bolt from the commons where the rabble stands. Renar would have men stationed where anyone might get a clear shot at the royal seating area, but targeting the combatants on the field was a far easier proposition.

I recovered my sword before the crowd really took in what had happened. A scuffle of some kind had broken out in the commons, a large figure in the midst of it all. Rike breaking heads perhaps.

I scooped up Sir James's axe and caught Alain's horse again. Once in the saddle I took axe and sword in hand. Townsfolk began to stream onto the field with some kind of riot in mind. It wasn't entirely clear where their anger lay, but I felt sure a whole lot of it rested on Sir Alain of Kennick.

A line of men-at-arms had positioned themselves in front of the royal stand. A squad of six soldiers in castle livery were angling toward me from their station by the casualty tent.

I lifted axe and sword out to shoulder height. The axe weighed like an anvil; it'd take a man like Rike to wield it as lightly as Sir James had.

From the corner of my eye I could see guards leaving their posts at the castle gates to help calm the disturbance and come to their lord's aid.

Corion found his feet, oddly reminiscent of a scarecrow, standing just below Count Renar's seat. The Count himself remained in his chair, motionless, hands in his lap, fingers steepled.

Did Corion know it was me? He had to, surely? When I'd broken his spell, when I'd woken from dark dreams after Father's tender stab, and finally remembered how he'd turned me from my vengeance, how he'd made me his pawn in the hidden game of empire, hadn't he known?

Time to find out.

I urged Alain's horse into a canter and aimed him straight at Renar, axe and sword in outstretched hands. I hoped I looked like Hell risen, like Death riding for the Count. I could taste blood, and I wanted more.

There really is something about a heavy warhorse coming your way. The stand began to empty at speed, the gentry climbing over each other to get clear. A space opened up around Renar's high-backed chair, just him, Corion, and the two chosen men flanking. A ripple even ran through the line of soldiers before the seating, but they held their ground. At least until I really picked up speed.

47

Alain's horse carried me through the soldiers, up the stands, like climbing a giant staircase, right to Count Renar's chair, and through it.

Had the Count not been hauled from his seat moments before, it could have all ended there.

'Get him away!' Corion said to the quick-handed body-guard.

The other chosen man came straight for me as the horse beneath me panicked at the strange footing. I couldn't control the beast, and I didn't want it to land on me when it fell, so I leapt from the saddle. Or got as close to a leap as a man in full plate can, which is to say that I chose where I fell. I trusted to my armour and dropped onto Renar's bodyguard.

The man cushioned my fall, and in exchange got most of his ribs broken. I heard them crack like sappy branches. I clambered up, with the horse whinnying behind me, hooves flying in all directions as it turned and bucked, threatening to fall at every moment.

I threw Sir James' axe at Renar's back, but the thing proved too heavy and ill-weighted for a clean throw. It hit his second bodyguard between the shoulderblades and felled him. Renar himself managed to reach the soldiers I'd scattered in my charge, and they circled around to escort him toward the castle.

I took my sword in two hands and made to follow.

'No.'

Corion stepped into my path, one hand raised, a single finger lifted.

I felt a giant nail skewer me to the spot, struck through the top of my head, driven into the bedrock far beneath my feet. The world seemed to spin around me, slow revolutions, measured by heartbeats. My arms fell, limp, hands numb, losing their grip on the sword hilt.

'Jorg.' I wouldn't meet his eyes. 'How could you think you might defy me?'

'How could you think I wouldn't?' My voice sounded far off, as if somebody else were speaking. I managed to fumble the dagger from my hip.

'Stop.' And my arms lost all remaining strength.

Corion moved closer. My eyes struggled to keep with him as the world turned. Behind me the sounds of the thrashing horse, muffled and distant.

'You're a child,' he said. 'You gamble everything on each throw, no bet hedged, no reserve. That's a strategy that always ends in defeat.'

He took a small knife from his robe, three gleaming inches of cut-throat.

'Gelleth, though! That took us all by surprise. You exceeded all expectations there. Sageous even left your father's side rather than face you on your return. He's back there now, of course.'

Corion put the blade to the side of my neck, angled between helm and gorget. His face held no emotion, his eyes empty wells that seemed to suck me in.

'Sageous was right to run,' I said. My voice reached up from a chasm.

I had no plan, but I'd had my moment of fear with Sir James and I wasn't about to reward Corion with any more.

I reached for whatever power the necromancer's heart had given me. I let my eyes look where the ghosts walk, and a cold thrill burned across my skin.

'Necromancy won't save you, Jorg.' I felt the bite of the knife at my neck. 'Even Chella doesn't trust in her death magic enough to face me. And whatever you stole beneath that mountain is just a shadow of her skill.'

It's will. In the end it always comes down to will. Corion held me, nailed within a treacherous body, because he willed it, because his want had over-written mine.

Hot blood trickled down my neck. I felt it run beneath my armour.

I threw everything I had against him. All my pride, my anger, an ocean of it, the rage, the hurt. I reached back across the years. I counted my dead. I reached into the briar and touched the bloodless child who hung there. I took it all, and made a hammer of it.

Nothing! All I managed was to flop my head forward so I no longer saw his face. He laughed. I felt the vibration of it in the knife. He wanted my death to be slow.

I could see my arms, metal clad, dagger held in loose fingers. Life pulsed through those arms, driven with each beat of my heart, mixed with the dark magic that had kept me from death at the King's hand. I saw Father's face again, in the moment of the blow, the bristle of his beard, the tight line of his mouth. I saw Katherine's face, the light in her eyes as she nursed me. And I reached with all of it, the bitter and the sweet, just to move the arms that lay before me. I put the whole of my life behind that plea.

It accomplished nothing but to turn the point of my dagger toward Corion.

'They're dying, Jorg,' he said. 'See with my eyes.'

And I was the hawk. Part of me stayed on the stands, being bled like a pig, and the rest flew, wild and free across the tourney field.

I saw Elban defending Rike's back amid the common crowd, Renar's soldiers closing on them from all angles, like hunting dogs knifing through the tall grass. A spear got him in the stomach. He looked surprised. Old all of a sudden, wearing all his years. I saw him shout, and spit blood over those toothless gums of his. But I couldn't hear him. A glimpse of Elban cutting down the man who speared him, and we moved on.

Liar stood out on the edge of the tourney field, a mean streak of gristle, bow in hand, arrows planted at his feet. He took the castle-soldiers down as they streamed toward the royal stands. Quick but unhurried, each arrow finding a mark, a tight smile on his lips. They got him from behind. The first soldier to reach him drove a spear through his back.

We swept closer to the gates. A tinker's cart. The sack covering shrugged aside, and Gorgoth rolled out, reaching the ground on two hands and one knee. He ran for The Haunt. The castle folk scattered before him, some screaming. Even soldiers turned aside, all of a sudden finding their duty to be on the tourney field. Two men discovered their courage and barred his way, spears levelled. Gorgoth didn't slow. He caught a spear in each hand, snapped the last foot off, and drove the broken ends through their owners' necks. He ran through the men before they fell. Three arrows hit him as he left my view.

Corion drew our sight back. On the cart the sacking twitched again. Something quick and mottled slipped out. Gog. The leucrota child ran in the direction Gorgoth had taken.

Our sight drew back. Across the tourney field where a score of soldiers closed on the royal stand. Burlow stood guard. A lone man between Renar's spears and the young Prince of Ancrath, yours truly. How he'd got there

I didn't know. Or why. But he had nowhere to run, and he was too fat to win free in any case.

Burlow took the first man down with an axe blow that sliced head from shoulders. A reverse swing put the blade between the next man's eyes. Then they were all over him. A single arrow looped in from somewhere and found a Renar neck.

Our sight drew back. I saw myself on the stand, face to face with Corion. Bleeding. Alain's horse still thrashing, as if it had been seconds rather than a lifetime since I rode up.

And we parted. I saw with my own eyes again. The knife in my hand, raised but impotent, the splintered boards beneath my feet. The sounds of Burlow dying. The scream of horse. I thought of Gog, chasing Gorgoth toward the gates, of Elban's toothless shout, of Makin out there somewhere, fighting and dying.

None of it made any difference. I couldn't move.

'It's over, Jorg. Goodbye.' The magus placed his knife for the final cut.

You'd think there was never a good time to get kicked by a horse.

The wild hoof hit me square in the back. I would probably have flown ten yards if I hadn't crashed straight into Corion. As it was, we flew about five yards together. We landed on grass, at the side of the royal stand, clutched in an embrace, like lovers. The eyes that had held me were screwed shut in pain. I tried again to lift my dagger.

It didn't move. But this time there was a difference, I felt the strain and play of the muscles in my arm. With a grunt I pushed him from me. The hilt of my dagger jutted between his ribs. What all my will, all my rage and pain, had been unable to accomplish, a single kick from a panicked horse had achieved.

I twisted the dagger, digging it in. A last breath escaped him. His eyes rolled open, glassy and without power.

The Count's bodyguard had fallen this way too, with the axe that had brought him down still bedded in his back. I wrenched it free. It's a nasty sound that sharp iron makes in flesh. I took Corion's head in two blows. I didn't trust him to be dead.

The soldiers that had taken Burlow began to boil around the side of the stand. I held Corion's head up before them.

There's an unsettling weight to a severed head. It swung on the grey hair knotted between my fingers, and I tasted bile at the back of my throat.

'You know this man!' I shouted.

The first three soldiers coming into view halted, maybe from fear, maybe to let the numbers build before the charge.

'I am Honorous Jorg Ancrath! The blood of Empire flows through my veins. My business is with Count Renar.'

More soldiers came around the corner of the stand. Five, seven, twelve. No more. Burlow had given good account of himself.

'This is the man you have served.' I took a step toward them, Corion's head held out before me. 'He made Count Renar his puppet years ago. You know this to be true.'

I walked forward. No hesitation. Believe they will step aside, and they will.

They didn't watch me. They watched the head. As if the fear he'd instilled in them ran so deep that they expected those dead eyes to swivel their way and draw them in with that hollow pull.

The soldiers parted for me, and I walked out across the tourney field toward The Haunt.

Other units broke from the left of the field where Rike and Elban had been fighting. They moved to intercept me. Two groups of five. They started to fall before they got within fifty yards. The Forest Watch were advancing along the Elm Road. I could see archers lining the ridge from which I'd first seen The Haunt.

I let Corion's head drop. I just opened my fingers and let his hair slide through. It took an age to fall, as though it fell through cobwebs, or dreams. It should have hit the ground like a hammer against a gong, but it made no sound. Silent or roaring though, I heard it, I felt it. A weight lifted from me. More weight than I'd ever imagined I could carry.

I could see the gateway ahead. The Haunt's great entrance arch. The portcullis had all but descended. A single figure stood beneath it, holding up an impossible mass of wood and iron. Gorgoth!

I started to run.

48

I ran for the castle gates. I had my armour on, save for the pieces I'd lost in the tourney, but it didn't seem to weigh heavy. I heard the hiss of arrows about me. Other men fell. The Forest Watch's finest archers kept my path clear.

I wondered where I was going, and why. I'd left Corion in the mud. When he died, it felt like an arrow being drawn from a wound, like shackles struck away, like the hangman's noose worked free from a purpled neck.

A few shafts reached me from guards up in The Haunt's ramparts. One shattered on my breastplate. But in the main they had too hard a time picking targets in the confusion of the tourney field to worry about one knight storming the castle single-handedly.

I let my feet carry me. The empty feeling wouldn't leave me. Where there had been an inner voice to goad me on, I heard only the rasp of my breath.

I met more serious resistance in the street running up to the gates, out of sight from the watch's positions.

Soldiers had gathered, between the taverns and tanneries. They held the road I had passed when I first came to The Haunt with the Nuban as a child seeking revenge.

Twenty men blocked the way, spearmen, with a captain in Renar finery, dull gleams from his chainmail. Behind them I could see Gorgoth holding up the portcullis. More soldiers milled in the courtyard beyond. There seemed to be no reason why they hadn't cut the leucrota down, and sealed the gates.

I pulled up before the line of spearmen, and found I had no breath with which to address them. A cold bluster of wind swirled between us, laced with rain.

What to do? All of a sudden, impossible odds seemed … impossible.

I glanced back. Two figures were pounding up along the path I'd taken. The first was too big to be anyone but Rike. I could see the feathered end of an arrow jutting from the joint above his left shoulder. Too much mud and blood on the second man to identify him by his armour. But it was Makin. I knew it from the way he held his sword.

I looked at the soldiers, along the points of their spears, held in a steady row.

What's it going to be then?

Another scatter of rain.

'House of Renar?' the captain called. He sounded uncertain.

They didn't know! These men had come out of the castle, without a clue what kind of attack they were under. You've got to love the fog of war.

I scraped a gauntlet across my breastplate to show the coat of arms more clearly. 'Sanctuary!'

'Alain Kennick, ally to the House of Renar, seeking sanctuary.' I pointed back toward Rike and Makin. 'They're trying to kill me!'

Perhaps Corion's death hadn't taken all of the wickedness from me. Not all of it.

I ran toward the line, and they parted for me.

'They won't get past us, my lord.' The captain offered a brief bow.

'Make sure they don't,' I said. And it didn't seem likely that they would.

I hurried on, up to the gates, feeling the weight of my plate-mail now. The air held an odd stench, rich and meaty, bacon burning over the hearth. It put me in mind of Mabberton where we torched all those peasants, a lifetime ago.

I could see squads of soldiers assembling in the great courtyard beyond the gates. Half-armoured men, some with shields, some without, many of them full of tourney-day ale, no doubt.

Coming closer I saw the corpses. Charred things, smouldering in their own molten fats, like bodies from a pauper's funeral with too little wood to make them ash.

366

Gorgoth stood with his back to me. Arrows pierced his arms and legs. At first I thought him a statue, but as I came closer I could see the quiver in those huge slabs of muscle across his back.

I moved past him, ducking under the portcullis. A hundred men in the courtyard watched me. Gorgoth's eyes were screwed tight with strain. He observed me through the narrowest of slits. More arrows jutted from his chest, standing among the reaching claws of his deformed ribcage. Blood bubbled around the shafts as he released a breath, and sucked back as he drew the next.

I kicked a smouldering head. It rolled clear of the charred body.

'That's one hell of a guardian angel you've got looking out for you, Gorgoth,' I said. Every soldier to have run at him lay in ashes.

The faintest shake of his head. 'The boy. Up there.'

Above Gorgoth, crouched in one of the gaps between the portcullis' timbers, Gog lurked. The inky voids that served him for eyes now burned like hot coals beneath the smith's bellows. His thin body had folded tighter than I believed possible. A few arrows studded the woodwork around him.

'The little one did all this?' I blinked. 'Damn.'

Gorgoth had told me the changes would come too quickly to Gog and his little brother. Too quickly and too dangerous to be borne.

'Bring this mad dog down.' The voice rang out behind me. It sounded familiar. It sounded like my father.

'Shoot him.'

It wasn't a voice to be disobeyed. But nobody had shot at me yet, so I turned from Gorgoth, and faced The Haunt.

Count Renar stood before the great keep, flanked by two dozen men-at-arms. To the left and right, bands of spearmen, a score in each. Other guards were coming down from the battlements above the gates.

I sketched a bow. 'Hello, Uncle.'

I'd only seen Renar in portrait before taking to the tourney field, and this was the best look I'd had at him so far. His face was rather thinner, his hair longer and less grey, but all in all he was the spitting image of his elder brother, and in truth, not that different from yours truly. Though far less handsome, of course.

'I am Honorous Jorg Ancrath.' I pulled my helm clear and addressed the men before me. 'Heir to the throne of Renar.' Not strictly true, but it would be once I'd killed the Count's remaining son. Wherever Cousin Jarco might be, he surely wasn't at home or I'd have seen his colours on the tourney field. So I let them think him dead. I let them picture him in the same pyre I'd set his brother Marclos on.

'You.' The Count singled out a man at his side. 'Put a hole in this bastard's head, or I'm going to cut yours from your shoulders!'

'This matter is between my uncle and me.' I set my gaze on the bowman. 'When it is done, you will be my soldiers, my victory will be yours. There will be no more blood.'

The man raised his crossbow. I felt a wave of heat sear my neck, as if a furnace door had opened behind me. Blisters rose across the man's face, like bubbles in boiling soup. He fell, screaming, and his hair burst into flame before he hit the ground. The men around him fell back in horror.

I saw the ghost leave him as he writhed, burning, clots of his flesh sticking to the flagstones. I saw his ghost, and I reached out to it. I reached with my hands, and I reached with the bitter power of the necromancers. I felt their dark energy pulse across my chest, running out from the wound I took from Father's knife.

I gave the dead man's ghost a voice, and I gave voice to the ghosts that hung smoke-like around the corpses at my feet.

The soldiers before me paled and shook. Swords dropped and terror leapt from man to man like wildfire.

With the screams of burned men echoing around me from beyond the grave, I took my sword in two hands and ran at Count Renar, my uncle, the man who sent killers after his brother's wife and sons. And I added my own scream, because Corion or no Corion, the need to kill him ate at me like acid.

49

And here I am, sitting in the high tower of The Haunt, in the empty place that Corion made his own. A fire crackles in the hearth, there are furs over the flagstones, goblets on the table, wine in the jug. And books, of course. The copy of Plutarch that I carried on the road now rests on oak shelves, with three score other tomes rubbing leathery shoulders. It's a small start but even the shelves themselves grew from a little acorn.

I'm sitting by the window. The wind is sealed away behind a dozen panes of glass, each one a hand's span across, and leaded together in diamond shapes. The glass came in by ox-cart across the mountains, all the way from the Wild Coast if you can believe it. The Thurtans make it so flat you can look out and hardly see the distortion.

I study the page before me, and the quill in my hand, and the ink at its point glistening with dark possibilities. Have I seen without distortion? Looking through the years, how much gets twisted?

The Nuban told me his people made ink by grinding up secrets. Here I am untangling them, and it's been a slow business.

Out in the courtyard I see Rike, a massive figure dwarfing the soldiers he's drilling. I'm told he has taken a wife. I didn't enquire further.

I spread the pages before me. A scribe will have to copy these out. I write in a crabbed hand, a tight unbroken line, the line I've followed from there to here, from then to now.

I see my life spread out across a table top. I see the course of my days, how I spun about, aimless, like a child's top. Corion may have sought to guide the destination but the journey, the murderous, random, broken journey, was all mine.

Gog is crouched by the fire. He's grown, and not just taller. He's making shapes in the flames, having them dance. He makes a game of it until it bores him. Then he goes back to his wooden soldier, making him march, running him here and there, charging at shadows.

I think about the road. Not so often now, but I still think about it. About life that begins new each morning, walking on, chasing after blood or money or shadows. It was a different me that wanted those things, a different me that wanted to break everything for the joy of breaking it, for the thrill of what it might bring. And to see who might care.

I was like Gog's little wooden soldier, running in wild and meaningless circles. I can't say I'm sorry for the things I did. But I'm done with them. I wouldn't repeat those choices. I remember them. Blood is on these hands, these ink-stained hands, but I don't feel the sin. I think maybe we die every day. Maybe we're born new each dawn, a little changed, a little further on our own road. When enough days stand between you and the person you were, you're strangers. Maybe that's what growing up is. Maybe I have grown up.

I said by the time I was fifteen I would be a king. And I am. And I didn't even have to kill my father to have a crown. I have The Haunt and the lands of Renar. I have towns and villages, and people who call me King. And if the people call you King, that is what you are. It's no great thing.

On the road I did things that men might call evil. There were crimes. They talk about the bishop most often, but there were many more, some darker, some more bloody. I wondered once if Corion had put that sickness in me, if I were the tool and he the architect of that violence and cruelty. I wondered if having taken his head, if having grown from boy to man, I would be a better person. I wondered if I might be the man the Nuban wanted me to be, the man Tutor Lundist hoped for.

Such a man would have shown Count Renar the mercy of a quick death. Such a man would have known his mother and brother would want no more than that. Justice, not revenge.

From my window I can see the mountains. Beyond them lies Ancrath, and the Tall Castle. Father with his new son. Katherine in her chambers, probably hating me. And past that, Gelleth, and Storn, and a patchwork of lands that were once Empire.

I won't stay here forever. I'll reach the last page and set down my quill. And when that's done I will walk out and it will all be mine. I told Bovid Tor that by fifteen I'd be King. I told him over his steaming guts. I'm telling you that by twenty I'll be Emperor. Be thankful it's just being told over this page.

I'm going down to see Renar now. I keep him in the smallest of the dungeon cells. Every day I let him ask for death, and then I leave him to his pain. I think when I finish my writing I will let him have the end he seeks. I don't want to, but I know I should. I've grown. The old Jorg would have kept him there forever. I've grown, but whatever monster might be in me, it was always mine, my choice, my responsibility, my evil, if you will.

It's what I am, and if you want excuses, come and take them.